To Kill the Past

'*Fear was back like a wild cat that had leaped on to her shoulders. Her body jerked and twisted as she fought the unnameable, the unidentifiable. The darkness never lifted. The fear never lessened. Gradually, she realized that she was in hospital. But the major part of her consciousness was grappling to come to terms with the appalling nature of her situation. She couldn't remember who she was.*'

After a terrifying car crash in which her two closest relatives are killed, Felicity Frear comes to in a Devon hospital blinded, burned and amnesiac. Even the news that she has been left Kingsleigh, the historic and beautiful family home of the Dashwoods, means nothing to her.

Discharged from hospital, Felicity heads straight for her new home, hoping that the sight of a place she's apparently known since childhood might bring her memory back. It doesn't. Felicity finds herself alone and vulnerable, unable to understand her hostile reception. Then her nightmare begins as the phone rings and a cold, detached voice says: 'Now you're back, I want what what's mine' . . .

Bit by bit, Felicity learns of the horrific sequence of events which took place at Kingsleigh the week before her accident. In a desperate attempt to make sense of the mysteries which surround her, Felicity sets about uncovering her past. But even in her worst imaginings she could never have guessed what might confront her there . . .

To Kill the Past

Janet Laurence

MACMILLAN
LONDON

First published 1994 by Macmillan London Limited

a division of Pan Macmillan Publishers Limited
Cavaye Place London SW10 9PG
and Basingstoke

Associated companies throughout the world

ISBN 0–333–62546–3

9 8 7 6 5 4 3 2 1

A CIP catalogue record for this book is available from
the British Library

Typeset by Intype, London
Printed by Mackays of Chatham PLC, Chatham, Kent

To
Tim
With Much Love

Chapter One

Fear filled her, its acrid stench invading her nostrils. Her heart raced and surging adrenalin brought desperate strength. She hit out, clenched hands punching, punching, punching. But it was like fighting shrouds, a ghostly foe. Agonizing pain racked her body and she couldn't see for the dark.

Through terror and bewilderment gradually swam the realization that the enemy was a tangle of tubes, that the punching connected with nothing, that she was safe in bed.

Nightmare, that was all it had been. She told herself there was no enemy but phantoms, nothing to be frightened of.

But that couldn't be true. All this pain, all this confusion must mean something more than a nightmare.

If she lay still and straight, here in the dark, would everything sort itself out?

But adrenalin was still pumping through her body, alerting every defence mechanism.

She could hear the breathing now, harsh and rasping, frightening in the quiet. Her mind said it couldn't be hers, her body knew it was. Knew but couldn't control, just as it couldn't control the fingers that plucked at the sheet or the rapid beating of her heart.

The dark began to trouble her. Laboriously, fighting the pain, she tried to raise herself in the bed, reach for a light switch.

Someone was beside her; there was a rustle of starched skirts, a sudden whiff of some pleasant-smelling toiletry overlaying an earthier aroma of stale sweat. She could hear tiredness underneath the quiet commands. Bedclothes were drawn back, she flinched from the sudden stab into the soft flesh of her buttock. Words tried to soothe but brought her no comfort. What was going on? Why was she here? What was wrong? She needed to ask questions, seek answers. All that came out was a slurred jumble that got more soothing noises in response. Her body was being expertly manoeuvred, the pillows rearranged, the bedclothes straightened, something being done to her arm. Then the fear started to slip away

1

as the pain lessened, her breathing quietened and the dark deepened.

Fear was back like a wild cat that had leaped on to her shoulders. Her body jerked and twisted as she fought the unnameable, the unidentifiable. Strangled, burbling screams issued from her mouth. Her punching fists were stronger now. Sounds of a door opening, rapid footsteps, restraining hands, more soothing noises, a quick command, bedclothes drawn back, another prick in her bottom, more disorientation, more darkness.

The darkness never lifted. The fear never lessened.

The fear never lessened but it changed character. Panic gradually ebbed away. Now when consciousness returned it wasn't to a choking terror. Now she could lie quietly in the darkness and hardly hear the sound of breathing. There were other sounds, though. Sounds that should have been reassuring: voices whose words were indistinguishable but whose tones spoke of normality; the cheerful clatter of a hospital going about its daily life; the squeak of wheels on polished flooring, the clashing of equipment, the rattle of trolleys. These were sounds that had nothing to do with nightmare, they spoke of care and comfort. And the pain was lessening. When she tried to move her lethargic limbs there was still pain but no longer agony. Why then was she still so afraid?

The question was the first rational thought she had had in a long time. She lay on the hard bed in the quiet room and repeated it in her mind. Then she tried saying it out loud.

'Why am I so afraid?'

Her voice sounded rusty and unused, strange.

'Why am I so afraid?' She repeated the question and could hear a puzzled quality now, an almost academic interest in her condition. It calmed her.

She lay quietly and felt the warmth of sunlight fall on her body. For a while it was enough to enjoy the sensation of life being gently restored. Then realization hit her. Sunlight had to be flooding the room, it couldn't be dark.

Panic returned, surging through her. It wasn't dark because there was no light, it wasn't dark because she always woke in the depths of night. She was blind!

She raised hesitant fingers to her face and felt bandages. The movements brought more pain but some of the panic slipped away. She couldn't see because her eyes were bandaged. The logic was soothing. It took time for her confused mind to formulate questions that removed the reassurance.

Why were her eyes bandaged? Why was there so much pain? And when the bandages were removed, would she be able to see? What had happened to her?

Now she was aware of other bandages. Most of her body seemed to be covered with them. How had she managed to wield her fists so frantically when her arms and torso were swathed like a mummy? Only her legs seemed to be free of the confining muslin. And she appeared to be connected to tubes, linked to some support system like an astronaut to his mother ship.

There came the sound of a door opening. Once again the pleasant toiletry smell and beneath it this time the body was fresh.

'Nurse?' she asked.

'Ah, you're awake, that's good. How are you feeling?' The voice was alert, interested, questioning.

'Am I blind?' It was the most important of all the questions that were fighting for articulation, much more important than what had happened or where she was.

The slightest hesitation, then, 'I'm sure you're not. And we'll soon know for certain.'

It seemed her brain was at last beginning to function, for she had no trouble interpreting the subtext. It gave her no comfort.

'Where am I?' That sounded impossibly hackneyed. She tried again, quickly. 'I mean, which hospital is this?'

'St Michael's.' There was relief in the voice, as though a tricky corner had been turned.

'And what happened to me?' She was tiring now, she could hear her voice trail away to a whisper.

'You were in a car crash. That's enough questions. You're alive and you're going to be all right. What you need now is rest.' The bedclothes were pulled back. She knew what would be coming and resented the thought of more oblivion just as she was beginning to make some sense of her situation, just when it seemed she might be able to fight off her fear. Her faint protest went unheeded.

This time when she woke her mind was clearer. She knew she was afraid but she also understood her fear was irrational. She had been in a car accident, had been badly injured if the extent of the bandages and the strength of the medication she had been given were any indication, but she was recovering. She tried to draw comfort from the fact but knew her unease was too deep-seated to be soothed away so easily.

It was essential to think clearly, to fight any further attempts to sedate her.

The door to her room opened but the battle she had prepared for never arrived. Now, she was told, she could be unhooked from her tubes; they thought she had recovered enough to obtain her nourishment from more conventional means. There was a quiet chinking and momentary discomfort then the sound of something being wheeled away. A moment later the nurse was back. But there was no pulling down of the bedclothes this time; it seemed another sleep-inducing injection was not thought appropriate. Instead, she was being shown how to switch the radio on and off.

'Classic FM? Is that what you'd like? Lovely music, isn't it? Really takes you out of yourself, doesn't it?' Meaningless phrases, uttered without thought. How many times had this woman said them to other patients? No matter, floating through the air came the side-slipping chromatic descents of music she knew and loved. For a moment she couldn't place it but as she listened she felt, for the first time, her fear retreat. The fact that her eyes were bandaged, the fact of the pain, muted but still there, the unfamiliar surroundings, all these acquired a less threatening aura. This music was something that belonged to her, something that was precious.

Mozart's Symphony No. 40; the information slipped easily into her mind and there was a brief glow of pleasure that she had remembered.

Then fear returned. Not a leaping fear now, something more insidious, sending icy ripples down her body, paralysing thought. However she tried, her mind couldn't get beyond the identification of the Mozart symphony.

She lay against the newly plumped pillows, tried to ignore the hurt in her body, tried to concentrate on her sense of gradually returning strength. It was no use. The music played on, blotting out the busy hospital sounds from beyond her door but unable to muffle the sudden blare of a car horn that penetrated her window. A tiny area of her mind registered that the hospital must be built alongside a main road but the major part of her consciousness was grappling to come to terms with the appalling nature of her situation.

She couldn't remember who she was.

Chapter Two

Now that she was properly conscious, a doctor arrived to explain her condition.

She lay in bed and listened to his voice. Even though it was so important that she learned everything he could tell her, she found it hard to concentrate on what he was saying. Her head still felt confused, the bright strands of lucidity that came more and more frequently were mixed with dark clouds that threatened her hold on reality.

And there was her lost memory. Up until now she had told no one, as though if she didn't acknowledge the fact, it didn't exist. But soon she would have to confess to the limbo in which her mind existed and the imminence of that moment made her shiver.

Was she a coward? The sort of person who preferred not to confront uncomfortable realities? Her reluctance to accept this possibility encouraged her to think she mightn't be totally spineless but when she couldn't remember anything about herself how could she be sure? Perhaps when she was really tested, she'd fail.

The doctor was quietly matter of fact but his voice sounded warm and concerned and she could sense him giving her his whole attention, not like the nursing staff who always seemed to be in a hurry to catch up with a part of themselves that was somewhere else. For the first time she felt a sense of reassurance. She could even find it encouraging that the doctor did not try to minimize her condition.

She was lucky to be alive, he said, after such a dreadful crash; it was no wonder her injuries had been so severe.

She forgot her hard-won equilibrium as questions tumbled out: 'How did it happen? Was anyone killed? Was it my fault?'

There was the briefest of pauses before he gently enquired, 'You don't remember the accident?'

'No,' she whispered.

'It's not unnatural.' The doctor was once more matter of fact. 'The mind has ways of protecting itself from facts too appalling to contemplate.' He then proceeded to give her a brief description of the incident.

She had been a passenger in a car that had crashed with an articulated lorry. Both vehicles had caught fire and only the courage and quick thinking of the driver in a car behind had saved her life.

'He managed to drag you out before the car exploded.'

'What about the others?'

'I'm afraid they died.'

Silence hung heavily between them, a silence peopled with faceless ghosts. Before she could summon up the courage to ask further questions, the doctor moved on to discuss her injuries. 'You may have a little difficulty recognizing yourself when we remove your bandages,' he said apologetically. 'Your nose and cheekbones were broken and,' he hesitated again then said, casually, 'I'm afraid rescue didn't come quite soon enough to save you from a certain amount of burning, on your back, arms and, I'm afraid, your face.'

She had already been able to work that out; her pain and the bandages told their own tale. But with one of her periods of total clarity her mind latched on to the implication behind what he said. 'You mean I won't be blind?'

Encouraging noises were made by the medical staff when the bandages and guards around her eyes were changed but all she could be certain of was that, without the protective guards, the quality of the dark in which she lived varied. It was as though deep velvet gave way to a multi-layered muslin that obscured rather than blacked out a faint source of light. And she was almost certain the layers of muslin were getting less.

'It's too early to be quite sure,' he warned gently, 'but you're young and the omens are good.'

The recovery of her sight was her main concern; she dismissed her appearance as unimportant. She had no doubt she could manage to cope with whatever the mirror would reveal had happened to her face.

It was only much later that she wondered if this certainty meant she might, after all, not lack courage.

Now, though, her main concern was her loss of memory.

'It's more than just the accident,' she brought herself to say. 'I can't remember anything. Nothing about my life or even who I am.' Not even what sort of person I am, she added to herself.

The doctor appeared unconcerned. He spoke of a postconcussive state that was not abnormal. It was a symptom of trauma, nothing for her to worry about. Her mind was unaffected, all her intellectual component functions unimpaired.

Her control, so recently reacquired, slipped. 'But I don't even know my name!' she shouted at him, then caught herself, disgusted at her hysteria, and stammered, 'I'm sorry, I apologize.' She tried to lighten her response. 'Life'll be a bit strange as Miss or Mrs X. And somewhere out there must be a family wondering where I am.'

As she said that there rose within her a sudden yearning for someone who could speak to her of familiar things, who loved her for what she was, who understood. She had no idea what it was that needed understanding but she felt the desperate want of a loving presence like a plant that needed water. Again she was brought to wonder about herself. Was there a husband, a lover somewhere? A beloved sister or parent? Who was it she was missing so badly?

The doctor was silent and tension built inside her. A slight rustle suggested he might be shuffling case notes. Then he cleared his throat and said, quite quietly, 'I have to tell you your closest family member, your cousin, died in the car crash with her husband.'

'Died?' There was an instant sense of loss then that was overwhelmed by a horror so strong it stank, filling her nostrils with feral odour. For a gut-wrenching second the world tilted and the dark whirled about her as fear reached out and brushed chill fingers along her skin. Through the clouds of uncertainty she knew without doubt that beyond the walls of this quiet room lurked danger and that until she knew who she was and how she came to be there, she was at its mercy.

'There were three of you in the car.' The doctor's measured tones cut through the confusion in her mind. She struggled for some sort of control, sensing him watching her, assessing how his information was received, whether it was jogging her memory. 'Your cousin Frances was in the passenger seat, her husband, Mark Sheldrake, was driving. You were in the back. The crash broke your nose and cheekbones and several ribs, one of which punctured a lung, and, as I said, if it hadn't been for that other driver, you would have lost your life as well.'

'But my cousin and her husband, they were killed?'

'They died at the moment of impact. They wouldn't have suffered.'

'But you said the car exploded. How can you be sure?'

His silence was not reassuring.

Her mind veered away from the image of bodies caught in the holocaust of a burning car. Later she knew she would have to grapple with it but not now, now it was too horrific. For relief, she repeated the names he had given her: Frances and Mark Sheldrake. Like a bell tolling funeral rites they echoed round her head, backwards and forwards, Mark and Frances, Frances and Mark, Sheldrake, Sheldrake, Sheldrake. Then she said them out loud, listening to her voice like a student of a foreign language attempting to find the meaning of a repeated phrase, but there was no frisson of half-remembered recognition. Frances and Mark Sheldrake could have been characters in a film or a novel for all they were to her.

'And me, who am I?' she whispered, terrified her own name was going to mean as little.

'Felicity Frear.'

For a tiny instant there was a click in her mind as of a distant door closing. For that one fraction of a moment she had almost caught something, nothing as precise as a memory, more an echo down a dusty corridor.

Frustration filled her. It was like living in a maze, not knowing which path led the way out.

'Felicity,' she repeated, tasting the name on her tongue. 'Felicity,' she said again, hoping that the sound would bring back that nano-second when something had shifted in the dark, bewildered world. There was nothing, the name now had no reverberations, meant nothing more than those of Mark and Frances Sheldrake.

'And where am I now, where is this hospital?'

'Devon.' He gave the name a questioning quality as though it might trigger some response but the clouds had rolled back into her mind and she was too tired to grapple any longer with where or who she was, what had happened or what menace it was lying out there in the real world.

Now she did indeed feel like a coward. She wanted to stay safe and warm in this bed with nothing to do but regain her strength, all decisions made on her behalf, protected, and even, in a way, cherished. She was alone and vulnerable and it was as much as she could do to cope with her blindness and the pain that still racked her body.

Chapter Three

Someone had come into her room; approaching her bed were heavy steps quite unlike the quick, soft, rubber-soled tread of the medical staff. Felicity lay listening as the steps came nearer. Her body tensed as she tried to reach through her blindness and assess her visitor. There was no word of greeting but something rustled as it was put on the bed. She flinched, then her nostrils caught a sweet waft of floral scents and a male voice said, 'These are for you.'

Seduced by the aroma, unthinking, she reached for the bouquet and buried her nose in soft petals, then gasped as the careless intake of breath burned up her damaged nose. But with the pain came a perfume that drowned out the antiseptic and scrubbed cleanliness that had surrounded her until now. Roses, jasmine, lavender, summer fragrances from a garden misty with greens, a myriad shades of pink, hazy blues and mauves and all the creams from pale apricot through buff to ivory. A summer garden; she could almost see beds, the lawns, the trees and shrubs, dipping and leading down, leading down . . .

The sensation was gone and so was the smell of the flowers; their fragrance had overloaded her wounded nostrils. Reluctantly she laid the bouquet back on the bed. 'Lovely,' she said to her unknown visitor. 'Thank you so much.'

'I asked for scented flowers. I hate the smell of hospitals.'

It was as though the aroma of the flowers had cleansed her mind, driven away the clouds and enabled her to catch every inflection of the voice.

It was dark, strong, reticent, reluctant even, as though, despite the words, he hadn't wanted to bring her flowers, hadn't even, perhaps, wanted to visit her. Her nerve ends still quivering with the pain brought by that injudicious sniff, Felicity felt threatened by the tension she could sense surrounding him.

'Who are you?' she asked bluntly.

He said nothing and she tried to imagine him standing beside her bed, taking in her bandaged appearance.

'I'm sorry you can't see,' he uttered at last in a tone that to

Felicity's highly tuned ears sounded grudging. He added quickly, 'I wanted to come earlier but the hospital said you weren't well enough for visitors.'

Could that be the reason no one had come to see her before this? Was she the sort of person who didn't make friends easily? So far she hadn't felt lonely in her hospital bed; perhaps she preferred not to get too close to people. Maybe it wasn't the sense of threat or her pain and weakness that made her feel awkward with this stranger. Or was he a stranger?

'Did they also tell you I've lost my memory?'

'No.'

Curious how one small word could reverberate with so many mixed emotions. In it she heard doubt and dismay overlaid with caution.

'So, you see, you are going to have to explain who you are.' She wished her voice didn't sound so faint, she desperately needed to appear strong, in command.

'My name's Sam McLean.' The voice was still stiff, distrustful.

Was she the problem or was it him? 'Have you got Burgess with you?'

'Burgess?'

'Don't the two always go together?' She could detect no reaction and what had seemed a happy feat of memory now faltered into absurdity. 'The two spies; you know, Burgess and McLean!'

'So, you can remember some things?'

The atmosphere of suspicion this person carried around him was exhausting and Felicity stumbled a little as she said, 'Only, it seems, for what affects me personally. I can remember Burgess and McLean and Mozart and who the Prime Minister is, I just can't remember who I am.' She tried to sharpen her faculties. 'Or if I've met you before.'

He picked up the cue, but with reluctance. 'I happened to be on hand when your car crashed.'

'On hand? You mean you were the one who pulled me out of the burning wreck?' His silence had to be one of assent. Her tiredness fell away, leaving her body humming like a taut wire. 'What happened?'

Still silence. It filled the room, pushing at her like a tangible force. Fiercely Felicity wished for sight. 'Tell me what happened, you *must* tell me.' She pulled herself up in the bed, ignoring the flaring pain in her body, and stretched out a hand towards where she knew he must be. 'Please?' It came out grumpy, like a sulky schoolgirl reminded of her manners, instead of irresistible as she had intended, and she suddenly realized exactly what it was he had done. His awkwardness now seemed explained. No wonder he was reticent, how difficult it must be to have to tell someone you saved their life.

Felicity dropped back on her pillows, her sudden surge of energy drained away. She wanted to cry. Everything was wrong with her world and she couldn't even be polite to her rescuer; her rescuer who was also her first visitor.

'I'm sorry,' she apologized weakly. 'I should thank you, not shout at you.'

'There's nothing to thank me for.' His voice was still stiff.

'Only my life.'

'That may not be such a gift,' he said and there was something grim in his tone.

She wondered if he was referring to her bandaged face and a first tremor of doubt about her appearance ran through her.

'Please, tell me about the accident,' she begged again.

'There's not much I can tell you.'

'You were there.'

There was a pause while he appeared to be making up his mind about something. When he started to speak, his voice was slow and deliberate. 'I was driving fast along a typical Devon road, narrow and twisting with high hedges, driving fast because . . . because I was late. Then, from ahead of me, came the sound of a crash; it was terribly loud, like a bomb going off.'

Felicity was so engrossed in what he was saying that she could ignore the flat, automatic delivery, the way the voice was drier than autumn leaves.

'I braked, came round a bend and saw it. A car smashed into a lorry; they were slewed across the road, locked in some terrible embrace of twisted metal, the car half in the ditch, both vehicles on fire. I stopped, got out and ran to the car. The front door was jammed, wouldn't open, but the rear one was all right and I managed to pull you out. I would have tried to reach the others but your hair and clothes were on fire and by the time I'd got you clear of the car and had beaten out the flames, the petrol tank exploded.' Sam McLean stopped abruptly.

Felicity had a sudden vision of a man fighting heat and the flames, working under the threat of an imminent petrol explosion, wrestling with recalcitrant metal before being able to pull her unconscious body from the wreck.

'Were you hurt at all?' she asked, managing to keep her voice as unemotional as his.

'A few burns on my hands, nothing much.'

'And your appointment?' It was an inconsequential question but something compelled her to try and reach behind his part in the drama as though she needed to know exactly why he had been in place to rescue her.

'Appointment?'

'You said you were driving fast because you were late.'

'Oh, that! It turned out it wouldn't have been any use my getting there anyway, I'd made a mistake.'

'Where were you going?'

'Just somewhere on the coast.' His voice was impatient.

'The Devon coast?'

'That's right.'

'North or south?'

'North.' She was having to drag the information out of him but now she knew that she, her cousin Frances and Mark Sheldrake must have been travelling in that direction too.

'What do you do?' she asked.

'I'm an insurance salesman, very dull, very boring.'

'I wonder if I have any insurance.' She gave a ghost of a laugh. 'You must give me your card; I may well be looking for some as soon as I get out of here.'

'I don't do that sort of insurance.' The comment came very quickly.

'What sort?'

'My business is all commercial.'

Was he saying he would prefer not to have any further contact with her? But then why this visit?

Felicity felt an overpowering need to retain some link with this man who had rescued her from a fiery grave. He was a contact point between her nothingness of now and the life that had been before. He had been following the same road as the car she'd been travelling in, when she had known who she was – when she had been terrified of what was to come. The thought slipped into her mind from nowhere and stayed, vibrating, making her catch her breath as the darkness in which she lived seemed once again to seethe with danger.

'I must be able to thank you properly, when I get out of here.'

'I need no thanks,' he said harshly. 'But I'll be in touch, some time.'

Footsteps and the closing of the door told her he had gone without saying goodbye. Only his promise to see her again reverberated in the air – had it been a promise or a threat?

For the rest of the day she pondered his visit, approaching his description of the car crash with the care of a timid circus artiste moving towards an unreliable lion, desperate to get on terms but terrified she mightn't be able to handle what lay in wait. That image he had conjured of screaming vehicles and licking, hungry flames whose heat distorted metal, blistered paint and burned flesh, how far could she trust it? There was something very disturbing about Sam McLean.

Her scorched body ached and throbbed, pain burned her mind as the flames had the car, she couldn't sort out what she had been told and could imagine from what might just be a returning memory. She had an overpowering need to believe that the veils were beginning to lift and that the accident was the danger she felt threatened her. If only her mind would clear, allow her to think rationally. Beneath the confusion, though, a cold and quiet voice told her that she could remember nothing. And that, whatever the danger was, it hadn't passed when she'd been dragged from that burning car.

*

Chapter Four

The next day Felicity had another visitor. This one came in on a click-clack of high heels, approaching her bed in a purposeful rush.

'Hello, Flick,' said a bright, determined voice, then the newcomer faltered, there was a hiss of indrawn breath. 'My God, I had no idea!' A pause, then, in a different voice, shaken and unsure, 'They said you'd been burned but I never realized . . . I should have come sooner but there was so much to do, the funeral, all the arrangements . . . and they said you were too ill for visitors . . .' The apologetic, shocked phrases stumbled to a stop.

'I think it looks worse than it is,' Felicity said. 'I'm much better,' she added, realizing as she spoke that her mind was already definitely clearer. 'The bandages will be coming off soon and they say I should be able to see.'

Silence. She heard her visitor take a deep breath. 'You always had courage, I'll say that for you, Flick.'

Another pause, sounds of a chair being dragged forward, her visitor seating herself and a bag being placed on the floor. 'I hardly like to ask how you are, it seems enough you're alive, you've obviously had a dreadful time. But I expect you'll want to hear about the funeral?' Just a moment of doubt came through at the end then the visitor rushed on. 'Such a lot of people and all so shocked. Everyone said what a tragedy it was; Fran and Mark were so happy and they'd been married such a short time. Everyone said how attractive he was. And, of course, with Fran has gone any hope of the Dashwood line continuing.'

Felicity nerved herself to interrupt the flow. 'Look, I've got to say it now, before you go any further. I've lost my memory.'

'That's what they told me this morning.' Her visitor sounded as though she could hardly believe it. 'Well, I suppose it's natural, you wouldn't want to remember anything as ghastly as that accident. Better you should remember Fran as she was alive – and Mark, of course.'

Felicity felt frustration building up. 'No, you don't understand, it's

14

not just the accident. I can't remember anything; not Fran, not Mark, not even who I am. And I don't know who you are.' She heard the note of apology in her voice and sensed an almost laughable resentment rising in her visitor.

'You can't remember anything?'

There was another silence.

Felicity forced herself to keep calm; shouting wasn't going to help her find her way through the maze. What would be the best approach?

'I know it seems odd, you can't imagine how odd it is to me, how lost I feel.' She groped for words that would soothe this graceless woman into a more co-operative frame of mind. 'It's wonderful to have someone who can tell me something about myself, you must be able to understand.' Would that work?

'You really don't know who you are?'

'No!' Felicity clipped the negative before it could become a wail. For an instant she felt like a child who had awoken in the dark, disoriented, wanting her mother to switch on the light and tell her everything was all right. She forgot all she'd been told as a terrible thought struck and wouldn't go away. 'You're not my mother, are you?'

There was a short bark of laughter. 'My dear Flick, now I know you've lost your memory. Not even you could think that one up.'

Indeed, anyone less motherly than this woman would be hard to imagine; what had made her dream up something so unlikely?

'No, you're no relation of mine. I am, I was, Frances's aunt, Belinda Gray. My brother, Tom, was her father. And her mother and yours were sisters.'

Felicity clutched at hope. 'Is either of my parents alive?'

A brief hesitation. 'They're both dead, you're an orphan, as was Frances.'

'Oh.' It was a tiny sigh of desolation. Then she heard again the doctor's voice as he announced the death of her cousin. She'd been her closest relative, he'd said. It seemed it was true, she really was alone in the world. The fact was forlorn but she found something familiar about it. Was she really such a solitary person?

Her visitor seemed disinclined to add further information; she didn't seem to realize how hungry Felicity was for someone to fill in her background. 'Do I live in Devon?' she asked.

A longer hesitation, then, 'No, you live in London. It was Frances who lived down here, at Kingsleigh, which has been our family home since the time of William the Conqueror.' There was something cold and alienating in the voice now.

15

'You mean you lived there as well?' Anything to keep this woman talking so Felicity might pick up a detail, however meagre, that could help to fill in a picture of her life before the accident.

'Before my marriage, I was a Dashwood.' Palpable pride filled Mrs Gray's voice. 'I was born and grew up at Kingsleigh, just like Frances. I lived there until I was married.' Her tone darkened. 'You tried to belong there as well. Tom never realized what you were trying to do, any more than Frances did. Sweet child that she was, she never understood.'

Back came the surge of terror, the invasion of her world by unknown forces. 'Understood what?'

There came from her visitor a sense of struggle, a repressed heaviness of breathing, a fidgeting of hands.

'You must tell me,' Felicity said desperately. 'It might bring back my memory. Any little fact could.'

Nothing was said.

'Why don't you like me?'

'I never said that!'

'You don't need to, it's obvious. What did I do to you?'

'Me? You did nothing to me.'

'You mean I did something to someone else? Who?'

No response.

'My cousin, Frances?'

Another pause that lengthened, then, reluctantly, 'There's nothing I can tell you. Frances wouldn't hear anything against you. That's why . . .' But Mrs Gray caught back whatever it was she had been going to say.

'Why what?'

Reluctantly, as though it was being dragged out of her, Belinda Gray whispered, 'Why she left you Kingsleigh.'

Chapter Five

Mrs Gray left soon afterwards. Felicity lay in her darkness and wondered about Kingsleigh. What sort of house could stimulate the repressed emotion she had heard in Belinda Gray's voice? There had been passion for the house and deep jealousy of Felicity because she was not its owner. Antagonism, even hate, had coloured that well-bred voice. How could a mere house stimulate such a response? Was it really that special? And how could she be expected to be thrilled when ownership had come through the death of someone who had been so close to her?

Then she wondered what her cousin had been like. It was incredible to Felicity that she couldn't summon up any memory of a girl Mrs Gray had insisted had been like a sister to her and now expected her to be mourning. But she was only a name; Frances, once Dashwood, later Sheldrake, owner of what was obviously a handsome estate, rich and newly married to an attractive husband, someone presumably to be envied. What sort of friends had they been, she and Frances?

Frances had been a girl who appeared to have everything to live for and now she was ashes, her body burned in that terrible crash. Felicity shuddered as the full force of how close she herself had come to death hit her. If it hadn't been for Sam McLean – with his name, thoughts of the cousin that was part of her lost past years were driven from her mind by memories of the enigmatic man who had been her first visitor. The cold, automatic tone of his voice as he'd related the details of the crash, the curious way he'd distanced himself from everything surrounding the accident. Why did she have the impression he'd been holding something back? He'd said he would be in touch; Felicity was torn between a desire to retain this contact with that dreadful event and a growing distrust of Sam McLean. Yet he had saved her life.

She pushed the thought of Sam McLean away and returned to her consideration of Kingsleigh. Here was a place she had constantly visited while growing up, must have spent many happy hours in; mightn't the sight of it prove the key to unlocking her memory?

*

mightn't the sight of it prove the key to unlocking her memory?

Interminable days went by. Days spent in the long battle to regain her health as physiotherapists worked with her, dressings were removed and replaced and the hermetically sealed life of a hospital enfolded her. Felicity felt cocooned, cut off from the real world. No one visited her, there were no cards or telephone calls, it was as though she had fallen through some black hole into an antechamber of death. She drew breath, gradually less and less painfully, but there was little else to suggest she had a life of her own. If it hadn't been for those two visits, the one from Sam McLean and the other from Belinda Gray, Felicity could have persuaded herself she had really slipped into some limbo land.

Then, as she grew stronger and the hospital more encouraging about her recovery, Felicity started to believe that the sight of Kingsleigh would jolt her into remembering her past.

Throughout the drive from the hospital northwards to the Devon coast, Felicity had been in a state of nervous anticipation.

The entrance to Kingsleigh was impressive. A long drive leading off into the distance was guarded by heavy wrought iron gates suspended from a pair of pineapple-topped stone pillars. When the taxi driver stopped his car to open the gates, Felicity got out as well and walked a little way along the tarmacadam surface for the first sight of what was now her estate.

Now, at last, Kingsleigh lay before her. Now was the moment one glance might bring memory flooding back.

Felicity looked down the drive towards the house, her pulse racing. But her eyes were dazzled by the sun and all she could see was an outline, dark against the glittering sea.

From behind her came the roar of a motorcycle swinging through the gates, its engine quickly killed to idling speed as the rider thrust a heavy leather boot into the ground, stopping the machine behind the taxi. ''Ere, these gates should be shut.' He lifted the visor of his helmet, revealing a thin sharp face covered with stubble that was a long way from designer. His green eyes narrowed in challenge as he took in Felicity's appearance. ''oo are you? We don't like trespassers on this land.' He couldn't be more than twenty-one or two but the aggression in his voice made him sound older.

Felicity looked at him from behind her dark glasses, glad it was bright daylight and that the taxi driver was with her. 'I'm Felicity Frear,' she said.

The youth wasn't impressed. 'Nah, I know 'er, you're nothing like 'er.'

'If you work here you must know I've been in a car crash.' Her voice was sharp.

The idling throb of the engine roared a couple of times as the youth gave the machine two sharp bursts on the accelerator while he scrutinized her more closely.

Felicity stood her ground, knowing this was merely the first of many such looks. At least he didn't appear to flinch at the sight of her face.

'Mebbe,' he said at last. 'Felicity Frear.' He repeated her name with a touch of insolence. 'So you're back. You'll find things a bit different.' For a moment it looked as though he would say something else but, instead, he brought up his engine into a shuddering roar and rode off down the drive.

Despite Belinda Gray's attitude, Felicity had been thinking of Kingsleigh as a healing place, somewhere she could come to terms with her situation in peace and comfort. Now, her mind jangling with the effects of this encounter, she found herself reluctant to go any further towards the house.

She closed her eyes and raised her face to the sun. Gradually her heart beats returned to normal but the heat proved too much for her scarred skin. She asked the driver to wait for a few moments and moved across the springy turf to the shade of a large oak tree, then she carefully lowered her stiff limbs to the ground.

The lightest of breezes set up a comforting rustle in the leaves above her head and cool, dappled light was all around her. Small insects buzzed, chirped and chattered busily and a bird was singing, pure, liquid notes pouring out. The grass was filled with small flowers: vetches, maids in waiting, eggs and bacon; where had she learned all these names? She bent her head to study the tiny petals more closely, so many different shapes.

Her sight was a daily miracle to Felicity. It wasn't perfect; she needed to wear dark glasses all the time and sun could dazzled her back into blindness if she wasn't careful but out of its glare she could see well enough and every day brought an improvement.

But the recovery of her sight had proved a mixed blessing. Though she had been warned, her first glance into a mirror had been a shock. Even if she hadn't lost her memory, she would have been unable to recognize herself.

Her nose was impossibly swollen. There were streaks of yellow and green bruising round her eyes and cheekbones; livid pink scarring round the edges of her face puckered the skin; her eyebrows were gone. Over her scorched scalp her hair was beginning to grow back into a fair frizz like an unkempt camel. Only a well-shaped mouth with tightly controlled corners and a pair of wary dark blue eyes, so dark they held a hint of purple, looked undamaged.

Felicity had gripped the arms of her chair. She had thought her appearance didn't matter but not even in her worst nightmares had she conceived anything as bad as this.

'As I said, it looks much worse than it is,' the doctor had soothed her. 'The swelling and bruising will die down, the scarring will settle, and, even though you broke your nose and cheekbones on the seat in front, it protected the centre of your face from the worst of the flames.' His voice became more cheerful. 'As I mentioned to you earlier, we've rebuilt your nose. As you were in no state to be asked, we took the decision on your behalf to make it a little straighter than the one in the photograph Mrs Gray sent us. If you hate it, we can rebuild again later but I'm willing to bet you're going to like the effect. There shouldn't be too much difference to your cheekbones, though, so your face won't have changed its shape dramatically.'

She had asked to see the photograph Belinda Gray had supplied.

Silently the doctor had extracted it from his files and handed it over.

It was a snapshot, a holiday memento, of a laughing girl in her mid-twenties. She was dressed in shorts and a brightly coloured short-sleeved shirt tied in a knot over her bare brown midriff. In the background was a native hut with a roof of leaves and dark-skinned children leaning interestedly over a primitive verandah. The girl's face was turned slightly away from the camera and the way the sun struck the side of her face showed clearly the bump in her nose; it made an oddly interesting feature, adding character to the good bones and fine skin. Her eyes were screwed against the sun, their colour hidden. A bush of short blonde curls gave a note of joyous abandon and there was an air of arrested motion in the stance of the long, slim legs that suggested she had merely paused for a moment on her way to something exciting. The snapshot said that here was a girl of energy, verve and fun.

Felicity felt she was none of those things now. The photograph, bumpy nose and all, was a cruel contrast to her present state.

There was a date on the snapshot. Comparing it with the doctor's desk calendar, Felicity saw it had been taken some eight months earlier, the previous November.

Once again Felicity looked at her apology for a face in the mirror. Then she handed the snapshot back to the doctor. 'At least I wasn't a great beauty.'

'A very attractive girl. And now that your nose has been straightened, you'll look even better. In a few months, that is, when everything has settled down.'

She gave him a crooked smile and said nothing.

It was one thing not to care much about your appearance, another

20

to know that your looks would turn off any normal person. Then she chastised herself for ingratitude. At least she was alive and hadn't suffered lasting damage to her body. And there the scars, if equally painful, were not nearly as noticeable as those on her face. Her ribs were healing well, her mind was, at last, clear again and she could think rationally. She had an identity and a home to go to, even if neither meant anything to her at the moment. Whatever her face looked like, the world would have to get used to it. As she would.

The feelings of panic Felicity had had on first regaining consciousness, the sense that danger was waiting for her, had gradually disappeared as she grew stronger. They had all been tied up with the accident, she decided. There could be no reason for feeling threatened by some unknown force. That could all be put behind her.

She had determined that Kingsleigh was going to mean a new life and now, sitting under the great old oak tree, she renewed her resolution. No stroppy youth was going to upset her, not when the weather was so wonderful and everything looked so beautiful.

She wondered if there was something about the peace of sitting here that was somehow rooted in the past; if, maybe, her memory was stirring. The breeze quickened and Felicity shivered slightly. Clouds were gathering, obscuring the sun, removing its glare. Felicity looked down the valley again towards the house and realized that, at last, she could see Kingsleigh.

Chapter Six

Felicity caught her breath as she looked at her inheritance. It wasn't Kingsleigh's size or its age that impressed but its beauty. The sun warmed the golden stone, caught the tangle of twisted chimney pots that crowned its long length and threw shadows where the entrance porch and side wings stood proud of the main sweep of the façade and made an E shape. What seemed like hundreds of symmetrically arranged windowpanes twinkled and sparkled, like the glittering surface of the sea spread in a shining cloth behind the house.

And the fields and trees she had admired before now acquired additional beauty as they provided a magical mix of subtly changing greens flashed with earthy browns to surround the house with a rich tapestry, weaving a spell to drag her into their depths so that she sank, drowning, down to a dark, dark centre that was both cool and warm together, where the golden stone, the shining sea and the leafy greens wound themselves into complex strands that held her fast.

Then she blinked and Kingsleigh was just a house. Still beautiful, still impressive but without any special powers. Not even the power to awaken her memory; the past was still locked away.

Felicity's taxi took her down the hill and pulled up at the front porch. The driver opened the boot and took out her case. 'Carry it inside for you?'

Felicity shook her head; it seemed important to enter Kingsleigh on her own. She paid the man, thanked him and watched the car as it turned, its tyres scrunching gravel before speeding up the drive. Only when it had passed out of sight did she walk through the stone archway into the porch.

The big, iron-studded, heavy wooden door was a little ajar. Felicity pushed it open and entered; first, a narrow foyer, then, down two stone steps to her right, into a medieval hall, flamboyant and splendid.

A hammerbeam roof soared above a flagstoned floor, the flagstones smooth and gleaming from years of passing feet. High above hung a series of ancient standards, tattered now, their colours faded.

The walls were dark, the polished wood panelling densely rich and sombre. A huge stone fireplace, a coat of arms carved into the overhead mantel, faced a big bay window. The shafts of light dancing through the mullioned panes did little to illuminate the sparse furniture and Felicity had the impression of a place that waited for some event long past.

At the far end of the hall, through another archway, could be seen a heavy, carved staircase that swung squarely round to reach a landing that looked down over the hall and might once have been a minstrel's gallery.

Then she saw that in the centre of the hall, standing on a large, oriental rug, was a round Regency table quite out of keeping with its surroundings. On its centre was an antique Chinese bowl, its pale blue glaze eerily translucent. Around it was arranged a miscellaneous collection of odd items: a set of old Ordnance Survey maps in a wooden box, its hinged top flipped open, a large visitor's book with a well-worn leather cover, a small pile of *Country Life* magazines, a pair of gardening gloves accompanied by secateurs, a silver tray that looked as though it was waiting for a letter, a riding whip and a set of poker dice. The table and its content should have seemed at odds with the spare grandeur of the hall but instead they provided a life-giving force that removed the heavy weight of history and made it a home rather than a museum.

Felicity flicked the stud of the dice's leather case and stood for a moment looking at the finely etched red and blue royal faces that were revealed. Then she tossed the case back on the table and, without thinking, walked the length of the hall, through the archway. Automatically she turned into a corridor running behind the hall. It was like moving into a different world, for here all was light, elegance and colour.

Opening a door, again without conscious decision, Felicity found a large drawing room filled with sunlight pouring in through high sash windows. Outside a paved terrace was edged with white shrub roses, the old flags stained with lichens. Inside, the sun sat, glowing, on the grand piano, the pale, damask-covered chairs and sofas, the golden parquet floor on which was spread an Aubusson carpet, its once-brilliant colouring faded to exquisite softness. Two glittering chandeliers hung from the ornately plastered ceiling; on the walls were a quantity of oil and water colour paintings.

Felicity felt adrift in sensation; she was bemused by the richness of everything that she saw, confused by the contrasting periods of the house and bitterly, bitterly disappointed to find she remembered nothing. The sensations resolved themselves into anger. She looked around her at the polished antiques sitting in the strong sunlight then walked determinedly over to the windows and started pulling down blinds, transforming the room into an aqueous world that swam in a filtered, dreaming light.

'Miss Felicity, I didn't hear you arrive!'

A woman of around sixty had entered the room by another door, thin, angular body wrapped in a flowered overall, face tense. She came across and irritably twitched the cord of the last blind out of Felicity's hand. 'This is why I came in.' She lowered the blind then went round the others, adjusting their levels so that all were at the same height. Throughout the process she maintained a massive silence.

Felicity's helpless anger rose, fuelled by the way she had been made to feel both interfering and clumsy.

The woman finished her task, surveyed the blinds and approved their arrangement with a nod of her head. Finally she turned to Felicity. 'I'd no idea you'd arrived. I expected you to ring the bell.'

'I hadn't realized I needed permission to enter.' Felicity was startled by the quick rise of words to her lips. It was as though someone else had taken over and it hadn't been her speaking at all. What would the woman think? But she was too busy registering Felicity's appearance to take in what Felicity had said. The slanted green eyes widened and the face flinched involuntarily. Then her features quickly arranged themselves into a smooth mask.

'And how are you now, Miss Felicity?' The restraint was admirable but there was a crack of uncertainty in the voice.

'Much better, thank you, Mrs Parsons.' Felicity took control of her temper and felt unexpected gratitude to Belinda Gray for filling her in on the housekeeper's name.

Mrs Parsons swallowed hard. 'It was a terrible accident. We still find it difficult to realize that Miss Frances, that is to say, Mrs Sheldrake, and Mr Sheldrake of course, are gone.' Warmth now coloured the slow, Devon accent and there was a sense of strong emotion held in check. Then expression was bleached out of her voice again as she added, 'I've made up your old room, Miss Felicity. No doubt you'd like to go up and have a rest.' Even the way she stood impassively before Felicity managed to convey a sense of distance between them.

All feelings of anger vanished and an overwhelming tiredness threatened to swamp Felicity. It was as though the house had sucked out her frail strength.

'Where's your case?' Mrs Parsons asked briskly.

'It's in the porch but there's no need for you to bother with it.'

24

'No call for me; I should say there is.' As though finding relief in physical action, Mrs Parsons set off at a rapid pace towards the front door, Felicity following some way behind.

Mrs Parsons picked up the leather holdall that stood in the porch, then led the way upstairs. Here was yet another period, wide corridors and nicely chosen pieces of furniture suggesting Edwardian country house comfort.

The bedroom Felicity was shown to was at the back of the house, overlooking the terrace. Spacious and furnished with large pieces of dark, highly polished mahogany furniture, there was little to suggest it was a room she had frequently inhabited. It looked like a particularly comfortable guest room, tastefully furnished and equipped with everything a visitor might need: biscuit barrel, small bowl of fruit, selection of magazines, a couple of shiny dustwrapper-covered hardback novels.

Then Felicity noticed a small bookcase under the window. It contained a number of children's novels, all connected with horses and well thumbed, a children's encyclopaedia and a few classic travel books, Eric Newby, Paul Theroux, Bruce Chatwin, evidently as well read as the pony club novels. She took one out and flicked through the pages without registering either title or content. Then she stood transfixed as her attention was caught by the view from the window.

An informal garden swept from the rose-edged terrace down to the sea, adrift with summer flowers and shrubs, green leaves interspersing the tumbling blossoms. Roses were everywhere, shaggy shrubs in every shade, mingling with herbaceous plants in blues, pinks and creams. The beds strayed through close-clipped grass in a series of random forays before reaching a shrubby area that provided a barrier between the garden and the beach.

Felicity's head started buzzing; she could feel her grasp on consciousness slipping and groped her way towards one of the armchairs that stood in the room. Sitting down, she closed her eyes and leaned her head against the buttoned back.

'You all right, Miss Felicity?' Just for a moment there was a hint of genuine concern from Mrs Parsons.

Felicity felt tears prick at the back of her eyes and was annoyed at this sign of weakness. 'I'm fine, or will be after I've had a little rest.'

Mrs Parsons placed the holdall on a webbed case-carrier by the wardrobe. 'Do you want me to unpack your things?' The offer was perfunctorily made.

Felicity shook her head, unable to summon enough energy for more speech. Mrs Parsons drew the curtains, shutting out the sun, making the room cool and dim. Then she took off the bedcover and turned down a corner of the sheet. 'Lunch will be ready at one, in the morning room,' she said as she left.

Felicity removed her trousers and top, left them lying on the floor and crawled into bed. She had hoped for so much from Kingsleigh. It had not so much disappointed as confounded her.

Chapter Seven

Felicity slept right through lunch and woke in the mid-afternoon feeling lethargic, as though she'd undertaken some hectic activity and needed time to recover her strength.

Her mouth tasted sour, her body felt sticky. She dragged herself out of bed, opened her case and found her toiletries bag. There was a basin in the corner of the room and she carefully washed all the skin that hadn't been burned. She longed to be able to soak in a bath; she had no trouble in remembering the delicious sensation of warm water next to healthy skin.

Naked, she stood wondering what to put on. She picked up her discarded trousers and T-shirt, sweaty from the heat of her journey, and put them in the clothes basket that stood next to the basin. How long would it take for Mrs Parsons to wash and restore them to her? Dare she ask for them to be done as soon as possible? She thought of the implacable face the housekeeper could wear and her courage failed.

Felicity turned out the cream leather holdall the housekeeper had placed on the suitcase carrier. Belinda Gray had brought it to the hospital on her second visit. She said it had been in the wardrobe in Felicity's room and she'd packed it with the small collection of clothes also there.

Felicity stood fingering the heavy, strong leather, trying to establish some connection with the case. Had she carried it often? Where had it been with her? It looked large enough to carry a useful amount of gear yet not so large that it wouldn't qualify as cabin baggage. A useful item but it yielded no vibrations in her mind. Then she noticed there was a stud missing from its base.

It was under the webbed case-carrier. Felicity picked it up and screwed it back on, admiring the skill with which the base had been constructed so that it seemed one with the sides, and the comfortable feel of the handles. It was an expensive item, much more so than the clothes it had contained.

Felicity placed the case in the wardrobe then arranged the collection of gaily patterned leggings, shorts, T-shirts and bright tops on the shelves. Most would be too tight for her to be able to bear the feel of them on her scarred skin. Then she came across a dress.

It was made from a light and silky cream jersey. The material slipped down her body, slithering smoothly over the sore skin. Felicity looked at herself in the long oval mirror in the centre of the wardrobe. She had obviously lost weight, the dress was designed to display curves, not hang like a shroud, and the scars on her arms spoilt the sleeveless effect but the high round neck was flattering and the dark glasses added a note of mystery somehow that went with the dress. It would have to do.

The morning room Mrs Parsons had mentioned surely had to be at the east end of the house. Felicity went down the stairs and along the corridor past the vast drawing room and then opened the next door. This belonged to a much smaller, corner room with a french door on to the terrace and an east-facing window. No doubt in the mornings it was cheerful but now the sun had moved away, leaving the room unattractively dim. Nor was it furnished in the same lavish style as the drawing room; here the pieces were of lesser quality and well worn.

On a table beside the small sofa was a tray with a chicken salad and a small bowl of strawberries with a jug of cream, all neatly covered with cling film.

Felicity eyed the tray, found herself unable to summon up any appetite and moved round the room, trying to absorb its atmosphere, make it prod her memory.

On a small table set against the wall was a collection of photographs. A couple in their early sixties she decided must be her Aunt Jennifer and Uncle Thomas. She picked the shot up, studying it with interest. Jennifer Dashwood looked very county, collected and amused. Attractive, too; she'd kept her figure, her skin was clear and the eyes were still deep blue, though the blonde hair might have received some help. Felicity thought she looked as though she had a sense of humour and would have been sympathetic, someone she would have liked to spend time with, both as a child and after she'd grown up. Tom Dashwood had a gaunt and faded look but had clearly once been extremely handsome. His face was strong and the grey eyes looked as though they could still flash fire. A more tricky customer, though, than his wife, Felicity decided. That autocratic look probably meant an uncertain temper and a sense of his own importance to match his sister, Belinda Gray's.

Then she picked up another photograph of the same couple but in this one her aunt had aged considerably, weight had fallen off her bones, her face looked strained, as though she held her smile with difficulty. Her husband, though, hardly seemed to have changed at all. Felicity found her hand was trembling and replaced the picture quickly.

She passed over a couple of individual shots of girls on horses in favour of a shot of the two girls together, perhaps eight or ten years old. Surely herself and Fran when young. As Felicity picked it up eagerly, the telephone rang. She went across and lifted the receiver. 'Hello?' she said. 'Felicity Frear speaking.' She didn't know what made her identify herself in this way.

'Now you're back, I want what's mine,' said a cold, detached male voice, emotionless and menacing.

Felicity stood holding the photograph in one hand and the receiver in the other, the words reverberating in her ears, her breath sucked away as though by some tremendous force. 'I don't know what you mean,' she managed at last as the silence filled with threat and her legs began to tremble. 'Who is this?'

'You can fool others but don't try to fool me; you know exactly what I mean.'

'Please, who are you? What do you want?' she stuttered.

'That not-remembering act won't wash with me and don't delude yourself into thinking that what we once had together means anything now. If you stand in my way, there's nothing I won't do. The past is over and the future is mine. Think about it.' There was a click and Felicity was left with the mechanical buzz of the dialling tone assailing her ear.

She replaced the receiver, trembling, her sense of imminent danger back in full force.

She sank down on to the sofa, once again haunted by menace.

The most sinister aspect of the caller had been that his voice was at the same time familiar and yet unfamiliar. Memory slipped and slid, eluding her.

Who was he? What did he want? What was he going to do?

She felt as though she was in some nightmare, where nothing made sense but everything threatened. Except that she knew she wasn't going to wake up.

Wasn't there someone she could turn to for help?

She could think of no one.

She still held the photograph she had picked up before the telephone rang.

The two young girls looked so carefree. Both in shorts and shirts, each with an arm around the other's shoulder, each grinning at the camera with identical dark blue eyes, they seemed like sisters, so close, so happy together.

Chapter Eight

The snapshot meant nothing to Felicity. Her mind was totally occupied with the telephone call.

Again and again she heard the cold voice and was taunted by its teasing hint of familiarity. Again and again she asked herself who the caller could be, what he wanted and, above everything else, how he had known she had returned to Kingsleigh. The air hummed with unanswerable questions, invading the quiet room with its undistinguished furniture and faded floral linen covers.

Felicity went in search of Mrs Parsons, passing through a green baize door and along a corridor that wound into yet another period of the house, probably late nineteenth century.

The kitchen was huge with a curious appearance that Felicity finally identified as due to the fact it had no windows. An elaborate overhead skylight illuminated the room more than adequately and left all the walls available for the cupboards, large Aga stove, long dresser and deep sink with which it was equipped. Mrs Parsons stood at a scrubbed pine table in the centre, icing a chocolate cake, spreading the glossy frosting with an expertly wielded palette knife. There was no sign she'd noticed Felicity had come into the kitchen as she finished smoothing the sides of the cake. Then she put it on the cupboard behind her and started to clear the table. Only then did she say, 'Yes, Miss Felicity?' and her tone turned the words into an insult.

Felicity stood awkwardly, absorbing the way she was made to feel an interloper. Once again anger flared. Kingsleigh was her house, she was recovering from a dreadful accident, she deserved better treatment than this. She groped for something to say that would make Mrs Parsons realize her mistake.

But before she could utter the sharp words that rose to her lips she remembered that this woman had had her life turned upside down as well. The family she had served, probably for many years, had disappeared. Perhaps, like Belinda Gray, she disliked the new owner. Felicity swallowed hard, stepped forward, drew out a chair from the table and sat down. She placed her hands together on the wooden surface. 'I expect you find all this a little strange, Mrs Parsons?'

The strong hands wielding the dish cloth stopped wiping up stray bits of chocolate frosting. After a moment, 'As you say, Miss.' Mrs Parsons took the cloth over to the deep stainless steel sink that occupied the middle of one wall and started rinsing it.

'And the strangest thing of all, to me, is that I can't remember anything before the accident. Nothing of my life here, for instance, and I understand I spent a lot of time at Kingsleigh, with my cousin.'

Mrs Parsons brought the cleaned cloth back to the table and started forcefully finishing the job of cleaning its surface. 'Not so often the last few years,' she said, then compressed her lips together as though she was determined to say nothing she might later regret.

'I shall need you to help me, Mrs Parsons.'

Again the housekeeper's vigorous hands were arrested and she looked across the table at Felicity. 'Me, miss?'

'Of course! You know the house and the estate. You can help me find out what has to be done, how we are to go on. I hope my memory will come back soon.' Felicity's hands gripped themselves a little tighter. 'But until then I shall need a lot of assistance.'

Mrs Parsons continued to look at her in astonishment, as though she were an automaton whose motor had been cut. Then power was restored and she gave a last wipe to the table. 'I think you'll find we have our routine, miss, and that Mrs Gray has everything in hand.' She surveyed the pristine table as though some alien force might suddenly erupt from its surface and need subduing then looked across at Felicity. 'Would you like a cup of tea, miss?'

'Oh, that would be nice, Mrs Parsons. I'm afraid I haven't eaten your delicious-looking lunch. I don't seem to feel very hungry, but a cup of tea would be lovely.'

She had said the right thing.

'You'll soon be feeling better here. It's all too restless in hospitals, isn't it? Never leave you alone, do they?' Mrs Parsons bustled about, filling a kettle and putting it on the stove.

'Quite,' Felicity said. 'And I can see I'm going to be happy here. Everything looks so beautiful, so well cared for, and my room is so comfortable.'

Like a cat who has been stroked in just the right way Mrs Parsons relaxed, her shoulders settling themselves into a more natural position, the angular line of her neck easing. 'You let me know if there's anything you're missing or you need,' she said.

Had Mrs Parsons been won over as easily as that? Felicity

wondered as she plunged on to ask the question that was burning inside her brain, the question that had brought her to the kitchen. She tried to make it sound natural. 'How many people knew I was coming here today, Mrs Parsons?'

The housekeeper's shoulders drew back into their previous rigid posture and Felicity knew there was a long way to go before Mrs Parsons' attitude towards her truly softened. 'What do you mean?'

'Mrs Gray obviously let you know I was coming. I wondered how many other people had been informed,' Felicity said easily, her head beginning to ache with the effort needed to frame her questions in a way that wouldn't antagonize.

The teapot was warmed, tea added from a red and black tin canister, and the boiling water poured on before Mrs Parsons spoke again. 'I'm sure I wouldn't know, Miss Felicity.' The words were clipped into a thorny hedge against further enquiry. The pot was placed on a tray, a cup and saucer added together with a small plate bearing three fingers of home-made shortbread. 'You always took your tea without milk or sugar?' Mrs Parsons turned the statement into a question.

Felicity had been given milk in her tea at the hospital. She had drunk it with no particular pleasure but without question. Now the smoky aroma of Lapsang Souchong filled her nostrils and her wayward memory bank was yielding up a wonderful sensation of unadulterated kipperish flavour. She nodded at the housekeeper.

Mrs Parsons picked up the tray. 'I'll take it through to the morning room for you.'

Felicity looked round the comfortable kitchen where a cat snoozed on a patchwork cushion in front of the stove. Despite the heat of the sun outside, the room wasn't overly hot; perhaps the open side vents in the big skylight provided efficient ventilation. But it seemed she was not allowed to remain here. What had raised the shutters again? Was it just that Mrs Parsons had no intention of letting her routine be disrupted?

Chapter Nine

Over the next few days Felicity found that Mrs Parsons made routine a rule for life. Mornings saw the arrival of a series of different women whose help was enlisted to attack the dusting and polishing and other cleaning. Felicity quickly learned to have her breakfast in bed then go out walking, otherwise she was continually dogged by coolly polite enquiries as to whether the housework was getting in her way. Had she more energy, Felicity thought, she could have dealt with the housekeeper with a few crisp phrases and no doubt found a replacement had that proved necessary. But she had no appetite for battle at present. She needed to husband all her resources and build up her strength.

Later she would have to try to fill in her missing past. Now, though, was a waiting time, a time to allow her bruised and battered spirit as well as her body to relax. So Felicity pushed away all the awkward questions that teased at her, and took herself out for gradually lengthening walks.

Getting out of the house also meant she couldn't hear the telephone.

So far that cold voice hadn't called again. But it could only be a matter of time. Then the insistent question would be repeated and the voice would require an answer. Time and again Felicity found herself braced for the telephone's ring, her mind desperately considering various ways of dealing with the caller. Outside it was easier to pretend nothing was threatening her.

Like the house, the garden was a series of contrasts. On the west side was a formal garden bound by tall, clipped yews. Inside were tiny box tree hedges snaking in complex patterns through carefully raked gravel, edged by flagstoned paths with occasional stone seats in recessed arbours. The shade of the yew hedges made it a pleasant place to sit in the hot afternoons.

On the east side of Kingsleigh were more formal gardens that offered a series of rooms leading one into another, some walled in stone, others bound by thick hedges of box, holly, escallonia, berberis

33

and viburnum. In these protected, hidden rooms, plants were allowed to drift and ramble, covering walls, erupting from their beds to fall gracefully over lichen-covered flagstones. There were different colour schemes, an all-white garden, one in creams and apricots, another in silver and blues.

For the first few days Felicity didn't move far from the house and paused often to sit in the sun on one of the plentiful benches. Then, venturing a little further, she found an elderly gardener bent over one of the beds.

He straightened as she offered a greeting. 'Morning, Miss Felicity,' he said. 'Nice to see you around again. Right sorry I was about Miss Frances and Mr Sheldrake.'

Apologizing for not being able to remember him, Felicity asked for his name.

'Rules,' he said. 'I been here on the estate since I were fourteen, near fifty year ago. I were too young for the war, just as Mr Foster, him as was 'ead Gardener, were too old. But I learned everything from 'im I did.'

Fascinated, Felicity led him on to talk about Kingsleigh's past.

'It were a struggle when I first come 'ere, just with Mr Foster and me. And things weren't much better after the war. Old Mr Dashwood said there weren't money for more 'elp. Then 'e died and 'is son took over. All change it was then.' Rules grinned at Felicity, leaning on his hoe, the sleeves of his check shirt rolled up above his elbows, revealing corded veins standing out on wiry arms, his brown eyes, half hidden by bushy eyebrows, alight as he remembered. ''e said it were time to turn the clock back, 'ave the place as it were before the war. Waal, the main lawn 'ad been ploughed up for vegetables when we were all told we 'ad to dig for victory and it still 'adn't gone back. 'e said it were a disgrace and what did we need to do the job properly? So Mr Foster told 'im and there were an 'ole team of us. Mr Foster planned the beds with Mrs Dashwood and we got 'em planted. Ah, them were good days. When Mr Foster went, I were in charge and 'ad three lads under me.' He stood lost for a moment in his memories.

Felicity waited, content for him to carry on when he wanted, feeling relaxed in the warm sun, enjoying the increasing strength of her legs.

Then the bright brown eyes, alert as a small bird's, lost some of their sparkle. 'But when the master died things were in a right old pickle, even worse than after the war. Master Tom said as 'ow 'e could only afford me.' He gave a sad little shake to his head. 'Eh, 'e was in a state, Master Tom was. Seemed as though 'e'd be ground down by all 'is problems.' Rules suddenly looked up at Felicity with a sly little grin, 'Then 'e met your ma and 'er sister and everything got better.'

Felicity felt a prickle of anticipation run down her arms. 'You remember my mother?'

'Aargh, I'll say I do! Prettiest lady I ever seen. 'er sister, as became Mrs Thomas, was a looker but your ma beat 'er. First time the two of 'em came 'ere I said to myself, Master Tom's got 'isself a real beauty. But then it turned out to be your aunty as became Mrs Dashwood.' Gordon Rules gave a perplexed little shake to his head.

'And you must remember when I came here?'

Another sly little grin. 'Right little scrap you were! Led Miss Fran a turrible dance. That first summer she told me she 'oped you wouldn't be coming again.'

'She did?'

'Waaal, you were a better rider, see. Looked as though you'd been born on a 'orse. And you beat 'er on the tennis court. And Mr and Mrs Dashwood were all over 'emselves over you. It was Miss Flick this and Miss Flick that. Put 'er nose right out of joint.'

'Poor Fran!'

'Yers, well, then there were all that commotion over you not being able to go back to Spain after your first stay 'ere. Seems your ma and pa's 'oliday business 'ad failed and they was splitting up. Never seen a kiddie take on so, seemed the 'ole of your world 'ad come to an end. Waaal, Miss Fran, she took it right to 'eart and you was best of friends after that.'

For the first time Felicity had been given a glimpse of her past history. She saw a small girl, until then extrovert and competitive, suddenly bewildered and heartbroken at not being able to return to her home, trying to cope with the news that her parents were separating. And her cousin suddenly forgetting her jealousy and open heartedly comforting the forlorn child, forging bonds of friendship.

'Maybe soon I'll be able to remember it all. It seems so odd visiting here as if for the first time when everyone can remember me so well.' Felicity looked around at the cool white flowers backed with a myriad of greens, the effect soft and remote. 'This is a lovely garden, you must work very hard.'

Rules ducked his head and shuffled the hoe among the soil. 'It's 'ard, not 'aving much 'elp, as you might say. But I does me best and it's nice the 'ouse 'asn't 'ad to be sold, even though the family's at an end . . .' He broke off abruptly and jabbed harder at the earth, avoiding Felicity's gaze.

'I know I'm not a Dashwood but I do appreciate Kingsleigh and

I'll do what I can to keep things going the way they should,' said Felicity.

Rules gave her a considering stare. 'Aye,' he said at last. 'I expect we'll manage between us.'

Felicity walked on feeling heartened. The gardener had made her feel she was welcome. For the short while she had been talking to him, she had forgotten the antagonism shown by Belinda Gray and Mrs Parsons, forgotten the telephone call, had lost any sense of danger. Not only that, she'd found someone she could talk to about her past. Tomorrow she'd find Rules again and ask him about her life here with Fran.

She was watching television that evening in the little morning room that Mrs Parsons had made clear was where she was expected to spend her time, when the telephone rang.

Felicity switched off the set and sat listening to the ringing. If she didn't answer it, surely it would stop? She stared at the instrument, its insistent ring drilling through her ears. The sound stopped abruptly and her body relaxed. Then she told herself she had been ridiculous, it had probably been Belinda Gray, ringing to see how she was getting on. She had been foolish not to answer.

She made a wry face and picked up the television remote control but, before she could switch the set on again, the phone rang once more.

Felicity went steadily across the room and picked up the receiver. 'Felicity Frear,' she said and waited for the nicely judged tones of Mrs Gray.

'Well? Are you prepared to give me what is mine?'

It was the same voice. Felicity felt her stomach turn with fright and revulsion. 'I don't know who you are or what you want and if you keep on ringing me I shall inform the police,' she said and found it difficult to believe the cool, controlled tones she heard were hers.

'Will you?' Only two words but how much they said! How could the caller be so certain she wouldn't go to the police, so certain that he was almost laughing at her? What did he know about her?

'You'd better believe it,' she replied tersely and put the telephone down, feeling the strength drain out of her legs. It was a long time before she could drag herself up to bed and even longer before she fell into a restless sleep.

In the morning, heavy eyed, Felicity abandoned any thought of a relaxed convalescence. She had to stretch herself, force her limbs into strength. Her walks must be longer.

36

She decided to start her more intensive exercise programme by tracing a path over the lawn and through the herbaceous borders to the scrubby area that led to the beach.

Felicity quickly discovered just how unfit she still was. By the time she reached the large, sharp-edged grasses decorating the dunes, her legs felt like cotton wool. Panting, she sank down on to the hot, softly yielding sand and watched the Atlantic rollers crashing in small, violent barrels of water and surf, gradually reaching further and further up the smooth golden beach towards her.

After she got her breath back, she started to look around her.

The small cove was embraced by two arms of land. The arm to the south-east was low, covered with gorse and bracken, but that to the north-west was a cliff that fell in a rocky sweep to the beach. Felicity looked at the way the point of the cliff finally broke down from a sheer face into a series of individual rocks falling into the sea, the water surging in frothing foam as the rollers beat their way around them. What was round that point? Another beach?

A voice behind her, trembling with shock, said, 'Frances, Fran?'

Chapter Ten

Felicity swung round to find a woman in her sixties standing at the end of the path, her face as white as bleached sand.

Then she saw Felicity's dark glasses and maimed face and gave a gasp of relief. 'Flick, I'm so sorry, it's that dress and the way you were sitting there. For a moment I thought, so ridiculous. Mrs Parsons said you were in the garden. I looked everywhere.' Her voice sounded aggrieved, as though Felicity had deliberately hidden from her. 'I could hardly believe you were strong enough to get down here.'

Felicity mightn't be able to recognize the face but the voice was unmistakable. 'I'm sorry, Mrs Gray,' she said, then asked herself why she should be apologizing. Why hadn't the woman rung before calling? She made no effort to rise to her feet.

'That is Fran's dress, isn't it?' Again that belligerent tone.

Felicity looked down at the faded blue shift she was wearing. 'I'm so short of suitable clothes I borrowed it from her wardrobe.'

There had been nothing left of her own she could bear to wear and laundry day apparently hadn't come round, for though the dirty clothes had vanished from the basket by the basin, nothing had yet reappeared and Felicity hadn't wanted to jeopardize her fragile relationship with the housekeeper by asking for them to be washed. Returning to her room from the bathroom along the corridor that morning, she'd opened the door to what she instinctively knew was her cousin's bedroom.

It was larger than the one she was in, built over the centre of the drawing room below. Facing the window was a huge bed with polished chintz in a blue and pink ribbon pattern cascading down from a gilded corona, the draperies swagged over gold holders either side of the bed and matched by an elaborately quilted cover. The room was full of light and graceful furniture; it was feminine yet the simplicity of the décor made it a room a man could happily inhabit.

Felicity couldn't see any wardrobes but there was a door in each of the side walls. The first led into a very masculine dressing room. There were few ornaments but on a chest of drawers stood a photograph of a beautiful girl with blonde hair, dark blue eyes and a charmingly straight nose. Felicity could see the resemblance to the photograph of herself but she could never have been mistaken, even at her best, for this lovely girl. She was smiling at the photographer and Felicity would have placed a large bet that behind the camera had been her husband; there was so much love shining out of the eyes. She had shut the door carefully. On the other side of the bedroom she found a bathroom with a run of mirrored cupboards. In them hung a large collection of clothes. Fran obviously had had difficulty in discarding garments she was fond of.

Felicity had quickly selected some shift dresses that had obviously seen many years' wear plus a couple of loose jackets and a pair of wide trousers.

Mrs Parsons had come along the corridor just as Felicity emerged from the master bedroom. Her mouth had pursed in instant disapproval. 'Those are Miss Frances's, I mean Mrs Sheldrake's!' Distaste dripped from her voice.

'And I'm sure she wouldn't have minded my borrowing them until I can go shopping. I have nothing suitable to wear,' Felicity had said firmly. Once again she reminded herself that life for Mrs Parsons was also difficult and that she was suffering a loss that, until her memory returned, Felicity could only imagine.

'We shall have to decide at some stage what to do with my cousin's things,' she added.

There had been a suspicious sniff as the housekeeper went on her way without further comment.

Now Felicity looked at Belinda Gray, still standing at the end of the path. Suppressing an urge to invite her to sit down beside her, she staggered on to her feet. Mrs Gray made no move to help her.

'How kind of you to visit me,' Felicity said.

Her visitor looked as though she suspected sarcasm. 'I would have come earlier, only . . .'

'I know, your life is so busy.' Felicity regretted her remark as Belinda Gray flushed. 'I've been wondering,' she added quickly. 'Is there another beach on the other side of that rocky promontory?'

'Oh, no, there's no sand there, that's where the boathouse is.'

'Boathouse?' Felicity was conscious of a feeling of pleasure. 'With boats?'

Mrs Gray's mouth fell open, shock and consternation on her face. Then it was as if a door had closed. Without a word she swung round and headed for the house.

Felicity hurried after her. 'What did I say?' With an effort she caught up with her visitor and looked into her face. She was astonished to see there were tears in Belinda Gray's eyes and her mouth was working. She put a hand on her arm. 'Please, tell me!'

The woman gave an angry little shake to her head. 'It's nothing, just me being silly.' A brief sniff and she had recovered her poise. She removed her arm from Felicity's grasp and continued up the garden. 'What a lucky girl you are to have all this.' An expansive gesture indicated the house and its surroundings. 'You must find it difficult to realize your good fortune.'

They were nearly at the house now. Felicity grimly forced herself to act the hostess. 'Can I offer you some coffee, Mrs Gray?'

'Oh, not that stiff Mrs Gray, please, Flick. I was always Aunt Belinda to you.'

'Well, Belinda, then, how about a cup of coffee?'

There was the merest hint of a bristle, then, 'That would be very nice.'

Mrs Parsons appeared at the door that led from the morning room on to the terrace. 'You found her, then, Mrs Gray?'

'She did indeed,' Felicity said quickly. 'Could we have some coffee, please, Mrs Parsons? And how about some of that delicious-looking chocolate cake you made the other day?' she added, for once feeling hungry after her exercise.

Mrs Parsons flushed a deep red. 'It's in the freezer,' she said after a minute and met Felicity's gaze steadily.

'Pity,' said Felicity. 'Never mind, your shortbread is excellent.' She bit off a request for the cake to be defrosted in time for tea. 'We'll have the coffee out here.' She waved her visitor towards the white painted iron table and chairs that decorated the sunny terrace.

'There are cushions for these.' Belinda Gray flicked at the seat with a handkerchief before sitting down. 'Mrs Parsons will know where they are.'

'I'll make sure they're out before your next visit,' said Felicity, carefully lowering herself on to another of the chairs, feeling her legs tremble after the effort she had put them through. 'Tell me, who do you think Mrs Parsons is providing with chocolate cake?'

'What do you mean?'

'Oh, come on! That freezer bit didn't fool you, surely?'

'You always were too quick to judge people, Flick. Mrs Parsons is an excellent housekeeper. I'm sure Frances never found any fault with her accounts and everything while I have been looking after things has been in apple pie order.'

Not for a moment did Felicity believe Belinda Gray had taken more than the most cursory of glances at the Kingsleigh expenditure.

'I don't mind her baking the odd cake for whoever,' she said impatiently. 'No doubt I can afford it and she certainly works hard enough in the house; it's her clumsy attempt at deception that bugs me.'

There was a sigh. 'You never mind how you speak to people, do you, Flick? No wonder you make so many enemies.' An undercurrent of grim satisfaction ran through Belinda's voice, as though a long-held suspicion had been confirmed. Felicity took a closer look at the woman who had been only a voice to her before this morning.

Belinda Gray was tall and gaunt with a strong resemblance to the photographs of her brother in the morning room. But the craggy features that had been handsome in the man were less successful with his sister. Nor was the long, square-jawed face flattered by iron grey hair arranged in rigid waves. The bumpy nose was badly powdered and lipstick attempted to give the thin lips a more feminine shape but turned them instead into a clown's mouth. She wore a nicely cut sleeveless linen dress that unkindly displayed flabby upper arms.

Felicity reminded herself that this woman had to be the nearest thing she had left to a relation.

'Thank you for arranging everything so well,' she said. 'Did you have to tell many people I was coming back?'

'Many people? Really, Flick, what do you expect, a party?'

Felicity swallowed hard and abandoned the roundabout approach. 'I've had a couple of strange telephone calls. I don't know who they are from but it must be someone you told I was coming out of hospital.'

Belinda's pale grey eyes bulged slightly. 'I don't know what you're talking about. I told Mrs Parsons when you were arriving but I can't remember mentioning it to anyone else; you're hardly headline material, you know. And even if I had, they wouldn't have been making, what did you say, "strange telephone calls". You must have got it all wrong.'

Mrs Parsons appeared and placed the coffee tray on the table in front of Felicity.

'Do you know anything about odd people ringing, Mrs Parsons?' demanded Belinda Gray.

The housekeeper's face went blank. 'We don't get many calls,' she said briefly, bending over the tray, her eyes checking its contents.

'Who have you told about my coming out of hospital?' asked Felicity.

Mrs Parsons straightened herself, her expression one of injured injustice. 'I expect I mentioned it to Rules and probably Johnny.'

'Johnny?' Felicity's voice was sharp.

She caught a brief exchange of glances between Belinda and Mrs Parsons.

'Johnny helps Rules in the garden,' Belinda cut in quickly.

The youth on the motorcycle, decided Felicity before remembering that the gardener had claimed he had very little help.

'I don't know who else would know,' Mrs Parsons continued. 'Will that be all, Miss Felicity?'

'Yes, thank you, Mrs Parsons.'

'Well, Flick, how are you!' asked Belinda after she'd been handed her coffee.

'Much better, thank you.'

'You don't look it.'

Felicity thought Belinda Gray's tactlessness had to rival anything she could produce herself.

'I feel much stronger inside, outside no doubt still looks pretty dire. Do you live far away?' There followed a long description of Mrs Gray's period house some twenty minutes' drive to the north of Kingsleigh.

'Nothing of course compared with Kingsleigh! But pure Queen Anne. This is such a jumble of periods. You've no doubt noticed the medieval hall; that was built by the first Dashwood. It was considerably added to in Elizabethan times, then the house doubled its size in the eighteenth century. The kitchen wing was added in the Victorian age. And there are all sorts of other bits and pieces, it's an architect's nightmare. But so much history!'

Even if she had wanted to, Felicity would have found it difficult to stop Belinda Gray's flow.

'It's hard to believe now but for a long period the Dashwoods were Catholics, kept the faith and wouldn't recant even when faced with burning at the stake. They had mass said regularly throughout the recusant period. Then a seafaring Dashwood married a wealthy Protestant in the middle of the eighteenth century and decided to convert. We've been Protestant ever since.'

Belinda Gray was happily involved with her story. 'But somewhere there's supposed to be a priest's hole. Tom and I spent for ever trying to find it when we were children and you and Fran had a go.' For the first time real warmth came through as Belinda smiled at Felicity. 'It was one Christmas holiday. You scoured the library for possible mentions and then tapped away at all the panelling.'

'Did we succeed?' Felicity found she had been caught up in the description of what sounded like a fun treasure hunt.

Belinda shook her head. 'No more than Tom and I did! There was a lot of teasing; you had been so convinced you were so much cleverer than anyone else!'

'How disappointing!'

'Particularly for you.' Oh, the satisfaction in that voice! 'Not that it seemed to dent your confidence; nothing seemed to get through your thick hide. You never showed proper gratitude for your life at Kingsleigh.'

Gratitude? If her mother had really lost all her money, as Rules had suggested, Flick would have been a poor relation, staying here as a charitable venture. No wonder she had been a prickly child. Felicity was sure she couldn't really have been as insensitive as Belinda seemed to think.

'Most unlikely it ever existed,' Belinda continued briskly. 'A nice legend, that's all. Anyway, even if it had, it wouldn't have survived all the rebuilding over the years.' Belinda looked towards the house. 'Kingsleigh's seen so much drama. There was a Lady Dashwood who suffered a terrifying interrogation at the time of the Civil War, while her husband was away fighting. For the king of course.'

'Why "of course"?'

Belinda's eyes bulged once again then she gave a short bark of laughter. 'Just like you, Flick, always the rebel.' She finished her coffee and Felicity offered a refill.

'I was talking to Rules yesterday and he mentioned my mother and my aunt's first visit to Kingsleigh.'

'Did he indeed? I always said very little passed that man by.'

'When would that have been?'

'Ah, let's see, it must have been well over twenty-seven years ago. Fran would have been twenty-six next week.'

'He said how pretty my mother was.'

'Huh! That was before she started drinking too much and indulging in, well, other things. She really let herself go after she divorced your father. But, yes, in those days, she was remarkably attractive. So was your aunt, and her personality was so much warmer than your mother's. It was no wonder . . .' Belinda broke off and drank from her refilled cup.

'No wonder my uncle turned his attentions away from my mother to her? Is that what you were going to say?'

'What has that wretched man been saying? As if he knew anything about it anyway.' Belinda wiped delicately at her mouth. She looked at Felicity then capitulated. 'I suppose Tom was first drawn to Sarah, your mother. It wouldn't have done, though, she was far too volatile for him. She always seemed to think, though, that she'd had a chance with him.' Felicity pictured a livelier, prettier version of the photo-graph she'd seen of Jennifer Dashwood. What had her mother really been like? And had she really fallen for Tom Dashwood?

From nowhere, into the back of Felicity's mind, came a peevish voice saying, 'Jennifer stole Tom from me, Kingsleigh should have been mine.' Imagination or memory?

Felicity told herself she'd think about that later. 'And your brother, Tom Dashwood, what was he like?'

Belinda smiled. 'Such an attractive and caring man. All the local girls were after him and it wasn't just because of Kingsleigh and the Dashwood name. But after he met the Powell sisters, they hadn't a chance.'

Felicity had a quick unpleasant vision of two beautiful sisters fighting for a young, well-heeled landowner.

'Did you know my father?' she asked abruptly.

'Alexander?' Belinda pulled a disapproving face. 'Yes, I met him a few times.'

'And?'

'I'm sorry to say I thought he was common, an adventurer. Always after the girls and no respect for anyone. I know Tom and Jennifer blamed him for the break-up of the marriage. Your mother met him in Kenya. She ran some sort of ranch there, I think she raised race horses.' She gave a derisive snort. 'I'm sure he was fortune hunting but his luck was out. Shortly after you were born the ranch went bust and next thing we heard was they were running that riding and tennis holiday place in the south of Spain.'

Which, according to Rules, had gone bust as well, leaving Sarah with nothing. While Jennifer had been queening it at Kingsleigh with the man who had first been attracted to her sister. It sounded to Felicity as though her mother had had a raw deal out of life.

'He was attractive, though, I suppose, if you like those obvious, film star sort of looks. Like Alan Ladd, if you can remember him, only taller. Looked his best on a horse or a tennis court.' It sounded as though, despite her earlier scathing words, Belinda Gray had actually been attracted to Alexander Frear. For a moment Felicity thought there'd been a flash of some old fire in her cold, pale eyes.

'Anyway.' Belinda put her cup down. 'I can't stay here gossiping, I've promised to sort out jumble for the Conservatives. I just dropped in on my way.' She helped herself to another piece of shortbread as she rose.

Felicity went with her to the front door and watched the ancient Rover drive up the hill. As it passed out of sight, Belinda Gray's distraught face as she'd asked about the boathouse came back to her. What was there about the place to make her so upset?

Chapter Eleven

As she passed back through the hall, Felicity saw the housekeeper was polishing the central table.

'Is the boathouse kept locked, Mrs Parsons?'

The woman looked curiously at her. 'I believe it is, miss. There's a key on the board outside the kitchen. But it's a fair step, all down the cliff,' she warned. For a moment it seemed as though she'd say something else, something that would put Felicity off any intended visit, then she gave a shrug of her shoulders and returned to her polishing.

Felicity looked at the items that had been cleared off the table. 'Don't you think we could return the secateurs and gardening gloves to wherever they're kept, Mrs Parsons?'

'But Miss Frances, I mean Mrs Sheldrake, left them there when she went to meet you at the station!'

Just like Queen Victoria, keeping Albert's bedroom unchanged after he died. No wonder the housekeeper was finding it difficult to accept Felicity as mistress of the house. Again Felicity found hasty words rising to her lips and managed to swallow them. 'I think it would be best to put them away,' she said, her tone gentle but firm.

She didn't wait for a reaction but went through the baize door towards the kitchen.

Amongst various keys hanging on the board was one with 'Boathouse' marked on its little ivory tag.

Felicity slipped it into her pocket and set off.

She took the path through the yew-hedged garden since this seemed to lead in the right direction. After emerging from the formal garden, it led behind the stables. Felicity had visited them the previous day. She had stood on the cobbled yard and looked at the names above the doors: Ninja, Prince, Paloma, El Cid, Jenny. Everything about the stables looked neat and well cared for; only the horses were missing. Felicity had sniffed the air and realized she missed the dusty, warm smell of horse sweat and was certain not only that she herself was an experienced rider but that horses had been here until very recently. Where had they gone? She couldn't see any in the fields around the house.

Felicity followed the well-worn path through a small pine wood. As she went, she puzzled over the way she kept snatching back angry words. Was she really so easily irritated? So quick to defend her ground as though she wasn't really sure of it? Things Belinda Gray had said, and something about Mrs Parsons' surprise when Felicity managed to change her approach to something more conciliatory, suggested she was.

Was it the accident that had removed a layer of skin, not just from areas of her body but also from her mind, so that she felt the reactions of others more strongly? As if the wind had blown away a layer of clothing and she shivered easily?

Under the trees it was indeed cool and dark. Felicity hurried her steps, eager to regain the sun. Too much in her world was unsettling at present and she couldn't enjoy the spring of the needle-layered ground beneath her feet or the scent of resin that filled the air.

Then she was out of the trees and standing at the top of a cliff looking down into a perfect natural harbour.

The bay was much larger than the bathing cove and the water came right up to the cliff. Part of the rocky face was almost sheer but just below where Felicity was standing it sloped less steeply and steps had been cut into the cliff. They led down to a natural rock platform. Here a boathouse and small jetty had been built.

Without considering the effort that was going to be needed, Felicity started down the stone staircase. Because the bay faced north, no sun warmed the cliff or the water. Felicity carefully negotiated the steps and wished she had worn a jersey. By the time she reached the boathouse, only the heat in her scars was keeping her warm.

The key turned easily in the Yale lock and the door swung open without a sound.

Felicity entered a large, airy room that appeared to have been designed both as a recreation area and somewhere to store equipment. Old rattan chairs and a sofa, their cushions covered in faded blue and yellow striped canvas, were arranged round a low table that held yachting magazines, a large glass ashtray with a yacht etched on its base and a pair of binoculars. Rag rugs decorated the varnished wood floor. Beside the door was a divan with deep cushions. A galley kitchen behind a counter was arranged along one wall with shelves of blue and yellow patterned china and glasses sporting signal flags arranged on shelves; high stools ran along the room side of the counter. Flanking the window opposite the kitchen area were ceiling-high cupboards, their doors covered with gaily coloured posters displaying knots, more signal flags and other marine lore. At the back of the room was a run of deep bins with sloping lips that looked as though they held such things as sails, ropes and other yachting impedimenta. Beside them was another door.

The room had a well-used air. Felicity sank into one of the rattan chairs, grateful for the chance to rest her legs, and looked around. The air in the room seemed fresh, not stale as it should have done if the boathouse hadn't been used since the car crash. The table with the magazines and ashtray was spotless, no dust anywhere. Did Mrs Parsons struggle down the steps to clean? Was that why she didn't want Felicity interfering down here? Or had she really been concerned that the way down might be too much for her?

Felicity looked at the door at the end of the room and struggled to her feet.

It opened into the boathouse itself, on to a small balcony with stairs that led down to a boardwalk edging three sides of the water. The end of the boathouse was open but there was little light inside. The ribbed roof soared above the dark water just as the hammerbeams of Kingsleigh's medieval hall soared above the flagstones. Felicity clutched at the balcony rail, for a moment disoriented.

Below, floating on the pitch-black waters, was a yacht, forlorn in a space that could have held several craft. There was light enough to see its name on the transom, *Seabreeze*. Its main mast was naked of sails, the cabin hatch securely closed.

Just as standing in the stables had convinced Felicity she was an experienced rider, now she was certain she had often been sailing and knew how to handle a boat. She looked at the yacht. Surely she and her cousin must have taken that out. She saw it bouncing over a sparkling sea, felt the bucking motion as the yacht lifted and fell over the waves. The dark red mainsail and jib were taut with wind, one girl was at the tiller, the other straining at the mainsheet, two pairs of dark blue eyes were screwed tight against the spray that flung itself over the deck into their faces.

With a small gasp Felicity spun round against the balcony rail. Had that been a memory, a tiny window into her past? She clutched at her arms; the shivers that were snaking up and down her body had nothing to do with the chill of the air in the boathouse.

She ran back into the living room and flung herself on the rattan chair again. She held herself closely, hunched forward, eyes closed, mind in ferment.

After a few moments her trembling gradually quietened and she lay back in the chair. Reality retreated.

She saw herself standing in this room with a man. He was taller than she and golden. Cropped hair glistened with life, golden lashes framed light blue eyes that held the sun in their depths, tanned skin was emphasized by the white creases that rayed out from his eyes; he was smiling with magnetic force. 'Don't you see, my darling, what this place can mean to us? It can give us everything.'

She was still standing there, her eyes fixed on his, and Felicity could feel the conflicting emotions that were running through her; how she yearned to reach out to him, be clasped to that warm body, respond to the urgency in his voice, in his eyes, in his pulsing life force. At the same time she felt the denial that fought with desire.

'Flick, darling, it's so simple!'

Oh, the power that radiated out from him. Surely it was impossible to resist anything that he demanded?

Then Fran rushed in, laughingly cross they hadn't got the sails for the boat ready.

Felicity shuddered as the scene shattered and she woke as though from a dream, wanting to recapture all the action and finding it was like water slipping through one's fingers. The images slithered from her and she retained nothing but an aching sense of loss.

There came again the picture she had had of *Seabreeze* and its red sails. Had that been just a fantasy? Could it have been a genuine memory?

Felicity looked at the run of lockers along the wall with their sloping lids. If she checked inside, would she find a pair of red sails?

Slowly she levered herself out of the chair and walked over, drawn by a dreadful fascination, both wanting to find the sails and yet half afraid to.

She lifted the hasp on the first of the lids and pulled it up. Only coils of rope and a couple of large flashlights. She went on to the next lid and lifted that. Heavy folds of white nylon sail. She struggled to burrow down, manipulating the stiff material, trying to see if underneath there wasn't a red version. She decided there wasn't and went on to lift up the lid of the third locker.

It crashed back from a suddenly nerveless hand.

Felicity stood gazing at it for a timeless moment, unable to scream, unable to believe what she had seen. Slowly she removed her dark glasses, her eyes flinching at the new brightness of the room. Her heart in her mouth, her teeth clenched tight, her lips forming a thin line of resolution, she slowly lifted the lid again.

She had not been mistaken. Stuffed inside the container was a body, corduroy-clad knees forced to chin, grizzled head skewed to one side, sightless bird-brown eyes staring resentfully up at her. It was Rules, the gardener.

48

Chapter Twelve

Horror filled Felicity's mind. It was impossible to act, impossible to think. She seemed doomed to stand here for eternity, staring at a product of hell. But her strength would not hold out that long.

Very slowly, her arm trembling, Felicity lowered the lid of the makeshift coffin. Then she dashed out of the boathouse. Supporting herself with a trembling hand pressed against the wall, she stood retching up scalding-hot bile. Even after there was nothing left to bring up, her stomach continued to heave convulsively. She leaned her forehead, streaked with sweat, against the cool side of the boathouse and made her mind a blank.

Gradually the upheaval in her body settled. Felicity dragged the back of her hand across her mouth and staggered on unsteady legs round the side of the boathouse and stared blindly at the water. Rules the gardener was dead and his body hadn't stuffed itself into that sailing locker.

Her mind refused to get beyond that fact and gradually the foul taste in her mouth overtook all thought. She looked around her. There were no pools of water and the surface of the sea was out of reach below the rocky platform on which she stood. She had no option but to go back into the boathouse.

Keeping her mind a blank, automatically skirting the pool of vomit, Felicity once again entered the recreation room. Refusing to glance towards the locker end, she made her way to the kitchen area and ran the tap of the small sink. She rinsed out her rank mouth, relishing the clean water, and splashed her clammy face. Then the flow faltered and gave out and she could no longer ignore the shaking of her body.

Beside the china and glasses stood a small selection of drinks.

The brandy bottle rattled against the edge of the glass as Felicity tried to pour herself a slug. The fiery spirit burned its way down her throat; she spluttered and coughed then felt warmth spreading through her veins. She leaned against the counter, closed her eyes and waited. When no more than the odd tremble ran through her, she opened her eyes again and realized she was no longer wearing her dark glasses. She had dropped them while she had been looking at Rules's body. It was impossible even to think of retrieving them.

Felicity drank some more of the brandy then set the half-empty glass on the counter. Wait any longer and she wouldn't be able to put one leg in front of the other, let alone start assailing the climb up the cliff that now loomed as terrifying as the north face of the Eiger. Wait any longer and she'd go mad knowing she was in the same room as that poor dead man.

Wait any longer and a murderer could be back to dispose of the body.

To Felicity it seemed she took years to haul herself up the steep steps. Her little strength quickly drained away and left her collapsed on the cold stone. She sat huddled against the cliff, trying to summon up the will power to mount a few more steps, then collapsed once again and rested her cheek against the rock, drawing new impetus from its inert strength. Finally she resorted to crawling, dragging herself up on hands and knees, the rough surface tearing at the scars on her legs, her face streaked with dust where she had wiped away the tears of exhaustion that threatened to blind her eyes.

Then, at last, Felicity reached the top. With a final heave she pulled her body on to the turf, into the sunlight. She lay for several more years bent in a prenatal curl, warmth slowly penetrating her chilled body, her damaged scars screaming with pain.

Eventually she got herself upright and staggered through the stretch of pines towards the house. From somewhere she picked up a dead branch to act as a stick. Then came the path behind the stables. Her breath coming in great, gasping pants, the blood pounding in her head, Felicity collapsed on to a stone seat just inside the yew-hedged garden.

Another period of eternity passed before she summoned up a last surge of energy and lurched into the morning room, her mind fogged with pain, her ears deafened by the rasp of her breath. For the first time since she'd arrived at Kingsleigh, she would have given anything for Mrs Parsons to appear.

The room remained empty. Felicity told herself it didn't matter what she felt like, she couldn't wait until the housekeeper found her.

She reached the phone and dialled 999.

She never knew whether she managed to give more than her name and address to the operator before she lost consciousness. Nor did she know how long it was before she was aware of Mrs Parsons standing before her, deep shock written clear on her face.

'Miss Felicity! Whatever's happened?'

'Rules, he's dead!' It came out as strangled gasps and Mrs Parsons stared at her as though unable to understand what she was saying. 'In the boathouse, in . . .' but she couldn't say more and once again darkness claimed her.

All was confusion after that.

In brief intervals of sensibility, Felicity understood the police had arrived, that she had been tucked up on the sofa, that a doctor was examining her.

'No hospital,' she rasped. 'Stay here!'

He soothed her, said all she needed was her broken scars dressing and to rest.

She heard him refusing to let her be interviewed.

'Surely you can see it's most important we talk to her as soon as possible?'

The speaker was behind her and Felicity was glad she couldn't see who owned that impersonal, chilly voice.

'And surely you can see she's in no state to talk to anyone at the moment? I'm taking her upstairs and administering a sedative. Mrs Parsons, will you help me, please?'

Felicity was gently raised to her feet, one arm placed round the doctor's shoulders, one round Mrs Parsons'. Automatically her feet took step after step, across the room, through the hall, up the stairs and into her room. Her dress was removed, then she was helped between the sheets of her bed, their cool lightness immensely comforting, and a syringe was stuck in her arm.

Just before she sank once again into darkness, she heard the doctor say, 'Is there to be no end to the tragedies surrounding this place, Mrs Parsons?'

A panic attack came in the middle of the night. As in hospital, Felicity awoke with her arms hitting out at an unknown assailant and fear sending adrenalin surging through her. Once awake, she lay with her heart racing, telling herself she was at Kingsleigh, safe.

But Rules's accusing eyes rose before her and she saw once again his contorted body. Again she heard the cruel voice on the telephone demanding what was his. There was no peace for her in this house and no safety either.

Her mouth was dry; switching on the light, she found a glass filled with liquid beside her bed and drank. A few moments later she was sinking again into sleep.

When next she awoke, daylight could be seen through the drawn curtains. For a moment Felicity felt disoriented, her eyes heavy with sleep. She couldn't work out where she was, then yesterday's events came flooding back and depression bore down on her like a tangible force.

Why had Rules been murdered? And who had killed him?

The questions were useless. Felicity sat up gingerly, eased her bandaged legs out of the bed and stood. She was stiff and very sore but her body seemed to be in reasonable working order. The hospital was going to be pleased with her when she went for her check-up next week. She slipped into a négligé and opened her door.

Outside stood a policewoman.

Felicity immediately closed the door again and stood leaning against it in a state of shock.

After a moment, she slowly opened the door once more. The policewoman smiled and gave a brief nod. 'Are you feeling any better?' she asked.

'Why are you here? Am I a prisoner?'

'I'm just making sure you're OK,' the WPC replied, her voice determinedly cheerful. 'Are you wanting the bathroom?'

Felicity flinched from the woman's curious gaze; without her dark glasses she felt naked. She wrapped her négligé round herself more tightly and walked off without answering. The policewoman followed. At least, thought Felicity, she stayed outside the bathroom.

After she emerged, the woman said, 'Chief Inspector Combe would like to interview you as soon as you feel strong enough.'

'I'll have my breakfast first,' Felicity said tightly. 'Perhaps you can tell Mrs Parsons I'm awake.'

She left the officer talking into a small radio and returned to bed.

Breakfast arrived shortly afterwards, Mrs Parsons carefully placing the tray on Felicity's knees.

'I hope you're feeling better, Miss Felicity.' Her tone was more sympathetic than usual but the swift jerks she used to draw back the curtains and let in another bright day said life was trying.

'I'm much better, thank you, Mrs Parsons.' Felicity blinked as the light hurt her eyes. She looked down at the tray. 'Scrambled eggs!'

'You had nothing to eat yesterday. I thought you'd probably be hungry.' Mrs Parsons sounded almost apologetic.

'I am!' Felicity said in surprise. 'It all looks delicious.' She shielded her eyes as she looked at the housekeeper and added, 'I don't suppose you could find me another pair of dark glasses, could you, Mrs Parsons? I've lost mine and the sun is so bright.'

'Of course, miss, I'll be right back. You get started on your eggs.'

It wasn't long before the housekeeper returned with an even larger pair of glasses than the ones Felicity had dropped in the boathouse. 'They belonged to Miss Frances, I mean, Mrs Sheldrake.' Was Mrs

Parsons's repeated inability to call her previous mistress by her married name a reflection on Mark Sheldrake? Or merely a habit that was hard to break?

Felicity slipped the glasses on, grateful for the dimming of the light. 'Thank you. Tell me,' she asked. 'Was Rules married? Has he any family?'

'No, miss. He had a wife once but she died and there weren't any children.'

'I'm so sorry about his death. We had such a nice conversation the other day.'

Mrs Parson's face worked. 'He was a lovely man,' she said. 'It's terrible him being killed like that.' For once there was nothing guarded about her tone. Eyes bright with unshed tears, she added, 'And I'm sorry it was you had to find him, miss.'

'I gather the police are waiting to interview me?'

'They talked to me yesterday, and Johnny, and I had to give them a list of everyone who comes in to work here. I don't know what people are going to think!'

'We have to help in any way we can, Mrs Parsons,' Felicity said. The words sounded hollow.

'I suppose so.' The housekeeper's voice was troubled and for a moment Felicity thought she was going to say something else. Then she left the room, closing the door decisively.

Felicity ate her breakfast slowly trying not to think about the coming interview. She washed and dressed equally slowly, choosing the long cream dress as the most formal she had available. Somehow she couldn't bring herself to raid her cousin's wardrobe for this event. Once dressed she stood in front of the mirror and tried to assess what the police would see.

Her hair had grown to the point where it almost curled instead of frizzing and was beginning to soften the effect of her facial scars. An outline of a nose was beginning to emerge from the swollen mess in the middle of her face and the bruising had faded. The sleeveless dress revealed livid scars down her arms and on the backs of the stiff fingers. Even with the dark glasses back in place, Felicity considered she looked repellent, particularly if you didn't know her present appearance was an improvement on her looks when she first arrived at Kingsleigh. Would her face be an asset or a hindrance in the ordeal that lay ahead?

She adjusted the set of the dark glasses and went out of the bedroom. 'Shall we go?' she said to her guardian.

Chapter Thirteen

The police had settled themselves in the library.

It was a large room in the north-west corner of Kingsleigh that the sun never reached. Despite the long sash windows arranged in a deep bay, the room was dark. The rows of leather spines with their gilded lettering gleamed dully along the polished shelving, their sombre erudition interspersed with more colourful modern editions and the occasional glossy dust jacket. The ceiling was covered in ornate plasterwork and in the middle of one wall was a heavy stone fireplace decorated with the Dashwood coat of arms. Despite its impressive appearance, though, it was a comfortable room. A large desk, obviously much used, sat in the window. Its rich green leather top was covered in books and papers, including several neatly folded sailing charts. Beside it stood an antique globe of the world. At the other end of the library were two solid-looking chairs covered in dark red leather and equipped with their own reading lamps. A long table with three more lamps down its centre stood in the middle of the room.

It was at this table, all the lamps on, that Chief Inspector Combe sat waiting for Felicity.

As she entered, followed by her faithful attendant, he rose; a bulky man wearing a badly cut lightweight suit, he had a patient, closed face.

'Morning, Miss Frear, please be seated.' He indicated a chair arranged on the opposite side of the table from his.

His voice was no warmer than when she had heard it the previous day, asking why he couldn't question her immediately.

'I'm Chief Inspector Combe. This is Detective Sergeant Haskins.' He introduced a younger, bullet-headed man sitting at one end of the table, wearing a short-sleeved shirt and jeans, a notebook in front of him.

Felicity sat down, arranged her hands in her lap and waited for what was to come.

'Thank you, constable. Can you please arrange for some coffee?'

The WPC smiled, nodded and left the room. Felicity wished he had asked what she was called. It was better to know the names of your enemies.

The police her enemies? What an extraordinary thought! Felicity snapped her attention back to Chief Inspector Combe and Detective Sergeant Haskins.

'Chief Inspector,' she broke in before he could get started. 'I would like to know why I am being kept prisoner in my house.' For the first time she claimed Kingsleigh with all its magnificence as hers. Yet, familiar though its aura might be, she felt a guest here rather than its mistress.

'Your house?' he repeated slowly. 'Yes, I understand it is indeed your house – now. You inherited it from your cousin, after she and her husband died in a car crash, didn't you?' His measured tones managed to surround the fact with sinister overtones.

'A crash in which I nearly lost my life,' Felicity said sharply. She raised a hand and adjusted the set of her glasses, drawing attention to the physical evidence of her suffering.

'Quite.' For an instant the chief inspector's glance fell and he shuffled a set of papers resting on the table before him.

'Then why, when, as a responsible citizen, I report a crime, am I treated as a criminal?'

'Hardly that,' he said smoothly, raising his gaze to meet hers again. 'WPC Bennett has merely been making sure you come to no harm. We do, after all, have a murderer on the loose.' His gaze hardened. 'Interesting you should assume differently.'

Felicity clasped her hands together under the table and bit back hot words of protest.

'Now, for the record, Miss Frear, may I ask if you feel well enough to be questioned? You wouldn't prefer to see the doctor first?'

'Thank you, I feel quite well enough,' she said steadily.

'Well, then, please tell us exactly how you found Mr Rules's body yesterday, starting with your decision to visit the boathouse.' He made it sound as though her little exploration was as bizarre as a trip to the North Pole.

Speaking quietly but clearly, Felicity gave a matter-of-fact account of her morning, finishing with the lifting of the bin lid. Towards the end of her recital, the coffee arrived. Only then did she realize that she had omitted any mention of the threatening telephone calls.

The sergeant busied himself with pouring out. She sipped at the cup he handed her and wondered whether telling the police would help the investigation or make the chief inspector even more suspicious of her behaviour. The brief, chilling phrases spoken by that voice on the phone were etched into her brain but when she considered repeating them to these sceptical ears, they couldn't help but sound ridiculous. Maybe, after this killing, with the police all around the place, the calls would stop.

The decision not to mention them had been made.

Felicity finished the coffee and hoped that the worst part of her interview was over. She looked across at the chief inspector. 'How, please, did he die?'

'Gordon Rules?' Combe looked straight at her. 'He was hit on the head with a winch handle, which was found underneath the body. At the moment we have found no evidence to show where the attack took place. Somewhere there must be bloodstains; his scalp seems to have bled profusely. The murderer would undoubtedly have had stained clothes.' He paused, then added, 'The dress you wore yesterday has been taken for analysis.'

Felicity stared at him. 'You can't think I killed him?'

His gaze never faltered. 'We have to consider every possibility.'

'Apart from anything else, I wouldn't have had the strength. I'm only just out of hospital.'

'You were strong enough to get down to the boathouse and to climb up again.'

'I only just made it!'

'Showing you'd been put to unusual exertion.'

Felicity went cold. It was ridiculous; he couldn't think she was capable of murdering a man and stuffing his body in that locker then climbing back up to sound the alarm, could he?

'When did Rules die?'

The chief inspector picked up a pencil and started drawing an elaborate set of inter-connecting boxes. 'We won't know for certain until after the post-mortem but preliminary examination suggests an elapsed period of some sixteen hours.'

It took Felicity a moment or two to work this out. 'You mean he died the day before yesterday, in the late evening?'

He nodded.

'So he'd already been dead some considerable time when I found him?'

'Only one set of identifiable fingerprints have been found in the boathouse. I need to take yours for comparison purposes but I think we are pretty safe in assuming for the moment that they do, in fact, belong to you.' He paused and looked straight at her. 'Your fingerprints, Miss Frear, are in a remarkable number of places if all you say you did was to enter, sit in a chair, go through to the boathouse then lift a couple of locker lids.'

Felicity closed her eyes behind her dark glasses. She remembered with pitiless clarity all her actions after discovering the body. Stumbling a little, she detailed them to the chief inspector.

'Never heard about the inadvisability of disturbing the scene of a crime, Miss Frear?' he asked when she'd finished.

Anger rose swiftly in her. 'I'm not trained in detection and I was in no state to consider whether I might be destroying evidence,' she retorted. Then she thought for a moment and added, 'I didn't wash away any bloodstains, if that's what you're worrying about. There weren't any there, I'm pretty sure of that. I studied the room quite closely.'

'And why would you have done that?'

'I was interested. As I told you, I've lost my memory. This is a place I practically grew up in; there's just a chance something here could jog my memory back into place.'

'Oh, yes, Miss Frear, we know of your connection with Kingsleigh,' Combe said quietly, 'and of your claim to a lost memory.'

'It's more than a claim, it's a fact!' Felicity found herself almost incoherent with rage. If only he knew how desperate she was to regain her past!

'Well,' the chief inspector continued smoothly. 'Let's see how good the memory you have at the moment is, shall we?'

It appeared that her ordeal had only just begun. The chief inspector and his sergeant proceeded to conduct a remorseless examination of her account of finding Rules's body. Again and again they made her describe the events of the morning, exactly how the room had looked, why she had gone down to the boathouse, why she had opened the locker. Whether she had seen anyone in the vicinity of the boathouse before yesterday. Whether she knew of anyone who could have had reason to kill the gardener.

As time wore on and the questioning continued, Felicity became deathly tired. She fought against tears as detail after detail was challenged and she was repeatedly asked for information referring to the time before her accident.

'Why can't you accept that I've lost my memory?' she pleaded at last. 'I've told you again and again that I can't remember anything that happened before my accident.'

The chief inspector looked at her, his eyes very cold and very steady. He got up and walked across to the desk in the window. After a moment standing with his back to her, he picked up the little pile of neatly folded charts and returned to the table, placing them in front of him.

'Nothing, Miss Frear?'

'No! I can't even remember who I am!'

'Nor how your father died?'

The room started to spin before her eyes. Felicity gripped the edge of the table till her knuckles went white. 'What do you mean?' she whispered.

Chief Inspector Combe sat down again and looked at her closely. 'Are you really telling me, Miss Frear, you remember nothing about that night?'

'Which night?' The words came out in a hoarse shout.

The chief inspector aligned the edges of the set of sea charts neatly. He seemed to be making up his mind about something.

'Thank you, Miss Frear,' he said at last. 'We shall probably want to speak to you again. Please don't leave the neighbourhood without letting us know.'

Felicity couldn't believe he wasn't going to tell her anything more. That he was sending her away not knowing.

'How did my father die?' she asked. 'You must tell me.'

'Miss Frear, if you really have lost your memory, it's better it stays that way. Now, if you don't mind, we have work to do.' The chief inspector rose, went and opened the door and stood waiting for her to leave.

The long-held-back tears began to pour down her face as Felicity struggled to her feet. 'Why don't you believe me?' she asked.

He said nothing, merely inclined his head slightly and waited for her to leave, then closed the door behind her.

In a daze, unable to think sensibly, careless of the tears now pouring down her face, Felicity found her way back to the main stairs and dragged herself up to her bedroom. She went across to the window and stood looking out. She could see the garden and the sea, a beautiful soft blue under the warm sun. No glimpse visible from here of the harbour or the boathouse.

'My father,' she whispered. 'My father?'

The mystery the detective had conjured around her father's death, her frustration at his refusal to tell her more, had vanished. What she felt now was a yearning for the man himself. For a father who would be protective, solve all her problems, call her 'his little girl'. This yearning, though, was for an idea of a father, not an actual person. She still couldn't remember what her father had been like, or her mother. Surely, though, they had cherished her? Cherished her in a way no one seemed to now. Tears sprang to her eyes again.

Felicity felt weak and spineless. She moved away from the window and its view of the sea, telling herself she mustn't be so gutless. It was ridiculous to mourn the loss of a loving pair of parents when you couldn't remember either.

Chapter Fourteen

Policemen swarmed all over Kingsleigh. From her window, Felicity could see ranks of uniforms examining the grounds, fanning out in every direction. She tried to feel outraged at the way the place had been taken over, its serenity blasted into outer space, but there was nothing, not even a sense that this was her home.

She stayed in her bedroom for the rest of the morning.

Mrs Parsons sent up a tray of lunch. Felicity picked at the fishcakes and considered her situation.

A voice was threatening her on the telephone, a voice that was unknown but yet nagged away at the edges of her subconscious, provoking her with its familiarity.

Murder had taken place at Kingsleigh. Harmless Gordon Rules, the one person who had seemed at all sympathetic to her, had been killed and the police appeared to suspect her of some involvement. The place she had imagined would give her shelter had been violated and now bristled with danger.

Suddenly Felicity wanted to get away from Kingsleigh, even if only for a few hours. Chief Inspector Combe had denied she was being kept a prisoner, well, then, she would leave here. If she just took her handbag they wouldn't stop her.

Felicity's thought processes jarred to a stop as she remembered that she had no handbag nor any of the normal things a bag held. No cheque book, no credit cards, no money. All she had at Kingsleigh were a few clothes and the leather holdall Belinda Gray had sent to the hospital. Everything else here had belonged to her cousin.

Along with the clothes, in response to a request from Felicity, Belinda had also sent some cash. With that Felicity had been able to buy some necessary toiletries, chocolates for the nurses and to pay for the taxi that took her to Kingsleigh. After all that, she had been left with less than a pound in her pocket.

A combination of irritation and impatience flooded Felicity. It seemed to her that she had done nothing since arriving at Kingsleigh but wait for her past to be unlocked. Yesterday might or might not have opened the door a tiny crack but she couldn't hang around waiting to see if it swung any further; it was time for action. She sensed she was a person who preferred action. The passive indolence that had been forced on her by her injuries was passing now; she felt her strength returning and with it came a longing to be doing something. At the very least, she told herself, she should be able to equip herself with cash and a cheque book so she could repay Belinda Gray.

After all, she owned Kingsleigh, she was a rich woman.

In the hospital she had received a letter from her cousin's lawyer informing her that she was Frances Sheldrake's legatee. It had closed by saying that she would no doubt want to go through the details of her inheritance with the writer as soon as she was well enough and he would be telephoning her in the near future to discuss matters.

No such call had yet been received. Felicity retrieved the letter from the drawer of the beside cabinet she had placed it in on her arrival and looked thoughtfully at the signature: Ian Rankin. The name appeared again at the head of the list of partners on the letterhead.

Then she looked back at the beside cabinet. Ever since she had arrived at Kingsleigh she had been behaving as though she was a guest. And that was how she was being treated by Mrs Parsons and Belinda Gray.

Felicity put the letter in her pocket, picked up the tray of almost untouched food and went down to the kitchen. There Mrs Parsons was looking none too happily at another tray loaded with cups and saucers.

'Have you taken any messages for me since my arrival?' Felicity asked baldly.

'No, miss, I would have told you.' Mrs Parsons appeared affronted, as though her efficiency was in question.

Felicity regarded her steadily. 'I thought maybe Mrs Gray considered me not well enough to be troubled with calls and asked you to protect me.'

Mrs Parsons looked wary and her eyes shifted uneasily. Felicity knew she was somewhere near the mark but it was too late now to get at the truth. If only she hadn't been quite so precipitate with her questioning. If only she could get the housekeeper on her side.

She pulled out a chair from the kitchen table. 'Do you mind if I sit?' she asked.

Mrs Parsons seemed unaware of this courteous acknowledgement of her territory. 'It's your house,' she said ungraciously.

Felicity sat. 'I'm still very shocked by Gordon Rules's murder, it seems so senseless.'

Mrs Parsons' gaze dropped and her mouth compressed itself. She took a large teapot from the dresser and went over to the kettle heating on the stove, added some hot water and stood, swirling it round the pot. Her green eyes were uneasy. 'Murder's a shocking thing,' she said finally, then added in firmer tones, 'Gordon was the last person to have deserved such a fate.'

'No enemies?'

'No more than that mulberry tree out in the courtyard.' That seemed to close the subject as far as Mrs Parsons was concerned.

Felicity looked at the tray of teacups. 'Is this for the police?'

The housekeeper nodded, poured the hot water out of the teapot and started ladling in spoons of tea.

'Don't you think it's a bit much to be expected to provide all this?'

Mrs Parsons looked at her, surprised. The uneasy expression in her eyes deepened and her hands shifted the china about the tray. Then she said, 'It's difficult to refuse the police, Miss Felicity.'

'You leave them to me, Mrs Parsons. I'll suggest you would be quite agreeable to have one of their officers come and use the facilities. Would that help?'

'I'm happy to do what I can, miss.' Mrs Parsons looked as though she would have liked to say a good deal more and Felicity waited but that was it.

'I'll go and do that right now, and you leave the teapot on the tray. No reason why one of them shouldn't come and collect it from here. It looks far too heavy for you to carry.'

Felicity swept out of the kitchen and along to the library.

Her weakness of the morning had vanished and she contemplated with pleasure a sharp confrontation with Chief Inspector Combe. In fact, she felt better and stronger than at any time since she had woken in the hospital after her accident.

It was therefore something of a disappointment to find the chief inspector was not in the library and to be told by his sergeant that he was down at the boathouse. Strong Felicity might feel but not that strong.

She therefore contented herself with telling the sergeant that she and her household wished to be helpful but providing large numbers of police with tea was a considerable strain and could they please depute one of their number to handle the refreshment side.

The sergeant was puzzled. 'But your housekeeper offered herself, Miss Frear. We wouldn't expect that sort of service.'

Felicity stared at him. Why hadn't Mrs Parsons said? Had she wanted to make her look a fool? 'I think she sometimes overestimates her ability to cope,' Felicity said smoothly. 'I would be obliged if the police didn't presume on her goodwill. Could you please collect the tea tray from the kitchen? It's all ready.' Leaving the sergeant speechless, she swept out again.

Felicity went to the telephone in the morning room and raised the receiver. A noise of clashing saucepans reached her. She replaced the receiver and considered the room's proximity to the kitchen. After a moment's thought she went through the vast drawing room and, on the other side, found a charming sitting room.

Smaller and more intimate than the drawing room, it was infinitely more attractive than the morning room. The early morning sun, working its way round the house, was nudging through the windows and the light décor was soothing to the eye. The television set was larger than the one in the morning room and was equipped with a video recorder; there was also a music centre. Beside the window, with its view over the garden towards the sea, was a small Georgian kneehole walnut desk. On it stood a telephone.

She laid the solicitor's letter on the desk and picked up the receiver.

'Mr Rankin, it's Felicity Frear,' she said when she got through.

There was a moment's silence then self-possessed, public school tones asked, 'What can I do for you, Miss Frear?'

Once again Felicity felt quick anger rise in her. Nobody, it seemed, was willing to be co-operative. The only person who had been at all kind since she'd arrived at Kingsleigh had been murdered and it had been she who had found him. 'I understood you were to ring me to discuss my cousin's estate,' she said crisply.

'Indeed,' Ian Rankin responded easily. 'I was waiting to hear your progress after that very nasty accident. Does this call mean you are now well enough to go through matters?'

'More than ready.' She waited. 'Well?' she said as the pause stretched interminably.

'Miss Frear, I don't think you understand. Mrs Sheldrake's legacy is not a simple matter. Kingsleigh is a large estate. There are tenants, there are trusts. It can't be discussed over the telephone and I need notice to get the files together before we meet.'

'Mr Rankin, what do you know about my own affairs?'

'I'm sorry?'

'I don't know if you are aware but the accident has left me without a memory.'

'I beg your pardon?'

'I can't remember anything that happened before the car crash and I need to organize my affairs. It would help if you could fill in some of the background for me.'

She could hear dismay and doubt coming down the telephone line.

'This is most unusual,' Ian Rankin managed at last. He cleared his throat. 'However, let's see what I know. Not very much, I'm afraid. Even though we handled your grandfather's business for many years, your mother preferred to use another firm so I know very little about your affairs.' A long-held rancour coloured the deliberate tone. 'I have, though, recently received some details on your travel agency.'

Her travel agency? She had her own business? Was that why she was now so impatient to regain control of her life? 'Perhaps you can give me its name,' Felicity said crisply as the solicitor waited for her response.

'The Paloma Travel Agency.'

'Address and telephone number?' pressed Felicity, opening drawers in the desk, searching for a pencil and paper. In her haste, her hands stiff from the scars, one of the drawers came right out, spilling its contents on the floor. Amongst them was a pencil. Grabbing an old envelope from the mess, Felicity with some difficulty scribbled down a telephone number and an address in Victoria, cursing the burns that had made holding a pen or pencil difficult. 'Thank you, Mr Rankin. Now, when can you go through matters with me? I'd like to do it as soon as possible. Are you able to come down here in the next few days?'

'I have a very busy diary, Miss Frear, but of course I will do what I can. Shall we say two weeks from today? My diary seems clear then and the trains are so good I should be able to manage it in one day. Of course, if you were well enough to come up to London before then I might be able to find an hour or so in my schedule to give you the salient details.'

Felicity fought down intense rage. 'Just tell me one thing, Mr Rankin. Do I have to have you as my lawyer now or are you just the lawyer of a deceased client?'

There was a startled silence from the other end of the telephone. 'My dear Miss Frear, I very much hope that you will want to retain me as your solicitor. My firm's connections with your family stretch back many years and I do understand the minutiae of what is a most complicated estate.'

'I'm sure you do, Mr Rankin.' She severed the connection.

Chapter Fifteen

Felicity remained sitting at the desk, thinking. Then she lifted the receiver and dialled the number of the Paloma Travel Agency.

A young voice answered.

'This is Felicity Frear.'

There as a gasp from the telephone before the voice said, 'Felicity, how are you? We were all so sorry to hear about the accident.' Not sorry enough to send a card, thought Felicity bleakly to herself. 'Hold the line a minute and I'll put Jane on.'

A moment later an older female voice said, cautiously, 'Felicity?'

'Yes, Jane, Felicity. Ringing to see how things are.'

'Oh.' An edge of relief appeared in the voice. 'Things are fine. We've had some nice bookings, South America this winter looks really good and I think we can say we're one of the leading tour operators there. The Spanish end is doing well, too; the tours round those small private hotels you found are going beautifully. No need to worry yourself about anything.'

'How are you managing without me?'

More relief in the voice. 'Fine, Felicity, fine. I've taken on an extra girl, just until you are back. Very experienced, she's couriered all over South America and worked behind the desk with Thomas Cook.'

'I expect there's some good reason why you haven't been in touch?' Felicity brought it out through gritted teeth and heard the gulp the other girl gave.

'I thought, I mean, we were told you weren't to be worried, that you were too ill. But I've sent a couple of reports to the Devon address we were given.' She sounded frightened.

'Reports? I haven't received any reports.'

'Well, I certainly sent them.' Aggression replaced the fright.

'You've got the Kingsleigh telephone number?'

'Of course, Felicity.'

'Well, ring it every morning and give me a status report, understand?'

'Yes, Felicity. Of course, Felicity.' Another gulp then Jane said, 'I'm glad, we're all glad you're so much better.'

Felicity put down the telephone feeling uncomfortable and ashamed. What she had done to that girl was close to bullying of the worst kind. Had Jane suffered the fall-out from her confrontation with the lawyer or was that how she normally behaved? Judging from Jane's reaction, Felicity was afraid her belligerent attitude hadn't been unexpected. Was this the sort of person she normally was? If so, no wonder she hadn't been sent cards or flowers.

Like spring rain falling on dry earth, a sadness soaked through Felicity. The fact that she owned a travel agency, seemed to be a successful businesswoman, was lost in the loneliness she felt. How wonderful it would have been if Jane had treated her as a friend instead of a boss she was afraid of.

It was another piece of the puzzle to be fitted in with those suggested by the attitudes of Belinda Gray and Mrs Parsons. Felicity wasn't liking the picture they made. What had happened to her while she was growing up to have turned her into such an unattractive person? Then she thought that if she had retained her cousin's affection she couldn't have been quite as bad as all that. Had she, though, shown one side to Frances and another to other people?

Felicity thought sadly of the fences she was going to have to mend, bent down to pick up the drawer that had fallen on the floor and started to fit it back in the desk.

Then she saw that a thick envelope had been taped to its back. Carefully she unpeeled it from the wood. The outside of the envelope was blank. She opened it, then gave an involuntary gasp as she saw that the contents were high denomination banknotes. Clumsily she spread them out and counted them.

There was a total of a thousand pounds in twenties and fifties. Nothing to say why it was there. An emergency supply, perhaps? Never mind, for the moment it was a gift from heaven for, after all, had not the house and all its contents been left to her?

For a moment Felicity continued to sit, thinking. Then she stuck the drawer back in the desk, replaced the spilled items and shut it. The money she put in the pocket of her dress. Picking up the lawyer's letter, she went upstairs to her cousin's room and searched for a handbag. Finding one in cream leather, she placed the letter and the money inside. Back in her own room, she added lipstick, a comb and the odd change from Belinda Gray's loan.

She went back to the kitchen, where Mrs Parsons was now involved in weighing out baking ingredients.

'There's no need to send my mail to Mr Rankin any longer. I'm well enough to cope with it myself,' Felicity said, not unkindly, and watched a defensive look come over the housekeeper's face.

'It was Mrs Gray's instructions,' she said, biting her lip.

'I quite understand, Mrs Parsons, but from now on we needn't worry her with such matters. Oh, and the police will be taking over their own tea-making, you won't be bothered any more.' She left Mrs Parsons looking lost for words.

In the corridor outside the kitchen Felicity stood for a moment studying the key board. A couple of days earlier she had found the garage. In it had been two cars, a huge, elderly Daimler and a drop-head, gleaming white Aston Martin coupé; either seemed a daunting prospect to drive. She took down the key for the sports car.

On her way to the garage, Felicity passed the stables. A mobile incident centre had arrived. As Felicity walked past, she saw banks of computers and short-sleeved officers organizing piles of papers. Could murders be solved by a series of entries on forms?

The Aston Martin's dashboard provided a bewildering array of instruments and it took Felicity a little time to sort out the controls; this was obviously a car she hadn't driven before. Eventually she found the ignition and the engine turned over first time with a satisfyingly powerful note. Carefully Felicity eased into gear, reversed out of the garage and set off up the hill.

It was a shock to find a police guard on the gate and humiliating to have to wait for the officer to confirm with Chief Inspector Combe that it was in order to allow her to leave. When at last he waved her through, Felicity's temper was at breaking point and the Aston Martin surged on to the road with a great leap of speed.

As the hedges ripped by her, unreasoning panic took over; a subconscious memory of screaming engines, crashing metal and spontaneous combustion made Felicity jam on the brakes. The heavy car went into a skid that nearly landed it in the ditch. Felicity released the brake pedal, fought the steering back under control and brought the car to a stop. She sat in the quiet lane with her heart thudding in her chest, her breath coming in short, convulsive gasps.

An irritated horn blared behind her. Cautiously Felicity restarted the engine. This time she drove slowly, learning the feel of the car, and gradually began to enjoy the way it held the road. Then she realized she had no idea in which direction she was heading. A sign-post at a crossroads told her she was eighteen miles from a town and she turned towards it.

It was an old market town built around the estuary of a river, picturesque with a mixture of period property and modern developments. Felicity found her way to the centre and looked for somewhere to park. A departing car offered her a space in the main square. She managed to ease the Aston Martin efficiently between two others, got out and locked it. She stood and looked around. Across the square a run of gracious Georgian houses converted into shops and offices looked promising. Sure enough, amongst them she found a brass plate proclaiming what she sought.

Inside the offices, a middle-aged woman typing behind a glass panel told her that Mr Biddulph would be free to see her in about half an hour. If Miss Frear cared to wait, the woman could get her a cup of coffee.

Felicity looked at the cramped little waiting area and said thank you but she had some shopping to do and would return in thirty minutes.

Outside a brisk wind was blowing off the estuary and she realized her surge of energy was ebbing and that she had no inclination to look at clothes. A small hotel at the corner of the square had a sign advertising Kenco coffee.

She went in and sat down. A waitress came across and stared at Felicity's face, wrote down the order and left with a last curious glance. Felicity forced herself to ignore it. If she chose to go amongst the public with a face like hers, she had to accept the consequences.

Felicity had chosen a quiet corner in the main foyer, just off the bar area. Dark red flock wallpaper, a red patterned carpet and red velvet upholstery was prevented from being overpowering by touches of well-polished brass. The atmosphere was quiet and relaxing.

The coffee when it arrived was fresh, hot and tasted delicious. Felicity sipped it with a relish that was new to her. She sat back and relaxed, finding that the anonymous surroundings of the hotel suited her. She felt free, safe.

From the bar area came a man's voice. Felicity felt the hairs on the back of her neck rise and her scarred skin pucker into gooseflesh.

'I'm not sure what this means,' the man hidden by the half-wall said. The words were innocent enough; it was the voice that resonated with terrifying associations.

Chapter Sixteen

Felicity fought the urge to expose her presence by moving so she could see the speaker.

'The girl's there now, you said?' A second voice, also male, was lighter than the first and struck no chords of memory in Felicity.

Chords of memory; she clutched at the phrase. Did the first man belong to her past? He spoke again, more quietly this time, as though he'd settled at a table – or become more aware of possible eavesdroppers – and she couldn't hear his words, only catch the timbre of his voice.

As she strained to listen, memory surged back. But it was of a time no further back than her hospital stay. The voice belonged to the insurance salesman who had pulled her from the burning car. What was he called? Sam and his surname had something to do with spies. McLean, that was it, Sam McLean.

The second man's voice came again, louder and clearer. 'He had to go, surely you can see that, Sam? Far too in the way.' He was casually authoritarian, in command. 'Look, time for a walk I think, don't you? All too public here. Where's that bill?'

Felicity heard him call to a waitress. She looked around and realized that they would have to pass her corner on the way out. Any moment now they would see her sitting there.

Acting on instinct, Felicity picked up her bag and her coffee and walked swiftly across the foyer to the ladies. She didn't dare look back but, if the men were still sitting down, she thought they couldn't have caught sight of her.

The cloakroom had a small armchair next to a tiny round table on which was a metal ashtray. Felicity sat down, shivering. Just why she was so convinced the two men had been talking about her, Kingsleigh and the death of Rules, she couldn't have said. There were, after all, any number of interpretations that could be put on those fragments of conversation. But for Sam McLean to be here, not twenty miles from where she was living, surely that was too much of a coincidence?

Or was it? He had said he was working in the area. He could be lunching with a client, talking about business. But it had been the other man who called for the bill. Could he be Sam McLean's boss? Maybe they had been going over Sam's client list and there had been nothing sinister about the conversation at all.

But back to Felicity came that unemotional description of the car crash. Something about the way Sam McLean spoke had struck false at the time; it had seemed forced, mechanical. This afternoon his voice had sounded very different, livelier, natural. That must have been why it had taken her time to place it.

Then for the first time Felicity wondered if it had been sheer coincidence he had been travelling behind the car she had been in, coincidence he had been so conveniently placed to drag her from that funeral pyre.

He had been behind her on the road. Now he was not twenty miles from where she lived. He had said in the hospital that he would see her again. When did he intend that to be? And exactly why would he come? In the hospital he had appeared reluctant even to talk to her. As though he disliked her as, it seemed, others did. Had he known her before, then?

It was an alarming thought. If he had, surely it had been no coincidence he had been so close behind that crash? But, then, surely he would have told her? Unless there was some very good reason why he didn't want her to know they'd met before. And what could that be?

Felicity rose and cautiously opened the door of the ladies just far enough to give her a glimpse into the foyer. It was empty. She opened the door wider so she could see into the bar area. That, too, was empty.

She was annoyed now that she hadn't been cleverer and managed to catch a glimpse of the two men. She would have liked to know what Sam McLean looked like, both him and his companion.

Felicity picked up her coffee cup from the little table and went to pay her bill. She toyed with the idea of asking if the hotel knew Mr McLean but decided against it. She didn't want them to mention the enquiry to him and her face was, unfortunately, only too memorable and easy to describe.

Felicity was now late for her appointment.

'I thought maybe you'd changed your mind,' said the woman behind the glass panel.

'I'm sorry, I got caught up and didn't realize the time. Can Mr Biddulph still see me?'

'I'm sure he can.' The woman smiled. She appeared to find

Felicity's face quite normal. She picked up the telephone and buzzed through to another office.

A few minutes later Felicity was being shown into an austere room with papers lying in piles all over an aged desk and side table. The floor was covered with a worn, rust-coloured carpet and limp net curtains screened a sash window.

'Malcolm Biddulph. How can I help you?' He came forward from behind his desk holding out his hand. He was younger than Felicity had expected, in his early thirties, with ginger hair, a friendly freckled face and hazel eyes that looked enquiringly from behind metal-framed spectacles. His eyes took in her dark glasses and damaged face but his manner never faltered.

She shook his hand, liking his firm grasp but not at all sure he was going to be the right sort of person to help her. She had thought an older man, experienced, someone with more, what? Gravitas?

'Please, sit down, Miss Frear, and tell me your problem.'

'My problem?' Felicity sat down in the chair he drew out for her in front of his desk. He shifted some piles of paper and perched himself on a corner.

'Young ladies who suddenly appear off the street wanting to talk to a lawyer as soon as possible usually have a problem.' He smiled at her in a way she found engaging.

Felicity had little to lose. She started on a brief and factual account of what had happened since the car crash, including her loss of memory.

Quite soon Malcolm Biddulph moved round to sit at his desk and drew a pad of paper towards him. 'Do you mind if I take some notes?' he asked.

Felicity shook her head. During her account he interrupted once or twice to clarify a point but for the most part he let her speak. She ended with the details of her telephone conversation that morning with her cousin's lawyer, opening her bag and passing Ian Rankin's letter across the desk.

Malcolm Biddulph read it quickly, then laid it to one side of his pad. He placed his pencil on the desk, lay back in his chair and looked at Felicity. The air of easy camaraderie with which he had greeted her had vanished and he seemed older.

'What, exactly, do you want from me?'

'I thought I should find myself a lawyer, one who had nothing to do with my cousin or her estate.' One whose loyalty would be to her, she added to herself.

'A very sensible decision.' He smiled at her. 'Let me tell you about our firm. I'm the junior partner. Mike Younger, despite his name, is the senior; he's been here for something like thirty years. We're both local boys, my father is a GP, practises just outside Tiverton. I did my articles in London but didn't want to be a hot shot legal eagle; like my old man I prefer something of everything and being a large fish in a small pond is more comfortable than the cut and thrust of the big time.' All the time he was talking, he was watching her. She understood his subtext; had he wanted it, a place amongst the hungry sharks could have been his; just because he practised in a sleepy Devon town didn't mean he couldn't mix it with the big boys.

'Let's see. You seem to have several immediate problems.' He picked up his pencil and began to make more notes as he talked. 'First, you need to have all the details of your inheritance from your cousin explained to you. As long as you don't desperately need a lot of money, that is not particularly urgent. Second, you need to know your personal financial position and I find it strange nobody has realized this and made some effort to sort things out for you. No doubt you also find this unsettling.' There was something very comforting in the matter-of-fact way he said this. 'Third, there is what appears to be your business, the Paloma Travel Agency. Again, it's been made difficult for you to be kept in touch with what is going on there. Fourth, there is the situation with the police *vis-à-vis* the murder that has occurred at Kingsleigh.' He looked straight at her. 'That must have been the most terrible shock for you. I think you are being incredibly brave.'

The unexpected sympathy unnerved Felicity and made her realize just how used she had become to tensing herself against hostility. She blinked hard.

'Has your permission for their presence in the house been requested?' Malcolm Biddulph continued.

Felicity shook her head. 'No one has asked me anything. I assumed they could do what they liked.'

'Far from it. Procedures have to be followed. I'm surprised at Bob Combe, he's usually pretty careful.'

'You know him?'

'Oh, yes, he's another local lad. I went out with his sister at one time. We lost touch when I went up to London; she's married to someone else now.' He was dialling the telephone as he spoke. 'Hello, Malcolm Biddulph here. I'm anxious to speak to Chief Inspector Combe. Can you ask him to ring me as soon as possible? It's in connection with the Kingsleigh case. Thanks.' He replaced the receiver. 'Well, that's one problem under way to being sorted out. Now, about your financial matters . . .' He thought for a moment, clicking the pencil against his teeth. 'The travel agency might be able

71

to help but I think we should use them as a last resort. Your banking records and that sort of thing are probably at your home address. Do you know what that is?'

Felicity shrugged helplessly. 'I'm afraid not.'

'Your manager at Paloma Travel must have it.'

'I should think Mrs Gray probably knows it as well. She's my cousin's aunt and seems to have been more or less in charge of everything after the crash.'

'Ah, yes, Mrs Gray, JP, Chairman of the Conservatives and local bigwig.'

'You know her as well?'

'Not many people around here I don't,' Malcolm Biddulph told her gently.

'Then you would have known my cousin and her family.'

His gaze continued to hold hers. 'I knew of them, though we never met. When Thomas Dashwood married Jennifer Powell, the Kingsleigh legal business was transferred to London.'

Felicity stared at him. 'You mean, you handled it before that?'

'This firm, yes. It was Mike's senior partner at that stage who was the Dashwood family lawyer. Mike said he was pretty cut up at the time but I suppose the move was logical.'

'Logical, why?'

Malcolm Biddulph looked mildly surprised. 'Because Kingsleigh was bought by your grandfather.'

Chapter Seventeen

'What do you mean, he bought Kingsleigh? I thought it was the Dashwood ancestral home?'

'It was, but Tom Dashwood was in the process of being drowned by his father's debts. Peter Dashwood was a profligate and a gambler; he lived up to the hilt and beyond. The debts he left behind plus estate duty meant Kingsleigh had to be sold. If an heiress hadn't come along, the Dashwoods would have had no more rights to their ancestral home.'

And how that would have upset Belinda Gray!

'Your grandfather was Clive Powell, big industrialist, made carburretors and other parts for cars and lorries. When his daughter, Jennifer, got engaged to Thomas Dashwood and he understood what the position on the estate was, he bought Kingsleigh as a wedding present for her.'

A handsome present indeed! And what had her mother got? Felicity remembered Belinda's reference to a ranch in Kenya raising race horses. Had Sarah been fobbed off with it as some sort of consolation prize?

'With the Powell money,' continued Malcolm Biddulph, 'went the Powell legal and financial advisers. No local firm was considered sufficiently expert to handle matters from then on.'

Even though he could not have been around at the time, the decision obviously rankled with the young lawyer.

'So you never met Frances or me?' For a wild moment there Felicity had hoped.

He gave a crooked smile. 'Afraid not. I wasn't that local and socially Kingsleigh was out of my orbit. Now,' his manner became brisk, 'do you feel up to tackling Mrs Gray regarding your London address or would you like me to do it? I can, you know, as your legal representative.'

Felicity straightened her shoulders. 'I'll go and see her on the way home, if you can tell me exactly where her house is.' After her confrontation with the police and conversation with Ian Rankin, the thought of coming to grips with Belinda Gray was actually stimulating.

'Good girl. I can give you directions but are you sure you don't want her to come to Kingsleigh?'

'Get her on my territory, you mean?' Felicity considered. 'It might be an advantage but I'd like to see where she lives and something tells me there won't be too many invitations coming my way.' It might also be an advantage to catch her unawares.

'If you like, once you know what your London address is, I'll drive you there, help you go through things.'

It was a heartwarming offer. Felicity knew that, even though she was feeling so much stronger, she wasn't fit enough yet either to drive herself to London or even to take the train. Somehow her recovery was going to have to be speeded along.

'Once we've got your personal affairs under control, we'll sort out your business. Then we can turn our attention to Mr Rankin.' Something in his voice told Felicity that Malcolm Biddulph was looking forward to that prospect.

His telephone rang. It was the chief inspector. 'Hi, Bob, good of you to ring back so soon. Look, I'm ringing on behalf of my client, Felicity Frear. She hasn't been approached for permission to have your men on the premises and I thought you might be able to throw a little light on the situation.' It was man-to-man stuff, friendly but direct. 'I see.' Malcolm Biddulph was doodling on his pad, circles and curlicues. 'Well, that clears that one up. Now, she seems to have some curious idea that you suspect her of the murder . . . Heavens, Bob, of course her fingerprints are all over the place! Have you taken a good look at her? Do you seriously think she is physically capable of lifting a dead body and stuffing it into a wooden locker like that? Talk to her doctor and the hospital, they'll tell you there isn't a chance in hell. You can't have it both ways, you know. And, chief inspector, I've told Miss Frear that I'm to be present at any future interviews you have with her.' He put down the phone and gave Felicity an encouraging grin. 'I don't think you'll have much more trouble from Bob Combe. He's only pursuing every possibility.' He glanced down at his pad. 'He told me Mrs Gray had given permission for them to use Kingsleigh any way they wanted.'

'But—' Felicity started to object.

Malcolm Biddulph held up his hand. 'I know what you're going to say. First of all, Bob Combe told me that they've more or less finished their initial investigation on the estate. He expects to move the incident room tomorrow. He's going to set up at the village hall, hopes that way they'll encourage information out of the villagers. As for Mrs Gray's role, Bob said he'd been put on to her by your housekeeper, Mrs Parsons, who told them Mrs Gray was trustee for the estate. I think I'd better have a word with Mr Rankin.' He picked up the letter Felicity had given him and made another telephone call.

While he was getting through, Felicity wondered whether the news that the police were leaving was actually good. Would she receive another telephone call? Even worse, would the caller come visiting? Perhaps she should have told the chief inspector after all. Then she realized that she hadn't mentioned the calls to Malcolm Biddulph either. Any more than she had mentioned the presence of Sam McLean in the hotel. Would it be wise to tell him everything, however paranoid it sounded? But Felicity was beginning to be afraid that paranoia would not be the worst interpretation.

Ian Rankin was unavailable but Malcolm Biddulph was put through to an assistant. He identified himself then said, 'I gather there is a trusteeship involved with the estate. Miss Frear would be grateful to have exact details . . . yes, of course, I shall look forward to receiving that as soon as possible but, in the meantime, can you give me the gist of it over the phone?'

A few minutes later he put down the phone. 'Well, we are gradually beginning to make sense of things, I think. Apparently when Jennifer Dashwood died of cancer just under a year ago, she left Kingsleigh to her husband. Thomas Dashwood's will left the estate in trust for his daughter, Frances, until she reached the age of thirty and the trust was to be continued should she die before that time and either her offspring or you inherited, again until the age of thirty. Mrs Gray is one trustee, Mr Rankin is the other.'

If Belinda Gray was working with Ian Rankin, it was no wonder he hadn't sounded particularly friendly. 'He never mentioned that!'

'He probably thought you wouldn't want to be bothered with the details. I'm sure he will go into everything when you have your meeting with him.'

'I bet if you'd been in his shoes, you would have told me.'

Malcolm Biddulph's gaze dropped to his notes. 'Probably,' he said quietly.

'And in the meantime, does it mean I have no control over the estate?'

'It depends what you want to do. The trustees would find it difficult to prevent you doing anything reasonable regarding the way you live there or spend the income.'

'But Mrs Gray felt it was up to her to give the police permission to operate from Kingsleigh?'

Malcolm Biddulph looked smug. 'Bob said Mrs Gray told them you weren't fit enough yet to take charge of things and she was invoking her power as trustee. Well, if you're not fit enough to run your home, you certainly aren't fit enough to bash someone over the head and haul his body into a locker the way you've described to me.'

'I only hope the hospital confirms that. I don't like being suspected of murder. But why did my uncle leave Kingsleigh in trust to the age of thirty? I don't know about my cousin but surely if I'm running a business I can understand the ramifications of an estate such as Kingsleigh?'

'I can't give you an answer to that, I'm afraid. Perhaps he was one of those out-of-date chaps who think women can't be trusted with money in their twenties.'

'How long ago did he die?' The question was idly asked and Felicity was surprised to see the good humour vanish from Malcolm Biddulph's face. He picked up his pencil and doodled some more, then flung it down, got up, came round and leaned against the desk, looking down at her with deep concern.

Something cold clutched at Felicity's heart. She didn't know what was coming but she knew it couldn't be good.

'However I tell it, this is going to be a shock, so hang on tight, Felicity. Thomas Dashwood and your father, Alexander Frear, were blown up in a yacht about a week before your car crash.'

Chapter Eighteen

The shock hit Felicity like a tangible force, knocking the air from her chest and leaving her gasping like a beached fish frantic for oxygen.

Don't you remember the night your father died? That was what the chief inspector had asked her that morning. And had then refused to say more on the subject.

How cruel, how bitterly cruel, to leave her to hear the truth like this!

'Blown up?' she managed, her hands clutching at the arms of her chair. 'How?'

Malcolm Biddulph was watching her carefully. 'They don't know exactly,' he said. 'Apparently your father and Thomas Dashwood decided to go fishing. Mark Sheldrake, your cousin's husband, was to have gone too but he didn't feel well or was too tired or something. All anyone knows is that an explosion occurred shortly after midnight, some distance off shore. The coastguard was sent out but all they found was an oil slick and debris – the remains of the *Seawind*, your uncle's yacht.'

'And it happened just before the car crash I was involved in?'

He frowned. 'About a week before. The local papers were full of both events.'

Felicity closed her eyes briefly. This was why Belinda Gray had been so strange when she'd questioned her about the boathouse. The death of her beloved brother must have been a dreadful blow; perhaps it was no wonder she was difficult.

But her uncle and father killed together, both she and her cousin made orphans in one fell night. Then Frances herself killed with her husband a week later. So many violent deaths within such a short space of time.

And Gordon Rules's murder made another.

'Boats don't just blow up,' she protested.

'Mark Sheldrake testified at the inquest that his father-in-law had complained of a smell of gas some time before the incident. He thought the matter had been looked into but it's just possible the trouble hadn't been located.'

'How many years had my uncle been sailing?'

'Ever since he was a boy.'

'And he went out in a boat possibly leaking gas? Do you really think that's likely?'

'What do you think?' Malcolm Biddulph whipped out at her.

Felicity blinked.

'You're questioning the official account of what happened. Why?'

'I . . . I don't know. It just seems odd.'

His expression softened. 'Your uncle was getting on; he hadn't been well recently. Several people testified he hadn't been himself since his wife, your aunt, died. Look, you're in a vulnerable state. People are going to be shooting all sorts of questions at you in the next few weeks. Bob Combe is going to get to the bottom of this Kingsleigh murder; he's as tenacious as a terrier with a rat, and he doesn't care who he rides roughshod over. I meant what I said to him. Next time he wants to question you, you insist I'm there to see fair play. Meanwhile, you've got to toughen up.'

'I'm no mimsy miss!' Felicity protested.

He smiled. 'That's the last thing I'd call you but you're a woman alone in a very difficult situation.'

'Do you think loss of memory can strike at random intervals?' she asked abruptly.

'What do you mean?'

'You don't think I could have killed Gordon Rules and forgotten all about it, do you?' The nightmarish thought was haunting her.

Malcolm looked at her curiously. 'You heard what I told Bob. It's physically impossible.'

He hadn't said that she, Felicity Frear, the girl sitting in his office, couldn't have committed murder, just that it wasn't physically possible for her to have done so. Well, for the moment it would have to do.

She summoned up a smile. 'I hear what you say.'

'Right! Now, over the next day or so I'll make some enquiries and I will need your authority to act on your behalf.'

He summoned in Mrs James from her outer cubicle and dictated a short statement of authorization.

Felicity picked up a pen, then found herself hesitating over the place for her signature.

'Having second thoughts about retaining me?'

'It's not that, it's just, I'm not sure anyone will recognize my signature. The scars make writing difficult.'

78

'Do the best you can, we'll fight that battle when we have to.'

She scribbled Felicity Frear at the bottom of the letter and looked doubtfully at the scrawl. 'That belongs to a demented spider, not a businesswoman,' she said, handing the letter back. 'There's another thing,' she added.

'What's that?'

'Your retainer; how much should I give you?' She started to scrabble in the cream handbag.

He waved such matters aside. 'Don't worry about that at the moment. Let's get you sorted out first. I'm sure you'll find you can afford our fees, they'll be a fraction of what Mr Rankin will be charging.'

But Felicity had managed to extract three hundred pounds and placed the notes on his desk. 'I've got this and I'd be happier if you took it.'

He looked at the crisp notes curiously. 'I thought you said you hadn't any funds.'

She told him about the envelope hidden at the back of the desk drawer. 'I thought since my cousin had left me everything, I was justified in taking it.'

'I'd rather not know anything about this and I'd prefer you kept the money yourself. Let's wait until we find out what Felicity Frear has in her bank account.' He gently took her bag from her, stuffed the money inside and handed it back.

'Now you want to know how to find Belinda Gray; I'll draw you a sketch map, it's not far from here.' He turned over to a clean page on his notepad and drew a neat, easy-to-follow map to Mrs Gray's house.

'Is there a Mr Gray?' Felicity asked while he was making the sketch.

'*Colonel* Gray died a number of years ago, shortly after he retired from the army; nagged to death is the general consensus hereabouts.' He tore the page off the pad. 'There you are. You shouldn't get too lost with that.

'Don't worry about not being able to remember the past either,' he added as she took off her dark glasses to look at the sketch, her damaged face thoughtful. 'Think of things this way. You've wiped the slate clean, lost the baggage of remembered faults most of us carry around, and can start again. Who wouldn't welcome such an opportunity?' He gave her a wry smile. 'Ring me tomorrow and let me know how things went, then we can make some plans.'

While he'd been drawing the map, Felicity's mind had been busily turning over something else.

'How much capital would I need to set up a travel agency organizing tours and things?' she asked.

He was startled. 'I have no idea! Why do you want to know?'

'I was just wondering.'

'Well, I think there's something about posting a bond with the Association of British Travel Agents, to ensure travellers can get home if you go bust. I don't know how much it is but it must be fairly sizeable. Then you would need a certain amount to cover your start-up expenses, the office and printing. You'd need lots of brochures, not to mention advertising, that would be heavy as well.'

'So it's not a business I could set up on a shoestring?'

'Without looking at the sort of outfit yours is I couldn't really say, but I wouldn't have thought so.'

'Thanks.' Felicity held out her hand and said goodbye.

What she was thinking as she went out of Malcolm Biddulph's office was that, if her mother had lost all her money, just where had the capital for her daughter to start the Paloma Travel Agency come from?

Chapter Nineteen

It didn't take long to find Belinda Gray's delightful Queen Anne house. Felicity spent the drive checking her direction and rehearsing what she needed to say to this high-handed woman.

Her arrival was an obvious shock. 'Are you fit to be driving that car?' Mrs Gray demanded on opening the door and seeing the Aston Martin parked by rose beds that flamed with salmon-coloured blossoms. 'Mark would hate it if you scratched the paintwork.'

The thought of paint scratches beside the wholesale destruction of the car's owner in a holocaust was ridiculous but Felicity felt no inclination to laugh.

'As you can see,' she said, looking Belinda Gray straight in the eye, 'I am very much better.' She waited. A doorstep conversation was not what she had in mind.

Mrs Gray remembered her manners, opened the door wider and invited Felicity in.

The small sitting room was charmingly furnished with a selection of nicely chosen antiques. Felicity recognized the influence of Kingsleigh in so many touches; the swagged curtains, the pale damask covers to chairs and sofa, the collection of Derby china arranged either side of the fireplace in back-lit recesses topped with shell mouldings. She felt a brief stab of sympathy for this woman who clung so fiercely to her background. No wonder she resented Felicity's ownership of her beloved ancestral home.

'I am, of course, delighted to see your recovery proceeding so well,' Belinda said stiffly, her gaunt face working itself into a semblance of a smile. She waved Felicity towards a seat. 'I must say, though, it's something of a surprise to find you here. Especially after the dreadful happenings at Kingsleigh.' She gave a small, embarrassed cough. 'I was, of course, coming over tomorrow to see how you were coping.'

Felicity ignored the oblique reference to both murder and neglect, sat down and arranged her legs neatly on the flowered tapestry rug. 'Now that I'm so much better, I'm trying to organize my affairs. It's proving a bit difficult and I don't know who else to turn to for help.'

Belinda visibly relaxed and sat herself down opposite her visitor.

Before she'd arrived, Felicity had been determined to confront this interfering trustee and demand she stay out of her life. But Belinda Gray's very tactlessness, the awkward way in which she betrayed her nervousness at what Felicity was going to do next, made her change her mind. She gave her a pleasant smile.

'First of all, I'm trying to find out my address.' Felicity gave a light laugh. 'Isn't it stupid? Not to know where one lives?'

'Oh, I can certainly help there.' Belinda rose and went over to a drop-leaf desk in a corner of the room, opened it and found an address book. 'You live in the same flat in Clapham that your mother bought when she came back from Spain and divorced your father. Dreadful little place, I thought.'

'I don't suppose she could afford much else,' Felicity commented tartly. 'Didn't you say she'd lost all her money?'

'She had an income from the trust fund.'

'Trust fund?' Yet another?

'Your grandmother left a small fortune in trust for you. Your mother had the income during her life. Still, I suppose if she'd bought a better place there wouldn't have been enough to send you to Fran's school – your grandmother had insisted on that – and provide her with enough to live on.'

For a moment the whirl of information confused Felicity. One part of her mind was registering the fact that she'd been the beneficiary of a sizeable trust fund and wondering if that was where the capital to start the travel business had come from but the other was trying to concentrate on the purpose of her visit; she couldn't afford to get sidetracked from that yet. 'The Clapham address?'

Belinda sat down at the desk, wrote down the details and gave them to Felicity.

Felicity put the piece of paper in her handbag. 'Talking of trust funds, I've had a chat with Ian Rankin. I gather both he and you are trustees of the Kingsleigh estate until I reach thirty.' Felicity preferred to keep Malcolm Biddulph's part in her affairs a secret for the moment. There was too much that was mysterious about Kingsleigh and, until Felicity could discover more of what was going on there, Belinda wasn't going to be told a jot beyond what was necessary.

'That is so, yes. I was happy to help my brother in that respect, though, of course, I hoped he would live long enough to make my role unnecessary.' Belinda drew out a small handkerchief and dabbed unselfconsciously at her eyes.

'I do appreciate the way you've helped ever since the accident.' Felicity was beginning to find being nice to people wasn't actually difficult. Again she wondered what had made her such a prickly person, so quick to react to any sort of disapproval with a hurtful remark. 'But I'm well able now to take care of most things myself. My mail, for instance. There is no need for Mrs Parsons to forward that to Mr Rankin in future.'

'We wanted to make sure you were free of all worries, so you could get well,' Belinda offered stiffly. 'Of course, mail addressed to the Sheldrakes or poor Tom will have to continue to be sent to the solicitor for attention but now you are so much better, I'll tell Mrs Parsons not to send on anything addressed to you personally.' She made it sound like a gracious concession.

From somewhere Felicity summoned a sweet smile. 'Thanks. And, while we're on the subject, I'm sure you have far too much to do to want to be bothered with supervising day-to-day matters at Kingsleigh. I can give Mrs Parsons any future instructions she may need.'

For a long moment Felicity's gaze locked with Belinda Gray's in a battle of wills.

Then the older woman bowed to the inevitable. 'If you are sure you are well enough,' she muttered, shifting in her chair and tugging at the little cover protecting an arm.

Triumph surged through Felicity. She opened the handbag. 'And I want to repay the loan you so kindly made me in hospital.'

She took out the wad of notes.

'Ian never sent you all that money!' gasped Belinda. 'How did you get hold of it?' Her gaze was transfixed by the sight of the cash.

Felicity explained.

'At the back of the desk? I can only think Mark put it there. It certainly isn't the sort of thing Fran would have done, or Tom. You must tell Ian Rankin how much you found. It will have to be entered in the probate.'

'Of course,' agreed Felicity smoothly. 'Why do you think Mark might have put it there? Was he, how shall I put this, perhaps in the habit of suddenly needing large amounts of cash?' The Aston Martin, to Felicity, suggested an owner who liked the good things of life.

'Not at all, I mean . . . I don't really know . . . That is to say, he was a bit of an enigma.' Belinda stumbled to a stop.

'An enigma?'

Belinda gave a little shrug. 'Fran met him in South America, on that trip with you after her mother died. The first we knew about it was when you both returned and said she was going to be married! Tom came over and told me he wasn't at all happy. Well, Fran was a considerable heiress and some drug company salesman operating in South America didn't sound at all suitable.' She made a little face that illustrated just how contemptible the Dashwoods considered such a pedigree. 'Then Mark came down to Kingsleigh and I have to say we were all charmed. Even Tom. Such a handsome and straightforward man. Blond, blue-eyed, quite an Adonis. He was very frank, explained that one of his few talents was for languages; he spoke excellent Spanish, and a career of some sort in Spain or Latin America had seemed obvious. And he was doing well with his company, expected to be made a director shortly.'

'Funny, I had the impression he was based at Kingsleigh.'

'Oh, that was after the wedding. I think it was Tom who suggested that it might be better if Mark resigned and helped him with the estate. Or it might have been Fran.'

'Perhaps she didn't like the idea of living in South America?'

'Fran would have lived anywhere Mark wanted to.' Belinda's voice rang with conviction. 'She was a girl in love, quite transformed. We hadn't seen her like that since . . . well, for a very long time. It was wonderful, especially after the terrible time she and Tom had had with Jennifer's illness, especially over the last year. That poor woman, what she suffered. It wasn't any wonder Fran didn't want to leave her father.'

'So it was all love's young dream?'

Belinda Gray regarded Felicity with a jaundiced eye. 'Just like you, Flick, to be flippant about things. I have to say, though, that you appeared to be as happy as anybody else about the match. It seemed odd to me because I thought you would have been the natural choice for Mark.'

'Me?'

'Yes, you speak Spanish, your business is connected with South America and, well, you were always laughing and joking with him.' She paused, then added, 'It wouldn't have surprised me if Fran hadn't been more than a little, well . . .'

'Jealous?'

'Especially after that other business.'

'What other business?'

'When you stole her fiancé.'

Chapter Twenty

'I don't believe it,' Felicity shot back at her, the denial instinctive.

Belinda bridled. 'How can you say that when you don't remember anything?'

'What proof do you have?'

'Fran said so.'

'Then she must have been mistaken.' Felicity's certainty on this point puzzled her but certain she was. 'And surely the fact that we went to South America together proves she discovered her mistake?'

'For two years you only came to Kingsleigh when Fran wasn't there, to see Jennifer. Then, when it was clear she was dying, you arrived one weekend out of the blue and said you were going to come regularly. Fran wasn't at all happy and Tom tried to throw you out. It was Jennifer who insisted you should come. They gave way to her wishes.'

'And was it her wish we went to South America together?' Felicity pressed.

'No,' said Belinda reluctantly. 'By then Fran seemed to have made friends with you again.'

'You see?' Felicity was triumphant.

'It proves nothing either way.' Belinda shrugged her shoulders.

'Do you think Jennifer felt guilty towards me, because she had Kingsleigh and my mother had been fobbed off with some twopenny ranch in Kenya?'

Belinda stared at her. 'Twopenny ranch? It was nothing of the kind, though the way that woman went on, you might have thought so! After they'd visited there, Tom said it was huge, far too big a concern for Sarah to handle. But Sarah always claimed Jennifer got everything and she nothing. As if her father hadn't always handed out money on her behalf to pay her debts or drag her out of one trouble or another. Like the time she was arrested on some sort of drugs charge. He engaged one of the leading silks in London to defend her. Got her off, too, Lord knows how.'

'If that happened before she went to Kenya, you can't know much about it,' Felicity protested.

'Jennifer never told me more than the bare facts,' Belinda acknowledged, 'but there wasn't much doubt about them. And I certainly knew about your mother's move to Africa because it was just after Tom and Jennifer got engaged.' Her gaze shifted from meeting Felicity's and moved to contemplate something on the wall. 'She was very emotional at the time, going round saying dreadful things.'

'No doubt she thought they were true!'

'Your mother never knew truth from a hole in the ground,' asserted Belinda caustically. 'She spent her whole life moving from one scrape to another. She begged and pleaded with your grandfather to set her up in Kenya. He spent as much money doing that as buying Kingsleigh, then she couldn't make a go of things. She was a superb horsewoman, I have to say that, but you need discipline and hard work to run a venture like hers. She was capable of neither. It was just the same with the Spanish venture and her marriage. While Tom and Jennifer were sublimely happy together.'

Felicity bit back the comment that Thomas Dashwood would have lost Kingsleigh if he'd lost his wife.

'Then she came back to England blaming her poverty on everybody but herself.'

Once again, unbidden, a bitter voice at the back of Felicity's mind said, 'I tell you, girl, if I hadn't been such an honourable person, Kingsleigh would have been yours. My fault has always been I think more of others than myself!'

'What about the income from my trust fund, didn't that provide her with enough to live on?'

Belinda gave a dry chuckle. 'I never saw Sarah madder than after she'd learned about your grandmother's will. She'd expected to get her hands on the cash. She went around saying she'd been cheated.'

Again Felicity heard the bitter voice in the back of her mind. 'I've been cheated and you've been cheated, never forget that, my girl!'

'When did I get the money? On her death?'

'That was what your grandmother had intended. But I'm afraid your mother managed to get her hands on it despite everything.'

'What do you mean?'

Belinda insisted on telling the story her own way. 'I can see Tom now, standing on that rug and telling me what a shock it had been for Jennifer. You see, she'd just had her first operation for cancer and, despite the doctor's advice, had insisted on going up to Sarah's funeral.'

'How did my mother die?' How strange she should hear about both her parents' deaths on the same day.

'Heart attack. You came back from work one day and found her

86

slumped in front of the television set. Lucky you weren't off on one of your couriering jobs or she could have sat there for days!' Belinda said with careless cruelty. 'But the doctor refused to write a death certificate without a post-mortem.'

'Why?'

'Jennifer said it was because he hadn't treated her for heart trouble but apparently the autopsy confirmed she'd been taking drugs and Tom told me they'd known for some time she was a cocaine addict!' Belinda made a distasteful moue. 'I always suspected she was on something. She was like a yoyo, you never knew whether she would be up or down or when some innocent phrase would set her off. And her language! I never knew how Tom could stand to have her at Kingsleigh. No wonder he kept out of her way as much as possible.'

'I expect my aunt liked seeing her sister,' Felicity said, carefully controlling her temper. She'd pushed the reference to cocaine to the back of her mind, as though it was something she was afraid to confront. 'After all, she wanted to come to my mother's funeral, she must have been very fond of her.'

'And you. That's what made it all so much more difficult.'

'Made what difficult?'

'The fact that your mother embezzled your trust fund.'

'Embezzled it? How could she have done that?'

'Tom explained it all to me but it sounded very complicated. Apparently she got the trustee to invest the funds in a shell company with associated holdings. There was some sort of chain with her at the end, drawing out the company assets. For a time the dividends provided the right sort of level of income. Then as the capital declined, that wasn't possible. By the time your mother died, there was practically nothing left.'

Felicity stared at Belinda. 'Wasn't it illegal?'

'Tom said not. He wanted to prosecute the trustee responsible but the lawyers advised him there really wasn't a case, it would just be a question of good money after bad. If only your grandmother had had the trust drawn up with her family lawyers, Ian's firm, instead of your mother's, it would never have happened.'

Felicity's ready anger bubbled up. 'It should have been my mother's money anyway! If I'd been consulted, I should have given it to her. She must have needed it very much.'

She had surprised her hostess. 'But you had been counting on that money to start your travel business! Ever since I can remember you, that was your ambition.'

'Well, I managed it anyway. I didn't need an inheritance!' But Felicity was back to wondering where she had got the capital from.

'Tom was never happy about how you did that. He said no bank in their right mind would back you.'

'Touching faith in me he had!'

'A girl in her early twenties, no business experience, no security, of course no bank would be interested!'

'What about my flat? Perhaps I could offer that as security?'

'Mortgaged to the hilt and your mother died two years ago, when the property market was at its lowest,' Belinda said with blatant satisfaction. 'No, it was a mystery. Tom said he just hoped you hadn't done anything really foolish.'

Felicity stared at her. 'Such as?'

'Oh, I don't know. What do young, attractive girls get up to?'

Felicity felt her hands tighten into fists. How could Belinda be so righteous, sitting in her elegant drawing room so confident in her Dashwood heritage that would have completely disappeared if it hadn't been for Felicity's grandfather?

She forced herself to relax. Carefully she counted out thirty pounds and pushed it across the coffee table. 'I think that is what I owe you. No doubt you will inform Mr Rankin I have repaid the debt. I'm sure you told him of the loan in the first place.'

Two red spots flared in Belinda Gray's cheeks.

'There is no need,' she started.

'Indeed there is. I have no intention of being beholden to you in any way.' Felicity rose. 'Nor need you bother coming again to see me.'

Belinda made a clumsy attempt to excuse herself but Felicity marched out of the house then channelled her pent-up indignation into the car. She shot out of the drive on to a quiet side road and forced the engine up through the gears, its powerful throb answering some deep-seated anger that reverberated through her on behalf of the mother she couldn't remember.

She came to a junction with a main highway and had to stop. Cars whipped past the long bonnet, their speed flinging them along the road like bullets; a huge lorry roared past, its exhaust quivering the air, the fumes assailing her nostrils. The anger suddenly drained away and Felicity's legs started to tremble; she missed an opportunity to pull out on to the road and had to wait for several more cars to rush past before, finally, she was able to make the turn. All desire now for speed had gone and it was with relief that she turned off on to a quieter road. Trees on either side met overhead and provided a soothing tunnel as she drove slowly along.

A clean slate was what Malcolm Biddulph had suggested she'd been given. A child had its personality tempered by experience. How it was treated by other people affected its development. The memory of that treatment travelled into adulthood. Now Felicity had lost her memories, had she also lost their tempering effects? Could she start again?

The car rounded a corner, the trees ended and the sea came into view. Felicity stopped the car in the entrance to a field and got out. A five-bar gate closed off ripening wheat, its pale gold interspersed with the odd red poppy like drops of blood on a satin gown. She scrambled up and sat perched on the top bar looking out to sea.

It was late afternoon but the sun was still bright and the sea was shades of blue, from aquamarine through pale to navy, broad sweeps of water colours, calm and serene. Felicity wondered how it had been the night the *Seawind* had exploded. Rough, stormy? Had her father been as experienced a seaman as Thomas Dashwood? How large was the yacht? Questions raced across her mind as a stiff breeze started up, chilling her and sending dark patches across the shining sea.

Chapter Twenty-One

By the time she arrived back at Kingsleigh, Felicity was exhausted. She identified herself to the constable on the gate then stopped the Aston Martin outside the front door; she had no energy left to drive it into the garage.

Mrs Parsons opened the door immediately the engine died. She held a duster in her hand. It was as though she'd needed an excuse to hover in the hall.

'Miss Felicity, you've been out so long, I've been worried.'

Her concern sounded genuine.

'I'm back, in good order, Mrs Parsons.' Felicity glanced up at the sky. That chill breeze had whipped clouds across its clear blue and more were arriving. 'Do you think it's going to rain?'

The housekeeper looked at the car. 'Were you thinking of leaving that there? Mr Mark . . .' She closed her mouth abruptly.

'I know, Mr Mark wouldn't have liked it,' Felicity said wearily.

'Don't you worry. I'll ring Johnny and tell him to come and put it away, you look done in.'

'Johnny?'

'The groom, that is to say, he used to be the groom, he's been helping Rules in the garden recently.'

Felicity remembered the empty stalls and the glance that Mrs Parsons and Belinda Gray had exchanged when Johnny's name had come up earlier. What had happened to the horses?

Everywhere she turned there were mysteries. It was like trying to speak a foreign language, thinking you had enough vocabulary to cope then finding the natives constantly using words you hadn't come across before.

Felicity left the key in the ignition, hauled herself out of the car and went inside. There were no signs of any police remaining in the house. Were they really moving out of Kingsleigh tomorrow? Leaving her unprotected?

Felicity stood uncertainly in the hall. She wanted to sit down somewhere relaxing and consider everything she had learned that afternoon but the idea of the morning room, always so dark in the afternoon, was unattractive. She remembered the sitting room where she had made her telephone calls.

Its blinds had been drawn against the sun. She raised them and saw the clouds from the sea were grey and threatening. The weather was probably going to break.

Felicity sat wearily in one of the armchairs and allowed the room's charm to soothe her battered spirits. Then she thought a whisky would help her even more. Her medication had finished, so why not? There was a bell beside the fireplace. She pressed it, wondering if anything would happen. A few minutes later a startled-looking Mrs Parsons appeared.

'Ask Johnny to bring the key of the Aston-Martin to me here after he has garaged it, will you, please? And, Mrs Parsons, I'll use this room after lunch in future. Could you see that drinks are always available on that table? And bring me a whisky and water now?'

The housekeeper gave a little nod and left the room with a curious expression on her face. It might have been respect.

The drink wasn't long in coming. Armed with it, Felicity went over to the music centre with its well-stocked rack of compact discs and chose one. A Chopin sonata filled the room with cool melody.

Then Johnny arrived.

As soon as she saw the dark stubble on the sulky face and recognized the aggression in the green eyes, Felicity wondered how she could have forgotten about the youth on the motorcycle. Just what had he been up to while she'd been here?

He came and stood in front of her chair, dirty trainers insulting the carpet, his body belligerent beneath a soiled blue sweat shirt and grubby jeans. An equally grubby hand extended car keys towards her without speech.

'Thank you.' Felicity took the keys. Behind her dark glasses, her eyes studied him. He shifted his weight from leg to leg uneasily and wiped a drip from his nose with the back of his hand. 'It's Johnny, isn't it?'

'Yeah. Miss,' he added belatedly. His truculence the day she arrived seemed to have seeped away. Did being inside the house intimidate him?

'I haven't seen you around the place.'

'No, miss.'

His hands fiddled with the belt loops of his jeans.

'I gather you're the groom?'

'Yeah.'

'But that you haven't any horses to look after?'

'Not at the moment, no, miss.' Well, that was at least three times the number of words he'd managed in a sentence up to now.

'Were the horses sold after my cousin died?'

He looked wary and wiped another drip from his nose. 'No, miss!'

'So where are they?'

A note of truculence reappeared. 'They was stolen.'

'Stolen? When?' Felicity was taken aback. She had assumed Belinda Gray had ordered the horses sold after the funeral and had been working out how to tackle her. Now warning notes sounded sonar-like deep in her consciousness. Family heirlooms or television sets could be burgled comparatively easily. To thieve horses was a different proposition.

'It was about two weeks ago, I think, miss.'

'You think? You must know.' Felicity stopped herself sounding as frightened as she was beginning to feel.

'Well.' Johnny chewed the side of one of his grubby fingers. 'It was a Monday, see, Monday two weeks ago.'

'Presumably the police were involved?' Johnny nodded. 'And what are they doing about it?'

'Dunno.' Johnny considered a bit longer, then said, 'They asked me if I heard anything, it was in the night, see, and I told them I heard nothin'. I'm too far from the stables, see?'

'Where do you live?'

'In one of the cottages by the kitchen garden.'

Felicity remembered noticing a pair of semi-detached cottages beyond the walled garden.

'Who lives in the other one?'

The youth swallowed convulsively. 'Mr Rules did.'

'Are you there alone or do you have a wife, or girlfriend, or something?' Cleaned up and without that surly expression, Johnny could possibly be considered attractive.

A not very pleasant smile split the youth's face. 'Nah, I'm on me own!'

Felicity returned to the subject of the horses. 'They were stolen in the night, you say. Do you know how?'

Johnny's feet in the dirty trainers shuffled uneasily and his gaze shifted round the room. 'The 'orse box was stolen as well. Police said they must have been loaded up in it.'

'How many horses were there?'

'Four. Prince, Mr Dashwood's stallion; Ninja, a big grey, 'e was Mr Sheldrake's; El Cid, that was Mrs Sheldrake's chestnut gelding; and Paloma, a roan mare.' Johnny's expression changed. For the first time he looked at Felicity as though he knew her. 'Mrs Parsons told me you don't remember nothing, miss. Well, Paloma was your 'orse. Not that you were down that often. Mrs Sheldrake often used to exercise 'er, or she'd ask me to.' He paused before adding, 'She's great.'

A pang of loss stabbed Felicity. Would she ever know how great Paloma was? 'Thank you, Johnny,' she said in dismissal, then called him back as he reached the door. 'Johnny, what have you been doing, since the horses were stolen?'

His face looked sulky as he took another swipe at his nose. 'Mr Rules said I 'ad to 'elp with the gardening. 'E 'ad me digging vegetables and weeding. 'Til 'e disappeared, like.'

Yes, Felicity would place a sizeable bet that over the last couple of days Johnny hadn't done a thing. 'Well, I think you should continue with the vegetables. In the morning ask Mrs Parsons what she needs and I'll come out and check on what you're doing. That's until we get the horses back or replace them,' she added and saw the sulky look lighten.

That night a storm arrived. Felicity lay in bed and tried to sleep through rain lashing against her window, lightning flashing through the curtains and the rumble of thunder. In the background the rollers crashing on the beech sounded louder than usual. They were nothing to the thoughts that were crashing round her mind.

Death and destruction were all around her. Violence was stalking Kingsleigh and those telephone calls she'd had must be part of it. Her panic attacks in hospital weren't a folk memory of her accident, they were caused by a danger that still lurked. What was going to happen when the police left? More telephone calls? More demands she didn't understand and couldn't fulfil?

If only she had a close friend. She needed someone to talk to, confide in and ask questions, someone who was close to her and could explain the sort of life she had been leading, even if there were gaps. But if she'd had such a friend, they would have been in contact with her, sent her a card at the very least. She remembered the lonely days spent in hospital, the flowers other patients had had, the cards that had covered every available surface except around her bed.

The storm lulled and Felicity blessed the impulse that had taken her into the office of calm, sensible Malcolm Biddulph. She should tell him everything, he would be able to advise her on what she should do. He might even be able to persuade Chief Inspector Combe she was in peril even if she couldn't say what it was that threatened her.

But what if he thought she was involved in something outside the law?

The thought had been creeping up on her ever since the second telephone call and had become insistent in Malcolm's office. It would explain the caller's attitude and could make sense of the chief inspector's suspicions.

Surely, though, she couldn't have murdered Rules, or had anything to do with the explosion on the yacht in which her own father had died? But she did seem to be involved in something mysterious going on at Kingsleigh. After all, if it was all straightforward, why didn't the man who was telephoning her just turn up and explain what it was he wanted?

If only she could remember!

Frustration fought with a new kind of panic as Felicity flung back the covers and started pacing the room, listening to the storm gradually moving away and trying to face the fact that if she told the forces of law and order about the calls she could be incriminating herself.

Until she knew exactly what she was involved in, she could trust no one. Somehow she had either to restore her memory or find some way of discovering what had been going on to bring all these disasters to Kingsleigh. Then and only then could she decide what should be done.

Towards dawn she tumbled back into bed and slept fitfully. She woke to an overcast and chilly morning, her body sweating with fear.

Chapter Twenty-Two

The demons of the night were placed in a more rational perspective for Felicity by the familiar sight of Mrs Parsons bringing in her breakfast and the sounds of the cleaning in progress around her.

As she ate muesli and drank orange juice, she wondered if she hadn't allowed a catalogue of dreadful incidents to prey on her mind. There weren't any sinister forces at work at Kingsleigh. Some tramp had killed Gordon Rules. Perhaps he'd dossed down in the boat-house, been disturbed and hit out with the winch handle when the gardener discovered him. He'd be miles away by now.

The yacht explosion and the car crash had been dreadful accidents and the horses had been stolen by smart professionals. The fact that all these events had happened within such a short space of time was unfortunate coincidence.

Felicity was still left with the telephone calls. The mysterious caller couldn't have mistaken her for someone else; she'd answered the telephone by announcing herself as Felicity Frear. Surely if what he wanted was something innocent, he'd have explained what it was?

Examining her conscience when she couldn't remember past behaviour might seem a pointless exercise but Felicity told herself that she didn't feel like a criminal. But then she supposed that there were many criminals who felt no guilt and thought their behaviour thoroughly justified.

She finally reached the conclusion that her present frame of mind might mean very little as far as her previous behaviour was concerned and that the only really helpful decision she had made in the last twenty-four hours was to find herself a lawyer.

Even just remembering her session with Malcolm Biddulph made Felicity feel more cheerful, dire though some of the things she had learned from him were.

A new decision got her out of bed and dressed. Downstairs, she took her tray to the kitchen, where Mrs Parsons was cooking. A casserole was standing on the kitchen table, filling the air with a wonderful, full-bodied meaty aroma.

'Oh, doesn't that smell good,' Felicity exclaimed as she put the tray on the table.

Mrs Parsons left stirring something on the Aga and moved into a flurry of activity, taking the casserole off the table and muttering something about stocking up the freezer.

Felicity couldn't let this go by. 'I must go through that freezer of yours some time, Mrs Parsons,' she said lightly and watched the way the woman's face mottled unpleasantly with colour as she took the breakfast tray to the sink. 'But I came down to say you needn't bring me up breakfast in the mornings any more. I'm well enough to come down now.'

'I, I don't think that'd be wise,' the housekeeper said, quickly recovering her poise. 'You need your rest and it's no trouble.'

'I'd prefer it,' Felicity said with finality.

'But it would be much better for you . . .' Mrs Parsons grimly stood her ground.

'No, Mrs Parsons, it wouldn't.'

Felicity held the housekeeper's gaze until the green eyes flickered.

'I only want what's best for you, miss.'

'I'm sure you do, Mrs Parsons.'

Felicity left, found an anorak and a pair of gumboots and went outside to the kitchen garden.

There she found Johnny, sulkier than ever, digging over one of the beds.

'What are you going to plant there?' she asked him cheerfully.

'Dunno,' he glowered at her. 'Only I picked the French beans for Mrs Parsons and you told me I was to work 'ere all day. The lettuces 'ad bolted and so I thought I'd better dig it over.'

'Excellent idea,' applauded Felicity, grimly amused at his dislike of the job. 'When you've finished, we'll decide what to plant.'

She moved on to the tennis court she'd glimpsed the other day. As she'd thought, there was a practice board along one end. A daily session with racket and balls should help get her back into shape.

Returning to the house, Felicity found Chief Inspector Combe coming towards her.

'Good morning, Miss Frear,' he called. 'No need to send for Malcolm Biddulph, I just wanted to tell you that I'm moving my men out of Kingsleigh this afternoon. We'll be setting up shop in the village hall.'

'Good of you to let me know, chief inspector.'

He stood firm on the lawn, a bulky man with a watchful face. 'Interesting you felt you had to run to a lawyer yesterday.'

'I didn't feel I needed to hide behind legal niceties, if that's what you're suggesting; it merely seemed a sensible course of action,' Felicity retorted crisply. 'Why didn't you tell me that the horses had been stolen?'

'So you've heard about that, then?'

'As I was bound to. It might have been better if you had informed me, chief inspector. As it is, I would be grateful to know what information there is on their disappearance.'

'It wasn't my case originally but I've called up everything available.' He looked at her enquiringly. 'How much have you been told?'

'Only that your colleagues apparently thought they were loaded into the Kingsleigh horsebox and driven away.'

'That's about it, I'm afraid. It looks like a professional job, no sign of the horses or the box. Or of any car that could have brought the thieves here.'

'It sounds as though whoever it was had some inside information.' Felicity hesitated then added, 'I take it you've thoroughly questioned the groom, Johnny?'

'Oh, yes, Miss Frear, we've certainly done that.'

'Have you asked him why the horses were in the stables? I would have thought, in summer, with nobody here to ride them, they should have been out in the fields.'

'That thought had occurred to us. According to the groom, he'd brought them in prior to the blacksmith arriving to check the shoes; he thought one or two needed attention. The blacksmith did, indeed, turn up early the following morning.'

'And you've no evidence that Johnny was connected with the crime?'

'No, Miss Frear, none.'

'I'd like to think that means he's innocent.'

'So would we.'

The chief inspector was giving nothing away. Felicity looked at him for a long moment. His eyes were guarded, his face politely blank.

What would it take to shake that bland self-assurance? Was there anything she could say that would really jolt him? What if she told him how frightened she was, that she believed someone was threatening her? But she could imagine how those watchful eyes would narrow suspiciously, how he would start to question her, ask for proof, reasons.

Felicity held out her hand. 'Thank you, chief inspector, and thank you for coming to tell me your movements.'

'Not at all, Miss Frear.' He shook her hand briefly. 'Just one little thing. You told me yesterday that your reason for searching the lockers was to see if you could find some red sails. That they would be proof you'd had a genuine flash of memory; that was the way you put it, wasn't it?'

'Yes, as I told you, it was the first faint sign I've had that my memory might be coming back.'

'Yet you haven't asked if we found any red sails in the boathouse.'

Felicity's mouth felt suddenly dry. 'Were there some there?'

He nodded, his gaze never leaving her. 'In the next locker to the one with the body. I believe they belong to the yacht in the boathouse, the *Seabreeze*. Your cousin's boat.'

Felicity gazed at him, stunned. Then it was true, she really *had* remembered something of her past!

'May I say you seem very much better this morning than you did yesterday?'

'I am better,' Felicity said, realizing that she did indeed feel much stronger.

'Strange, many women would feel worse after what you've been through in the last couple of days.'

'Some of us thrive on crisis, chief inspector!'

'I hope you don't need many more to recover your health completely, Miss Frear.' He lifted his hand and touched his forehead in a salute that she saw as sardonic and left.

Before looking for tennis equipment, Felicity decided some telephoning would be a good idea.

Malcolm Biddulph was her second call. He sounded delighted to hear her voice, particularly when she reported that she had the address of her Clapham flat and had spoken again to Paloma Travel. Apparently she kept a spare flat key in her desk there and they were posting it to her, first class. With luck it should arrive the next day, Friday.

'Well done, you are coming on,' he said admiringly and Felicity felt her sense of achievement made sweeter by his praise. 'How about I call for you early on Monday and we drive up then?'

She replaced the receiver with an unusual sense of something to look forward to. A moment later, as she sat looking through the window at the grey sea, the telephone rang. Malcolm, with something he'd forgotten to tell her, she thought, and picked it up happily.

'You'll be on your own once the police have left,' said the now all too familiar voice. Slivers of ice slipped down her spinal cord. 'You know what I want. Why can't you be sensible?'

'I don't know who you are or what you want!' Felicity cried. Fear edged her tone razor-blade sharp. 'Unless . . .' Inspiration suddenly struck. 'Is it the money that was hidden in the desk?'

'What money?'

'I found it yesterday, in an envelope, a thousand pounds.'

His laughter was genuine. 'Good God, girl, what's a thousand pounds? A drop in the ocean.' The amusement vanished, leaving his voice colder than ever. 'Now stop trying to act clever.'

'Why can't you understand? I can't remember anything before the accident!'

'Make yourself! I'll give you a little longer, then . . .' He left the words hanging in the air before cutting the connection.

Felicity clutched at the dead receiver. All her sense of well-being vanished and she was once again fighting panic. What did he mean by 'a little longer'? A few hours, several days? Was he coming to Kingsleigh? If so, when?

What was she to do?

The only practical answer she could think of was to get fit.

Chapter Twenty-Three

Felicity found a pair of tennis shoes in her wardrobe and balls and rackets in a downstairs cloakroom, then went back to the tennis court.

She quickly found that her impression of returning strength was something of an illusion. Running quickly exhausted her and even patting the ball against the wooden wall so that it returned to her feet made her arm feel like a tired piece of rubber.

Gritting her teeth, Felicity persisted and gradually worked her way through some sort of exhaustion threshold to a slightly more energetic state. Feeling she might be getting somewhere, she continued for another ten minutes or so, then knew she really had had enough. But, walking back to the house, Felicity realized that much of her sense of oppression and threat had been lifted.

She ate her lunch wondering if most of her problems wouldn't be solved by leaving Kingsleigh. She had, after all, a flat in London and a business to look after. But during her call to Paloma Travel earlier she had received her progress report from Jane. It had been brief and to the point. So many bookings received for such and such tours, a cancellation here, some problem solved there. It had all meant very little to her. Unless her memory suddenly returned, she had weeks of hard work ahead of her before she could make any contribution to the business.

The idea that whoever was calling her on the phone wouldn't have the number of her flat in London when he seemed to know everything else about her was laughable. She couldn't escape him by moving back there but might it not jolt her memory back into place?

Being at Kingsleigh hadn't.

Except there had been that brief moment on the balcony in the boathouse when she had seen *Seabreeze* with its red sails. And afterwards, hadn't there been something else? A memory that had vanished as soon as she'd brought it to mind, leaving only that devastating sense of loss?

Were there perhaps other parts of Kingsleigh that would bring back other moments? There were many rooms she hadn't even entered, others, such as the library, where she had been under pressure that must surely have prevented any memory getting through. Now that she thought about it, Felicity couldn't believe she'd spent so many days here without looking properly round her house. It was an indication, if any were needed, as to how weak she'd been feeling.

She began a tour, room by room, of her inheritance, trying to open herself to the atmosphere of the house and imagine herself exploring it as a child.

The police had removed all their papers from the library but a faint air of bureaucracy still hung around the stacked shelves. Felicity gave the globe by the desk a twirl and fingered the spaces marked 'unexplored'. That was what she was, a map labelled Felicity Frear, with known boundaries neatly drawn and blank spaces marked 'unexplored'.

In the billiard room she took a cue from the set hanging on the wall, pushed the marker board to zero and set up a frame of snooker balls. She sent the white ball spinning down the full-sized table, then aimed it at a convenient red ball, pocketing first that then two more. Felicity Frear seemed to have quite an eye for snooker.

The dining room, where Mrs Parsons had yet to serve her a meal, was large, dark and impressive, liberally decorated with precious items. A Georgian wine cooler stood in the window, a pair of elegant knife boxes and some pieces of antique silver were on a Sheraton sideboard, oil paintings of Dashwood ancestors hung on the walls. Felicity looked at their bony faces and wondered whether they'd been tight-fisted or profligate; had they increased or squandered their heritage?

She went upstairs and started looking through the bedrooms.

Thomas Dashwood's was grand. A heavily carved four-poster bed with crimson hangings, a huge cheval glass reflecting a variety of antiques, more oil paintings.

Further along the corridor, next to hers, Felicity found another room with signs of occupation.

A suitcase was sitting on the webbed case-carrier and on a table by the window, overlooking the front of the house, were papers.

She went over and found a small pile of brochures for a polo establishment in Argentina.

Curiously she picked one up and glanced through it. The name 'Frear' jumped out at her.

She sat down by the table and looked through the pages more carefully.

The Buena Vista Ranch offered a range of services from breeding polo ponies to breaking them in and training them, plus access to the best equipment in the world for every aspect of polo playing. The pictures of the ranch suggested it was luxuriously appointed and offered every convenience to both ponies and riders. No expense seemed to have been spared.

The owner of the Buena Vista appeared to be one Alexander Frear. Fortune hunter, Belinda Gray had said. His ranch looked prosperous enough. Had it been her father who had provided the capital for her business?

The suitcase was empty but hanging in the wardrobe were some clothes, including a suit with a Savile Row tailor's label in the jacket, a smart-looking pair of casual trousers and a supple leather jacket. In a chest of drawers were several shirts and some underwear. On the dressing table a set of silver-backed brushes bore the initials AF.

Felicity held one of the brushes in her hand for a long moment and tried to reach out to her father. What had he been like, this man her mother had divorced, who ran an up-market polo pony establishment in Argentina? What had he been doing at Kingsleigh when he and her uncle had been blown up? Visiting her or the Dashwoods?

Belinda Gray hadn't liked him, which in Felicity's eyes could be a positive recommendation, but Thomas Dashwood must have at least tolerated him, otherwise why would he have taken him sailing?

Felicity ran her fingers over the finely patterned silver back to the brush and traced round the A and the F. She balanced it on her palm, feeling the soft prickle of the natural bristles. Morning after morning they had groomed her father's head; his scalp had felt their passage. Had his hair been short, long or balding? Grey, dark or fair? She remembered Belinda's description, 'Like Alan Ladd only taller.' Dimly she recalled seeing the star's old films on television. He'd had a sleek blond head so her father must have been fair as well.

She held on to the brush more tightly – but no impression of Alexander Frear came through to Felicity, the brush could have belonged to anyone. She replaced it gently on the dressing table, left the bedroom and continued along the corridor, opening door after door into bedrooms that waited for the next house party. None of the others had any personal items.

Nowhere gave Felicity a particular frisson. Nothing suggested her memory was about to return.

At the kitchen end of the first floor was a narrow staircase. Treading lightly, Felicity continued to the top of the house. Here the corridors were uncarpeted and ran through a variety of levels. Steps went up and down, the corridor snaked and twisted. Felicity moved along, opening and closing doors. Small windows looked out to the sea or on to the roof. Some of the rooms were sparsely furnished, contrasting with the opulence of the rooms on the floor below, some were empty. It was obviously the servants' quarters. 'Capitalist exploitation,' said a little voice at the back of her mind. Felicity ignored it and wondered where Mrs Parsons lived. There was nothing up here to suggest one of the rooms could be hers. Perhaps she had a cottage in the grounds. It wasn't a pleasant thought, that every night she was left in this huge house on her own. Surely that couldn't be possible?

Felicity arrived at the west end of the house to find another staircase. It led down to the balcony landing overlooking the hall.

Reaching the landing, Felicity saw, leading off it, another, short staircase she hadn't noticed before.

It took her into a small, dusty panelled room with a window overlooking the hall. A solar room, where medieval ladies would retire after dinner, much as ladies later left the men to their port and withdrew to the drawing room. She turned slowly round, took off her dark glasses and let her eyes accustom themselves to the gloom. There seemed no source of light beyond that interior window and the hall was so dark on such a murky day it didn't offer much illumination.

But there was nothing to see beyond the panelling; an empty wooden torchère stand and a plain, planked floor. Something, though, held Felicity. She stood and felt despair come welling up from somewhere deep inside her. It was a profound sensation, raw as pain, and it had nothing to do with the feeling of menace and fear that had dogged her ever since she had first woken after the accident.

Tears started welling in her eyes and she knew if she remained in that room she would break down. With an immense effort of will Felicity forced herself out and down the little staircase, yanking the door shut behind her. By the time she stumbled on to the landing, the despair had receded so completely that Felicity wondered if she could have imagined it. She glanced over the balcony towards the interior window that looked over the hall and shuddered. No, she hadn't imagined it.

The front door bell rang.

Felicity stayed on the landing and waited for Mrs Parsons to attend to it.

A few minutes later she saw the housekeeper pass along the foyer and heard the front door being opened. 'Yes? Can I help you?' Her voice floated across the hall towards the landing.

Then Felicity moved involuntarily, flattening herself against the wall beside the balcony as she heard the visitor ask if Miss Frear was there.

It was Sam McLean.

Chapter Twenty-four

Felicity heard Mrs Parsons say, she was sorry, she didn't think Miss Frear was available.

The housekeeper was taking too much on herself! However much Felicity shrank from meeting Sam McLean again, she wanted to make the decision herself. She almost called out that she was there, then heard her visitor politely ask Mrs Parsons if she mightn't be mistaken.

'Well, sir, I'll check,' the housekeeper said grudgingly. 'If you'd like to wait in the library.'

Felicity heard their footsteps come into the hall and pressed her back against the wall, heedless of the pressure on her still-sore scars, knowing only that she was terrified of betraying her presence before she could decide whether to see this man or not.

Why such reluctance when it was he who had saved her life?

Felicity couldn't rationalize it, she only knew that ever since his visit to her in hospital, she had been suspicious of his part in the tragedy. The brief conversation she had overheard in the Golden Lion the previous day had increased her wariness. Sam McLean was another, sinister facet of the strange and unexplained goings-on at Kingsleigh.

The footsteps moved in the direction of the library and Felicity felt her heart beats gradually slow. She made up her mind and went down the stairs. Until now Sam McLean had only been a voice. Now she must come face to face with him and try to discover what it was he wanted.

Mrs Parsons was standing in the hall, almost as though she was waiting a suitable length of time before she went back into the library to say that Miss Frear was not at home.

'Who has called?' Felicity asked.

Once again brick-red colour erupted on the housekeeper's face in painful-looking patches and she sounded flustered as she said, 'A Mr McLean, miss. I've put him in the library. Are you at home?'

Felicity nodded. She would face dealing with Mrs Parsons later.

'Bring him into the sitting room and organize us some tea, would you, please?'

Mrs Parsons moved towards the library with painful dignity.

Felicity ran nervous fingers through her fluff of hair as she went through to the sitting room. She chose a chair with its back to the window and sat down, adjusted her dark glasses and hoped she looked frail but composed.

'Mr McLean,' said Mrs Parsons.

Sam McLean's appearance was a shock. Listening to his dry, clipped voice in the hospital, combining it with his role as an insurance salesman, Felicity had visualized an academic type, slight and thin with stooped shoulders. The man who came into the room looked like a rugby player. He was tall and burly and his face seemed moulded from strong rubber, its contours all rounded and flexible, apart, that is, from his nose. At some stage, perhaps in a scrum at Twickenham, it had been broken and allowed to mend without benefit of plastic surgery; it had ended up crooked with an oddly flattened bridge.

'Good of you to see me, Miss Frear. I was passing this way, realized I was close to Kingsleigh and thought I would come and see how you were getting on.'

The voice was as she had heard it in hospital, closed, careful. No hint now of the lively quality it had displayed when she'd overheard him in the hotel. The eyes were wary too but their gaze was very direct, too direct; who was it said con men always looked you straight in the eye? His were grey eyes with a peculiar quality of depth, and the eyelashes, as dark as his short, curly hair, were long and thick, out of place on his rugged face.

Felicity made her voice hesitant. 'It's very kind of you. I'm much better, as you can see. Please, won't you sit?'

The grey light struck him squarely as he lowered himself into the chair, his eyes studying her as though trying to assess the truth of her words. He was wearing a dark business suit with a pale blue shirt and paisley tie. They didn't suit him; he looked uncomfortable in their formality.

'Mrs Parsons is going to bring us some tea. I hope you can spare a few moments?'

He smiled. 'You're very kind.' For the first time he sounded natural, almost charming, and his smile was so open that Felicity thought she could fall through it.

'How's business?'

'Business?'

'The insurance world!'

106

'Ah, the insurance world. Quiet at the moment. Lots of calls but not many customers signing policies.' Charm was breaking out all over; the open smile had even reached the grey eyes.

'Do you work for a big firm?'

'No, we're specialists.'

'What in?'

'A form of marine insurance.'

'Is that to do with cargo ships, huge tankers and things?' It sounded a most unlikely kind of business to employ a local man travelling round the southwest.

'I'm concerned with a much smaller area, sailing boats, motor yachts, that sort of thing.'

The room's temperature suddenly dropped. 'Did you insure my uncle's boat, the *Seawind*?'

'I don't recall it. What's your uncle's name?'

'Dashwood, Thomas Dashwood.'

Again that charming smile displaying nothing more than his excellent teeth. 'Not to my knowledge, no.'

Was that an answer?

'It was lost at sea just before my accident.'

'I'm sorry to hear that,' he said easily. 'I hope without loss of life?'

If this was really his area, how could he not have heard about the explosion? She stared hard at him through her protective dark glasses as she outlined the few details she had.

'Another of your family dead, that's rough!'

Felicity could hear no real sympathy in the easily spoken words.

Could Sam Mclean just possibly be a simple, rugger type, not too intelligent? Was that guarded quality because he was not at ease with women, perhaps even shy?

Mrs Parsons knocked at the door and brought in a tea trolley.

Sam Mclean leapt to his feet and helped her wheel the trolley towards Felicity. As well as tea there was a small plate of smoked salmon sandwiches and a Dundee cake.

'This is a nice surprise,' her visitor said after the door closed behind the housekeeper. He took the plate and small napkin Felicity handed him and helped himself to the plate of sandwiches offered. 'Don't often have the chance of tea.'

'I suppose with all the driving you do it must be difficult to eat properly.' She busied herself with the teapot.

'Usually subsist on a sarnie in a local pub,' he agreed. He took another of the sandwiches.

'Don't you ever take clients out to lunch, or get taken out by your boss?' Felicity handed him a cup of tea and offered the sugar bowl, almost willing him to say he'd had a business lunch yesterday at the Golden Lion.

He shook his head and found a place for the teacup on a small side table. 'Not often. I can't remember the last time.'

Felicity thought how valuable it had been to have met Mr McLean whilst she'd been unable to see. Had she first encountered him today, she might easily have thought him harmless.

Sam McLean put down his empty plate. 'But tell me how you are really,' he said. 'I can see you're far from fully recovered, though you do look a little better.'

'Tact must be your strong point, Mr McLean.' Felicity raised an apologetic hand to the scars on her face and her still-swollen nose. 'But of course when you saw me in the hospital I was so bandaged even my own mother wouldn't have recognized me. Anything would be an improvement on that.' She put a large slice of Dundee cake on his plate.

'How's the memory? Back in place yet?' He picked at the cake.

'Not yet.'

'Returning here didn't bring anything back to you?'

'How did you know I used to stay here?' Felicity could not prevent her voice sounding sharp and suspicious and for a brief moment his eyes narrowed.

'The hospital said you'd gone back to your old home,' he said easily. 'I rang a few days ago to see if I could visit you again. And how are your eyes?' he added.

It sounded plausible enough. 'I can see a certain amount but my sight hasn't fully returned and I shall have my dark glasses for quite a while.' Felicity arranged herself to give an impression of an invalid struggling bravely to appear fitter than she was.

Sam McLean refused more tea and moved his big body in the chair to take in the room, seemingly fascinated by his surroundings. Then Felicity saw his gaze caught by something on the desk by the window. 'What a lovely place this is,' he said. 'What a lucky person your cousin was.'

'Until her car met that lorry, I suppose she was.'

She was surprised to see him appear genuinely embarrassed. 'Stupid thing to say, I'm sorry.' He got up with an awkward twitch of his shoulders, walked to the window, stood beside the desk and looked out. 'Fantastic view, all that garden and the sea.'

Felicity remained in her chair with her back to him and watched his reflection in the mirror above the mantelpiece. 'I can't think of a nicer place to convalesce,' she murmured. She saw him glance at her, then coolly and quickly turn and read Malcolm Biddulph's card as it sat where she had placed it that morning on the desk as she made her call to the lawyer.

'But I don't seem to be able to keep away from trouble,' she added, resting her head against the back of the chair as though she was tired, and slowing the pace of her voice. 'You probably heard that I found the body of our gardener the day before yesterday.'

'No!' he said quickly. 'How dreadful!'

'I'm surprised nobody told you. They can't be talking of much else around here.'

'I've been in London until this morning.'

She let out a breath she hadn't been conscious of holding. The bit about lunch might have an evasion but that was an outright lie.

He sat down again. 'What a terrible shock it must have been for you.' He was more relaxed now, his expression engaging, even his voice sounding livelier. In other circumstances she might have found him attractive. If only his eyes weren't so watchful. If only he wasn't such a liar. How much of what he'd told her was true?

'The police have been all over the place. You weren't stopped at the gate?'

He shook his head. 'There was nobody there when I came down. But, police? Was your gardener murdered?'

'If you don't mind, I'd prefer not to talk about it.' He wasn't going to get her relating the grisly details. Let him find out whatever it was he wanted some other way.

'I'm sorry, really sorry.' He sat forward in his chair, arms resting on his legs, hands clasped between them, a picture of concern.

'Look,' he said casually, 'You've been terribly kind and I'm very pleased you're so much better. Perhaps next time I'm in the area, I could call again, take you out to lunch or something?'

What *was* he after? 'I don't know.' Felicity made her voice sound as weak as it had in the hospital. 'With everything that's been going on, I'm not sure I'd be up to it.'

His glance was even sharper. 'I'll call anyway, check up on your progress. If I can get by your dragon of a housekeeper.'

'You've no need to worry about Mrs Parsons,' Felicity said grimly, forgetting for a moment her pose of weakness. 'She's only trying to protect me. I get tired so easily,' she added quickly, giving her words a dying fall.

'I won't allow her to put me off,' he assured her.

She was willing to bet he'd be back within the next few days.

She rose and pressed the bell beside the fireplace, then gave an artistic stagger. In a moment he was by her side and helping her back into the chair. 'I'm sorry,' she said weakly. 'I find every now and again my strength just seems to vanish.'

He stood looking down at her. Felicity lifted a hand to her forehead as though she might have a serious headache, shielding her eyes from a gaze that seemed as though it might bore through the dark glasses and into her very soul.

Then Mrs Parsons was there.

'Mr McLean is leaving. Please show him out,' Felicity said.

Chapter Twenty-five

A few minutes later Mrs Parsons returned and, after a quick glance at Felicity, started piling the tea things on the trolley, her movements quick and decisive. 'If you don't mind my saying so, miss, you look terrible. Can I get you anything?'

Felicity sat up straight. 'I'm quite all right, thank you, Mrs Parsons. I was wondering, do we have a daily paper?'

'I take the *Daily Mail*. Mr and Mrs Sheldrake took the *Independent* but that was stopped after the accident.'

'Ask for it to be reinstated, would you, please? And do you still have yesterday's paper? And today's?'

Mrs Parsons brought them to her.

Felicity started to search for coverage of the murder. It took her a little time before she discovered a story on an inside page regarding the body of a gardener found on an estate in north Devon. The police were treating the death as suspicious, the report said, and followed it with a brief paragraph detailing the chain of mishaps that had befallen the estate. In earlier years no doubt the story would have hit the headlines; these days there was too much crime and too many murders; pop stars, football players, politicians and drugs were what interested the media.

It was a story Sam McLean might easily have overlooked. But it wasn't true that he had only just come down from London. It had been he she had eavesdropped on in the hotel, she had no doubts whatsoever about that. And he had denied having lunch out in the recent past.

Another unsettling thought occurred to her. Was Sam McLean staying in the Golden Lion? Had he been there the night Gordon Rules had been murdered? So near to Kingsleigh?

Felicity deliberately wiped from her mind a vivid picture of those strong-looking arms wielding a heavy metal winch handle and replaced it with those same arms pulling her from a burning car. She found that the first picture remained, a palimpsest beneath the second.

There were no follow-up details in that day's paper on the murder inquiry. She took them back to Mrs Parsons then stood and watched while the housekeeper stacked a dishwasher with the tea things.

'Where do you live?' Felicity asked. 'In a cottage, like Rules and Johnny?'

'No, miss. In the flat.'

'There's a flat? Where?'

'At the back, here.' Mrs Parsons went over to a door at the far end of the kitchen and opened it, displaying a short corridor. 'It was built on about twenty years ago, very nice, no nasty stairs to climb, and makes me quite independent. It's got its own entrance, you see. I go in there, shut the door and I'm on my own. After-hours I needn't worry about anything in the house. I don't answer the telephone or anything.'

'Yes, I see, very convenient.' So she wasn't completely alone in the house at night. Felicity hardly felt reassured.

'What sort of security does Kingsleigh have, Mrs Parsons?'

'Oh, the best, miss! All the windows have security bolts and we keep those locked when the windows are shut. I check them all before I do supper. And the doors all have special bolts as well as regular locks. I check those as well.

'No alarm system?'

'Mrs Dashwood wanted one and I believe she got a firm to quote just before she got so ill but Mr Dashwood said it would cost too much. It's such a large house, you see, miss. And he said it was so tucked away nobody hardly knew it was there.'

Felicity looked around the well-organized kitchen. 'How long have you worked here, Mrs Parsons?'

The housekeeper closed the dishwasher and started wiping down the trolley. 'Nearly ten years, Miss Felicity.'

So when Mrs Parsons had first arrived, Felicity reckoned she herself must have been about fourteen. 'It must be strange for you, me not being able to remember anything when you know me so well.'

'As you say, miss.'

'I gather this was a second home for me?'

'People would sometimes think, those as didn't know, that you and Miss Frances were sisters.'

'What were we like as girls?' Felicity sat herself down at the table.

Mrs Parsons wiped her hands on a cloth and started stringing beans.

'I can do those,' offered Felicity.

'You will not! You never knew your place as a child but, as Mrs Dashwood used to say, with your upbringing, it wasn't to be expected.'

112

'What do you mean, my upbringing?'

'Well, as I understand it, miss, your first home was in Spain, racketing around with horses, mixing with grooms and things. As Mrs Dashwood explained it, you never had no discipline, your parents were too busy. Then, when Mrs Frear was back in London, well, the company she kept! We 'ad one or two of her young men down here, not that Mr Dashwood liked it. They never lasted long, though. She was very attractive, your ma, but young men like that only ever want one thing, don't they?' Words poured out of Mrs Parsons as though they had been kept dammed up for too long. 'We all thought it was no wonder Mrs Dashwood wanted you here with Miss Frances most of the holidays. Well, it was no life for a kiddie up in that London flat, with a mother who had no idea of how anyone should behave! It's not surprising your poor dad... well, that was none of my business.'

Mrs Parsons' view of her father appeared very different from that of Belinda Gray.

'But when you were at Kingsleigh Mrs Dashwood said she never knew what the two of you would be up to next, she was that worried at times.'

'Why, what did we do?'

'Well, once you both took Miss Frances's boat out and never came back till next day. Had the police out and everything, Mr and Mrs Dashwood did. Then in the two of you sail as though nothing 'ad 'appened.'

'Where had we been?'

'You said the wind had dropped and you couldn't get back. And you weren't at all sorry, just shouted at them that if only anyone had looked at the weather, they'd have known what had happened.'

'My God. You mean we spent the night in the Bristol Channel on a dead calm sea waiting for wind? We could have been run down by something!'

'That's what Mr Dashwood said. He was that angry! Said you'd sailed much further than you should 'ave and you'd been criminally careless. Right to do, there was.'

'I bet.'

'Then there was the time you invited the gypsies to camp in Long Acre field. Except they weren't really gypsies, more a load of 'ippies. And once in they wouldn't budge! Mr Dashwood wrote to parliament and everything. There was such a fuss and you just said there was so much at Kingsleigh why couldn't a little of it be shared!'

'What happened in the end?'

'Two of them was accused of burglary and Mr Dashwood offered to get them a good lawyer if they'd move on and they did.'

113

'Sounds like youthful high spirits to me.'

Mrs Parsons sniffed. 'You didn't have to deal with it yourself, is all I can say.' Her voice was sour and bitter.

'Just before he was killed, Gordon Rules told me that Mr and Mrs Dashwood were so kind to me when I first came here that my cousin was jealous. Yet what you've said suggests maybe I tried their patience too much.'

'I don't know too much about that. When I came here there was no favouritism that I could see. Bit on the contrary, I thought. Mr Dashwood was always coming down on you, you could never do right in his eyes, not that you tried very hard as far as I could see!'

'You don't sound as though you liked me, Mrs Parsons.'

'It's not my place to comment as to that, miss.'

Felicity lost patience. 'Oh, come on, Mrs Parsons. All that "my place, your place" disappeared years ago. I haven't forgotten that! Why don't you spit it out, whatever it is you've got against me? You've made it plain that I'm not fit to polish my cousin's shoes but you haven't explained why.'

Mrs Parsons's mouth pursed firmly. 'I shouldn't 'ave said what I did. I was trained in the old ways and I 'old with everyone knowing their place. Anyway,' she hesitated for a moment then plunged on, 'your cousin's gone now and it seems as though you might have improved your manners. Sometimes it's almost as though I had Miss Frances back, poor thing. Let the dead bury their dead, that's what I say, and what you did to her that time don't matter no more.'

'What time? What do you mean? What did I do to my cousin?' Felicity was almost pleading.

But Mrs Parsons wasn't going to tell her anything. She put the colander of sliced beans on one side, rolled up her sleeves and started washing lettuce, tight little heads with crisp leaves that had to be disentangled from each other.

'All right, Mrs Parsons, let's talk about your freezer stock, shall we?'

The woman went on washing the lettuce and tucked her head down over the sink. 'I don't know what you mean, miss. I've always used my time well, cooking ahead, then when it's needed something's available. Where do you think the sandwiches for tea came from? I buy smoked salmon ends when they look good and find a few minutes to turn them into pin wheels and triangles. Always go down well, they do, and a moment in the microwave defrosts them nicely.' She straightened her back into a righteous line. 'If you want to check, do, the freezers are through there.' Mrs Parsons pointed towards a door beside the Aga, her arm quivering with virtuousness.

114

Even before Felicity opened the door of the store room or lifted the lid of one of the two long white freezer cabinets, she knew it would be useless. She was going to find a chocolate cake in there and a meat casserole.

Sure enough, there they were, amongst a range of other neatly packed and labelled dishes, dated correctly.

But would they have been if Felicity hadn't made her pointed remark this morning?

Too late to wonder that now. She went back into the kitchen.

'I've never been questioned about my activities before.' The housekeeper was full of indignation.

'Mrs Parsons, I have no complaints about the way you run Kingsleigh. But you know and I know that you do not like having me here. I find that difficult to live with.'

'I wouldn't say that, quite, miss,' the housekeeper muttered, her eyes downcast, the lettuce ignored.

'Well, what would you say?'

'Everything's different, that's what!' Mrs Parsons burst out. 'I like my routine and knowing what's 'appening. It's all this uncertainty that's so difficult.'

The words seemed to hang in the air.

'What uncertainty?' asked Felicity softly.

Ugly colour once again mottled Mrs Parsons's face.

'Mrs Parsons, what is going on here?'

The housekeeper stared at Felicity and the bright colour drained away, leaving the bones standing out beneath the pale skin like a portent of death. 'I don't know what you mean,' she said finally.

'Yes, you do, Mrs Parsons.'

But the woman wasn't saying anything else. She stood by the sink, distressed but mute and obstinate.

'We've had murder here, Mrs Parsons.'

Fright leaped into the housekeeper's eyes. 'I know nothing about that, miss, I promise you.' Her hands clasped themselves, twisting tightly.

Felicity looked at her. 'You must see that I can't continue like this. I would very much like you to stay but I have to be able to trust you.'

'I only want what's best for everyone!' insisted Mrs Parsons.

There was something more here than distress at losing all the family within such a short time and the harrowing effects of the gardener's murder.

'I'm glad to hear that. Then I can rely on your loyalty?' Felicity took off her dark glasses and fixed Mrs Parsons with an unwavering stare.

The housekeeper appeared to shrink inside her flowered overall. Felicity knew that never again would she be treated as a guest but also that she had not got to the bottom of Mrs Parsons's behaviour.

'I'm sure everything will come all right soon, miss.'

'It had better, Mrs Parsons,' Felicity said grimly and left the kitchen.

Chapter Twenty-Six

It was a more than usually taciturn Mrs Parsons who produced Felicity's supper that evening.

Nor did Felicity feel like making conversation. The various confrontations of the day had left her battered. She allowed the housekeeper to serve and clear away in silence while she considered her next move.

Various aspects of her past were slowly coming together but she had learned very little about what she had been involved with just before the accident. And it was surely there that the key to the mystery must lie. If she could only remember what had happened then, she would not only know what was going on here but also what that voice on the telephone wanted.

Wasn't there anything she knew about the time before the car crash?

Apparently that day Frances and her husband had met her at the station and they all seemed to have been driving back to Kingsleigh when the collision occurred.

It sounded as though she'd been on the train from London. Had she been there when the *Seawind* had exploded?

The chief inspector's words, though, suggested that she had been at Kingsleigh. For a weekend, perhaps? With a travel business to run, she couldn't have had much time for coming down here. Yet the car crash had occurred mid-week and was supposedly only a week after the explosion. What had brought her down here then?

Would Belinda Gray know?

Felicity didn't think so. The woman didn't appear to have been closely involved with Kingsleigh. Her brother seemed to have visited her rather than Belinda constantly popping in on him.

Surely Frances must have had a friend down here, someone she talked to apart from her cousin? After all, according to both Belinda Gray and Mrs Parsons, the cousins hadn't had much to do with each other for a couple of years. However close and self-sufficient they had been before that, Frances must have had someone else to turn to then.

Felicity went over to the desk. In the middle drawer she found an address book. It was full of names, nothing to pick out one from another. Glancing through, Felicity found her own name and London address. How ironic; it had been under her nose all the time!

There was no personal correspondence in the desk. Had that all been sent up to Mr Rankin?

Felicity sat back and looked around the room, seeking inspiration.

In a set of bookcases running under the windows she saw several volumes of photograph albums.

She pulled them out and placed them, beautifully bound in white leather with gold tooling, on the large coffee table that stood in front of the sofa.

She found one that was only half full and seemed to be the latest. She started looking through it. Quite soon she found several of a tennis party. Frances looked stunning in her short white dress. There were shots of her with an equally attractive-looking man in his mid-thirties, tall and as blond as she, the short hair glinting in the sunlight, his arm around her shoulders. He had a bony nose that gave his face a hawk-like look, which added to his appeal. The other couple looked more ordinary, a plump girl with an interesting face that had no pretensions to beauty and an intelligent-looking young man. Felicity flipped over the pages and came across snaps of a sailing expedition on a large yacht that must be the ill-fated *Seawind*. There was one of her uncle, looking even gaunter than in the photographs she'd seen in the morning room, and several group shots that included the couple who had been playing tennis.

Felicity looked at the names printed neatly under the photos. The couple were called Denise and Charles.

She went back to the address book.

It didn't take her long to find an entry for Denise and Charles Comstock.

She lifted the telephone and dialled the number.

Denise answered.

Felicity took a deep breath and introduced herself.

'Oh, Flick, how are you? I feel awful about not ringing or anything. We've been up to our eyes and I gathered you weren't fit enough for visitors.' She sounded warm and concerned.

'I'm much better and longing for some company.' Felicity tried to sound lonely but not self-pitying. She received a ready response.

'Of course you are! Look, shall I come over tomorrow?'

'Would you really?'

'Now that it's the holidays I'm dying to get away from the house; all the things I should be doing are just screaming at me!'

'Come to lunch,' Felicity offered, thinking it would do Mrs Parsons good to have more than one to cook for.

A moment later it was all arranged.

Felicity rose earlier than had been her habit at Kingsleigh so far. Meeting the housekeeper coming along the corridor with her breakfast, she took the tray.

'Thank you, I'll take this down to the dining room. I meant what I said about getting up for breakfast, Mrs Parsons.'

'I think you'd feel much better for the extra rest,' the woman said. 'It's no trouble to bring you a tray.' She sounded anxious and Felicity wondered if she was genuinely concerned about her health or worried that her morning routine was going to be upset.

'Downstairs in future,' she said with finality. 'Oh, and Mrs Parsons, I've got someone coming to lunch today.'

'Lunch? I never knew nothing about lunch!' Her tones expressed curiosity combined with unease. Felicity noticed, as she had the day before, how Mrs Parsons' command of English slipped whenever she was seriously disturbed.

'It's Mrs Comstock, I spoke to her last night.'

Mrs Parsons' face cleared. 'Oh, her! Right, I'll see you get a nice lunch. One o'clock suit?'

'That'll be fine. Mrs Comstock said she'd come around twelve-thirty.'

'I've got some nice soup in the freezer and the butcher's calling this morning. I'll get a piece of steak. If I'm quick, I can get the milkman to leave some cream and Johnny can pick some raspberries from the garden for dessert.'

'That all sounds very good,' Felicity said as Mrs Parsons hurried away, good intentions bursting out of her.

What a contrast with yesterday!

After breakfast, Felicity had another session on the tennis court, then had a shower before getting ready for her guest.

It was still overcast and too chilly to be out on the terrace. Felicity checked that Mrs Parsons had filled the ice bucket and had the drinks ready in the sitting room, then sat nervously awaiting Denise Comstock's arrival. How well had she known her? Did Denise know about her loss of memory? Would she be able to answer any of the questions that beat so desperately at her brain?

By the time the door bell rang, Felicity was walking up and down the sitting room in an agony of impatience.

The moment she heard the bell, Felicity hastened to the door, calling to an advancing Mrs Parsons that she would deal with it.

Denise was tall, as tall as Felicity herself, and her kind, pleasant face was one that didn't photograph well, as she looked more attractive than some snapshots had suggested, with warm brown eyes and a captivating smile that more than made up for the mouse-brown straight hair. Felicity couldn't remember ever having met her before.

As she took in Felicity's appearance, Denise's eyes widened and she swallowed hard but she gave no other sign of either horror or curiosity and her expression became concerned and sympathetic. She held out a small round melon. 'I am sorry for not coming before. I've brought you this. Charles is so proud of them; it's the first time he's tried melons.'

Felicity took the fruit and automatically raised it to her nose, savouring the sweet, cantaloupe aroma. 'How wonderful, I'll have it for supper,' she said. 'Come through and have a drink before lunch.'

Denise sat down on the sofa. She looked around and her brown eyes filled with tears. 'It's the first time I've been here since the funeral,' she apologized, brushing them away. 'I still can't get used to the fact that Fran has gone.'

'I can't cry.'

'Poor you.' Denise gave her a watery smile. 'It must be worst of all for you; you were so close.'

'It's not that. I've lost my memory. I can't remember anything before I woke up in hospital.'

'That's terrible! How awful for you.'

The ready sympathy was almost too much for Felicity. She turned to the drinks tray. 'What can I offer you?'

'Something non-alcoholic? I hate drinking in the middle of the day – and when I'm driving.'

Felicity found a bottle of apple juice, poured out two glasses and gave one to Denise, who was now looking at her with a puzzled frown.

'But if you've lost your memory does that mean you can't remember me?'

'I'm afraid so.' Felicity was apologetic. 'I rang because I was looking through Fran's photo album last night and I saw these . . .' She drew Denise's attention to the book that was still lying on the coffee table. 'And I had an overpowering need to talk to someone who knew Fran and me. So I looked in her address book and found your telephone number.'

It was close enough to the truth and it satisfied Denise.

'Oh, I quite understand. How very disconcerting for you, losing your memory on top of everything else!' Her glance acknowledged

Felicity's injuries. 'That makes me feel even worse at not getting in touch.' Denise's calm forehead wrinkled slightly. 'I don't really know why I didn't, except Mrs Gray said you were very poorly, but I could have telephoned.'

'Except you've never liked me all that much,' Felicity heard herself say.

Denise looked shocked. 'Whatever gave you that idea? It certainly isn't true.' Felicity didn't answer and after a moment Denise added, 'I suppose, if I'm honest, I never felt there was any real friendship between us. But that was your fault, not mine. You were . . . not cold, exactly, more . . .' She searched for the right word. 'Steely. You were always so bright, so sharp. I felt you were . . .' Again she hesitated. 'Self-contained. That's really why I didn't get in touch. But, today . . . it's funny, perhaps because we've both lost Fran, today I feel much closer to you, while you can't remember me at all!'

Felicity liked Denise's straightforward approach. 'I'm truly sorry if I wasn't more friendly before. Perhaps I was jealous.'

'Of my friendship with Fran? I can see perhaps you might have thought she was getting closer to me but I could never have taken your place, not with Fran.' Denise settled herself more comfortably on the sofa and started slowly turning the pages of the album, occasionally studying a snapshot. 'It's strange to look at these again. We all look so happy. If only we'd known what lay round the corner. Just as well we didn't. It's been one tragedy after another with the Dashwoods. Before *Seawind* blew up we thought maybe everything was coming right for Fran, what with finding Mark, I mean. Such an attractive man.' Her smile acknowledged the fact without envy.

'You mean life was difficult for her before our trip to South America?' As Denise shot her a curious look, Felicity added, 'I have managed to find out a bit about my life. There are, however, a lot of gaps.'

'And you'd like me to try and fill some of them in?' Denise sounded matter of fact.

'The doctor at the hospital said my memory could come back at any time. I thought if I tried to remind myself of the past, it might jog it into place.'

'And you thought a chat with a friend could help? I'm flattered you called me.'

Mrs Parsons appeared at the sitting room door to announce that lunch was ready and Felicity took Denise through to the dining room. It was gloomy and the two places elaborately laid at the top of the long mahogany table looked lonely. There were no flowers on the table; instead two silver pheasants decorated its polished surface.

'My, how magnificent it all is,' laughed Denise as she sat down and shook out her damask napkin. 'I always thought coming to Kingsleigh was like visiting royalty or at the very least the aristocracy. Your Uncle Thomas behaved just like a duke.'

As Mrs Parsons served the soup Felicity got Denise to talk about her life as an English teacher at a local girls' school.

'It's just the sort of job I was looking for. Fran and I both wanted to work locally. She found a post at a small public school not far from here. Philip, of course, wanted her to work at a London school in a job involving immigrant children. He would! Fran said she had enough doubts about her ability to control a class of children without adding racial difficulties and kids struggling with English as a second language.'

'Philip was her fiancé?'

'I keep forgetting you can't remember what happened.'

'Belinda Gray mentioned something about a broken engagement,' murmured Felicity.

Denise gave her a keen glance. 'Has she been giving you a hard time over that? Don't listen to her. Philip was great fun but weak. His great attribute as far as Fran was concerned was that he was totally uninterested in her money. In fact he hated everything about Kingsleigh; he never came here if he could help it. He would never have done Fran any good but she was like a mother hen with him. Without her he'd never have managed to get his degree. And the fact that he got a 2:2 instead of a third was a miracle! As was the fact that she got him to cut down on his marijuana smoking. Perhaps if he'd stayed in Devon instead of going to work in London he'd have been all right.'

'What happened?'

There was a slight pause as Mrs Parsons came in, cleared away the soup and served the steaks.

As she door shut behind her again, Denise picked up her story. 'Philip fancied himself as a poet. His work was dreadful! But he managed to get a job with a publisher. Fran said he seemed to spend his time reading something called the slush pile – unsolicited manuscripts from people who could hardly write a coherent sentence. Maybe it was that that sent him overboard.'

'Overboard?'

'Mind you, Fran must have had her eyes shut not to see what was going on. Mmm, this steak is good and the potatoes must be from the garden. I think there's nothing like them when they've only just been dug up.'

Denise ate with eager appetite and it took a little time before Felicity could get her to continue.

'Well, Fran was always complaining about how Philip was so thin and how volatile his temper was. He always seemed to be either in a fit of depression or ecstatic about something. She should have gone and seen him more often but she thought he should come down here. Maybe she should have gone and worked in London, then she would have realized what was going on.'

'And what was going on?'

'He was living in this terrible flat in north London with Clive who worked for a pop band. Not that Clive was ever there, he was mostly on a gig. But I bet it was him who introduced the stuff to Philip. I don't believe you did it, I'm sure you wouldn't have done.'

'Denise, please! I'm completely lost. What was the matter with Philip and what was I supposed to have done?'

Denise put down her knife and fork with a contrite expression. 'Flick, I'm so sorry, Charles is always telling me I let my tongue run away with me.'

But before she could say anything more, Mrs Parsons brought in the raspberries and cream.

'Mmm, these are delicious,' Denise said and gave Felicity a wicked little smile. 'I know, don't worry, I'll tell you everything.' The smile died as quickly as it had arrived. 'It's not a pretty story, I'm afraid. Fran went up there one weekend after he'd stopped answering his telephone and found him dead. He'd overdosed on cocaine.'

Chapter Twenty-Seven

Felicity felt the room swim about her. She put down her spoon and reached for a glass of water.

'Are you all right?' Denise sounded worried. 'I'm such a fool, I should never have told you right out like that.'

'It's OK, really.' Felicity drank some more water. Her senses steadied until there was only a slight buzzing at the back of her head.

Denise was still looking anxious.

Felicity tried to marshal her wits sensibly. 'Are you saying I'm supposed to have supplied this Philip with cocaine?'

Denise sighed. 'Fran never believed that! She was just desperately hurt. Philip was supposed to have told her he was in love with you and couldn't marry her. You had a terrible row and you stopped coming down to Kingsleigh. Until Mrs Dashwood was dying, that is.'

'Why don't we go and have coffee in the other room?' Felicity flung down her napkin and rose, her mind in a ferment.

Cocaine!

Then she wondered who else had mentioned cocaine to her recently.

They'd reached the sitting room and she was pouring out the coffee Mrs Parsons had left there when it came to her. Belinda Gray, when she'd been telling Felicity about her mother's death.

'Are you sure Philip Bishop was supposed to be in love with me?' she asked, handing Denise a cup of coffee.

Denise regarded her curiously. 'I don't think I mentioned Philip's other name.'

'How strange. I didn't think about it at all, it just popped out.' Felicity felt uneasy.

'Philip had told Fran he was crazy about you.'

'What did I say about it?'

'That it was a passing phase and he'd grow out of it.'

'Nice of me!'

'Don't be like that! Fran was desperately insecure. You'd think with all this behind her' – Denise gave the sitting room a comprehensive glance – 'she'd have had all the confidence in the world. Instead she thought everyone liked her for her money. As I said, one of the reasons she was attracted to Philip, I'm sure, is because he was so contemptuous of it. He'd never let her pay for anything.' Denise smiled sadly. 'He didn't have any of his own so they never went to a nice restaurant or to the theatre or anything. I can't imagine what would have happened if they'd ever got married.' Denise paused for a moment then said, 'Fran knew Philip was weak and that she should have made more of an effort to be with him. I think what hurt her was that you hadn't protected him from himself. Worse, that you'd taken advantage of him.'

Felicity looked at her. 'Denise, do you think I deliberately made a play for him?'

The other girl shook her head. 'Philip wasn't your style at all. I don't suppose you could have done anything about it unless you'd stopped seeing him. Away from Fran, he probably just latched on to the nearest strong female he could find. He was a parasite!'

'How do you know he wasn't my style?'

'Oh, Flick, it was obvious. The only men you ever showed an interest in were strong with charisma and usually rather older. Men like your father.'

'Alexander? You met him?'

'A couple of times. The first was just before Fran's mother died. It was mid-week in the summer holidays and you were in London. I was visiting and he sailed into Kingsleigh's harbour on a friend's yacht. He went up to see Mrs Dashwood and Mr Dashwood showed his friends around. Then he came down and we all had tea together. I thought he was marvellous. So attractive and such a character. He told us all about his polo ponies and life in Argentina.'

'I found a brochure on his ranch. It sounds quite a place,' said Felicity. 'I hadn't thought before but I was his only child. It could well be mine now.'

Denise looked slightly embarrassed. 'I don't want you to get your hopes up. After he left, Mr Dashwood told us your father lived on a knife edge and was always dunning his friends and relatives for loans.'

Felicity looked at her in dismay. Did this mean that she still didn't know where the capital to start her travel business had come from? And that her father hadn't been nicely settled and prosperous?

'Then I met him again a few days before the *Seawind* exploded. We all went for a sail together, at least Fran and Mark and Charles and I and your father did. I don't think Mr Dashwood actually liked Alexander very much.' Denise smiled bleakly. 'I think we all had a very much better time without Fran's father, actually. It was a wonderful day. Fran, Mark and Alexander did the sailing and Charles and I just lolled about. We all had such fun; everyone got on so well together.'

'You liked Fran's husband, then?'

Denise nodded. 'I think he was a bit of a playboy but he obviously adored Fran and she was so happy. I couldn't understand why Mr Dashwood kept picking on him.'

Mrs Gray gave me the impression he liked his son-in-law.'

'He did to start with. I don't know what happened; perhaps he was beginning to go to pieces, without Fran's mother. That last time we went sailing, he was really uptight, he almost refused to let Mark take *Seawind* for a sail. But we all begged and he relented. But when we got back Fran wasn't feeling very well and he was furious with Mark for taking her along.'

Denise blinked hard. 'That was the last time I saw her. I wanted to come over after the explosion but you were here and she said she wasn't feeling up to much and could I wait a few days.' Now tears were falling down Denise's cheeks. 'She was terribly upset there weren't any bodies to bury. I said there could always be a memorial service.' She got out a handkerchief and gave her nose a good blow.

'Was I at Kingsleigh when the boat blew up or did I come down afterwards?' Felicity asked.

'No, you were down here. You'd taken a few days off, I think to see your father, and you'd arrived the day after we'd all been out together.' Denise looked down at her fingers, twisting the handkerchief. 'I thought, afterwards, you would stay here, be with Fran, but when I rang again, a few days later, you'd gone back to London. I said I'd be right over but Fran wouldn't let me come, said she still wasn't feeling up to much.'

'Did she say anything else?'

'Just that Mark was taking the tragedy very badly. She thought he was in a worse state than she was. She was afraid he was going to have a nervous breakdown.'

'And that was the last time you spoke to her?'

Denise gave a big sniff. 'No, I rang her the day she died. She said she was much better but that you were coming down and she thought you had more bad news for her. She said she'd ring when she knew what it was.' Denise blotted away more tears. 'But, of course, she never did.' She looked at Felicity. 'And you can't remember what it was you were going to tell her?'

Felicity shook her head.

'It must have been something important,' Denise said slowly.

Felicity, frustrated beyond measure, could only agree with her. Why did tiny little facts like Philip Bishop's surname come back to her, but the important details remain hidden?

'And Fran didn't tell you she was worried about anything else, or say that anything strange had been going on here?'

Denise thought for a moment or two. 'I can't think of anything,' she said. 'That last time she was in rather a state; she wasn't making a great deal of sense. I was afraid she might be breaking down herself. She was beginning to sound just like she did after Philip's death.' She looked at her watch. 'I'm sorry, Flick, I shall have to be going. I promised my mother I'd call in on her on the way back.'

Felicity rose. 'It's been great to see you,' she said.

'I can't think I've been much of a help; all I seem to have done is tell you about terrible things. I'll come again next week and go through all the nice times we had together.'

'Promise?' Felicity thought she'd like to see sensible Denise again. Despite all the dreadful events she had related, Denise had provided a sane interval in what seemed an increasingly anarchic world.

She led the way out.

As they passed through the medieval hall, Denise looked about her. 'This hall always gives me the willies, it's so sombre, full of ghosts. The first time I came here I was terrified. I'd hate to have to spend a night alone in this place.' She looked at Felicity. 'Doesn't it worry you?'

'Ah, but I'm not alone. The redoubtable Mrs Parsons is here.'

'I've never thought she was a particularly cosy person. And as for that nephew of hers!' Denise gave a little shudder.

'What nephew?'

'The groom, Johnny, isn't that his name?'

'He's her nephew?' Felicity was astonished. 'Nobody's told me that!'

'It's probably hard to remember that you don't remember, if you see what I mean,' Denise said comfortingly. 'I'm being naughty. I'm sure he's perfectly ordinary really, it's just the way he looks at you. I'd hate to meet him on a dark night.'

Chapter Twenty-Eight

Felicity closed the front door behind her and leaned against it, hammers pounding against her temples.

Thoughts were clashing inside her head. Johnny and Mrs Parsons, bound in a malevolent partnership, lies about her involvement with Fran's fiancé, insinuations about cocaine addiction. None of it made any sense. It was all irrational.

Why shouldn't Johnny be Mrs Parsons' nephew? What was wrong with that? No doubt if she accused the housekeeper of keeping the relationship from her, Mrs Parsons would point out that she didn't know she was interested.

And how could Felicity be sure she hadn't tried to steal her cousin's lover? Perhaps she'd been overwhelmed by an instant attraction. Who was Denise to know the sort of man Felicity went for?

Felicity ran her hands lightly down her body, feeling through the loose cotton the unscarred breasts, the flat stomach, the long thighs, flinching as she disturbed the scabs on her knees from the climb up the cliff. That body knew passion, somehow she was sure of that. Had it been with Philip Bishop? How had his surname slid into her mind so easily?

Or had she loved, did she love, someone else? Someone, as Denise suggested, more charismatic, more like her father?

And could she ever have been a cocaine addict like her mother? Surely that had to be impossible?

The pain and confusion she'd suffered when she first awoke in hospital, the irrational fears that had threatened to swamp her, came back. Cold sweat broke out down her back as Felicity recognized all that could be put down to withdrawal symptoms.

Then she told herself that that was ridiculous; the doctor would have said something to her.

Unless he was waiting until she was stronger.

Unless he thought she would be in no danger of temptation at Kingsleigh.

Unless he believed she brought in her supplies from South America and until she went back there she wouldn't have access to more anyway?

Is that what that voice on the telephone wanted – cocaine?

Cocaine commanded high prices. Somebody desperate for a large sum of money, who often visited South America, might think it could provide the capital that wasn't available from more legitimate channels.

But how could she have been regularly smuggling an illegal substance through customs?

A thought, horrifying in its implications, struck Felicity and wouldn't disappear.

She tore herself away from the solid, reassuring feel of the heavy wooden door and walked upstairs on legs that threatened to give way. She told herself what she was thinking was impossible but she knew it had to be checked.

The leather holdall was still sitting on the case-carrier by the wardrobe.

Felicity grabbed it by the handles and dragged it over to her bed.

Sitting on the quilted polished chintz cover, she loosened and took off the stud that had come off, then tried to unscrew the others.

They didn't move.

Felicity carefully inspected inside the holdall but all was smooth and innocent, no loose flap that could conceal a hidden compartment. She sat and looked at the case, her breath coming quickly. Could she be sure there wasn't a false bottom? It had only been the loose stud the day she'd arrived at Kingsleigh that had suggested the idea.

But if it was to pass customs' scrutiny, the studs wouldn't be that easy to unscrew anyway.

Felicity left the holdall sitting on the bed and went downstairs, forcing her unsteady legs to carry her outside to the garage. There she found a pair of pliers, a thin screwdriver and a Stanley knife.

Back in her bedroom, her head swimming with all the effort she had put herself through, Felicity once again attacked the studs. Gradually, stiffly, they yielded and eventually she was able to unscrew all of them. They lay glinting on the bedcover, shiny nuggets of metal, the scratching of the pliers lost in the scarring inflicted on the studs whenever the case had been put down on a rough surface.

Felicity forced the screwdriver between the base and the sides of the holdall and tried to force it out. It appeared to be fixed firmly in. Had the studs no more purpose than to prevent the leather getting scratched when the holdall was put down?

Once again Felicity inspected the case and finally was convinced that the thickness of the base could conceal a hidden compartment.

She gritted her teeth. If necessary, she would use the Stanley knife to tear through the tough leather. Before that, though, she would see if there wasn't some other way.

It took a long time before Felicity found the secret. Pushing and pulling at the leather produced nothing. Eventually, by working the thin, sharp blade of the Stanley knife between the base and the sides of the case and trying to run it right round, she discovered that there appeared to be four pieces of metal running from the base into the bottom frame of the holdall. Finally, by balancing the case on one end on the floor, pushing down with her knee on the other end and pressing with each hand on the two sides where the locking metal appeared to be, all the shafts suddenly and smoothly withdrew into some central knot and the base came loose.

Felicity sank, breathless, on to the bed. The handsome holdall lay collapsed on the floor, its sides sagging. Then, frightened beyond measure, she reached out, lifted off the base and saw that it had concealed a shallow space lined in unpolished leather.

The hidden compartment was empty.

Felicity let out a long sigh. She didn't know whether she had expected the case to contain anything or not. It was enough that it was capable of carrying illicit goods.

She picked up the holdall and studied the inside of the compartment. Adhering to one part of the rough leather was what looked like white powder.

She licked a finger, picked up some of the tiny granules and placed them on her tongue. Minute explosions took off inside her mouth.

Cocaine! It must be.

She closed her eyes as the implications dug deeper into her agonized mind. Then she opened them again and forced herself to consider practicalities.

How much cocaine could be fitted into that space? Enough, surely, to be worth the risk. Especially if the smuggling was done on a regular basis.

Felicity drew up her legs and lay on the bed in a miserable huddle. Life seemed very bleak.

After a little she started shivering. She got off the bed and picked up the case and its base. Almost by accident she found that pressing the middle made the metal struts spring out again. With the base in place the case looked no more than a particularly handsome leather holdall. She chucked it into the bottom of the wardrobe and went downstairs.

Something drew her into the central hall. She stood under the tattered standards that hung down from the hammerbeam roof, symbols of Dashwood chivalry, and felt very vulnerable. The police had left but that didn't mean they still weren't suspicious of her; the voice on the telephone could materialize at any time and somewhere around was Gordon Rules's killer.

The police had said the gardener had been murdered in the evening; what had he been doing, wandering around then? His cottage was at the other end of the estate from the boathouse. He surely wouldn't have climbed down there late at night, and the police seemed convinced he'd been killed elsewhere anyway.

Johnny lived in the cottage next to Rules's. He was thin but wiry, used to hauling heavy bales of hay around. He could easily have wielded that winch handle and stuffed the body into the locker. But why would he? Had the gardener discovered him involved in some sort of suspicious activity? Something like the theft of the horses? But that had happened several days earlier and the winch handle made Johnny an unlikely candidate for murderer, anyway. Why go all the way to the boathouse for a weapon when there was bound to have been something nearer to hand?

There were no rational answers to the unending series of questions that haunted Felicity.

She walked slowly into the foyer and checked the front door. Mrs Parsons had obviously done her security check. The strong iron bolts and sturdy old lock looked comfortingly efficient.

How efficiently secured was the rest of the house?

Felicity started checking the windows of the ground floor. All had security bolts and as she found each was fastened, some of the unease began to lift.

The library was the last reception room on the ground floor to be checked. Automatically she moved round the windows, unsnibbing the traditional locks and checking if the bottom sash would rise. As with the others she had tried, window after window resisted her pressure and Felicity's confidence rose. Then she came to the last and almost lost her balance when the big sash moved easily on its cords. Here the security bolts had not been screwed into the window frame. Felicity gently pushed the window back into place.

Had it been an oversight? Had Mrs Parsons perhaps not got round to checking the security yet?

Fighting panic at the way the house had been left vulnerable, Felicity walked rapidly to the kitchen.

Mrs Parsons was preparing supper.

'I was wondering about the security bolts,' Felicity began, feeling duplicitous, but Mrs Parsons flushed in the unbecoming way she had.

'I've checked them, miss,' she said.

How stupid of her, thought Felicity. Why hadn't she said she hadn't had time and was going to do it after Felicity had eaten?

'I've been going round and one of the windows in the library is open.'

'Open, miss?' Mrs Parsons' green eyes flashed. It was difficult to say whether she was indignant or suppressing guilt but Felicity wondered how she hadn't recognized the housekeeper's resemblance to Johnny before this. Dread at what she herself might be involved in and terror of what might be lying outside waiting to invade and confront her combined in an overwhelming rage at being left vulnerable in this way.

'This is the end, Mrs Parsons. I can't trust you and I have to ask you to leave.'

The housekeeper's jaw sagged. Suddenly she was just a frightened, elderly woman.

'Miss Felicity, please! I haven't done anything. All I want is for the best.'

'You have a funny way of showing it!'

'But I've nowhere to go.'

As her rage died in the face of the woman's consternation and patent despair, Felicity began to feel sorry for her. Whatever her failings, Mrs Parsons worked extremely hard and had made her very comfortable. Then she remembered the unsecured window and hardened her heart. 'You can share your nephew's cottage until you find somewhere else.'

Mrs Parsons's eyes narrowed suddenly. 'That's it, isn't it? You think Johnny's been responsible for what's been going on here and you're making me part of it.'

'Do you think he's responsible?' Felicity asked, suddenly alert.

Mrs Parsons' gaze dropped to the dish of chicken she'd been about to put in the stove. 'Course I don't,' she said stoutly. 'Johnny's straight, always 'as been.' But there was no conviction in her voice.

'Show me where all the security keys are kept,' Felicity said wearily. 'Then you can give me supper and start packing. You're to leave in the morning.'

'You've never been nothing but trouble to this house!' Felicity was startled by the viciousness in the housekeeper's voice. She stood back and let Mrs Parsons pass well in front of her then followed her through to the library.

Once she had collected all the keys, Felicity locked the library window then continued checking, listening to her footsteps and the creaks and groans of the ancient house, and it seemed to her as though she was listening for something else. But everything else on the ground and first floors was secure and there was no one hiding in wardrobe or cupboard.

When she reached the end of the corridor, Felicity looked up the narrow staircase that led to the top floor. Was it really necessary to check the windows up there? She almost decided it wasn't, then remembered the venerable wistaria that grew against the back of the house, its thick, sturdy stem and branches providing a perfect ladder.

Felicity went up the staircase and moved lightly along the uncarpeted corridor, negotiating the different levels and awkward corners. There were no security locks here but these windows couldn't be opened from the outside. She passed swiftly in and out of the rooms; something in the atmosphere made her edgy but she could find no clue to any occupants other than mice and flies.

She regained the main staircase and avoided looking at the short flight of steps that led to the solar room. Nothing, she thought, would take her into that room again. And surely it wasn't necessary; the room had no outside window. Then she gazed thoughtfully across the balcony to the inner window that overlooked the hall. If anyone wanted to hide in the house, what better place?

She forced herself up the steps and pushed open the panelled door. It was so dim inside the room that she had to stand in the doorway for several minutes before her eyes could be certain no one else was there, not even behind the door, and by then the same despair she had felt the first time she'd been in this room had filled her and tears were streaming down her face.

With a shaking hand she closed the door and ran back to the main landing, then waited for the despair gradually to drain out of her.

She went down to the sitting room, turned on all the lights and drew the heavy cream curtains, blotting out the early evening light, before sitting far back in the chair she usually chose. She clutched at its arms and told herself she was safe. Nothing and nobody could creep in and hit her with a winch handle, or anything else.

Chapter Twenty-Nine

That night Felicity took one of the sleeping pills the hospital had supplied her with and woke late, her head muggy. She opened her eyes slowly, at first not sure where she was.

Then yesterday surged back with terrifying clarity.

She hastily dressed herself and went downstairs.

Yesterday evening Mrs Parsons had produced supper on a tray and slammed it down on the coffee table in the sitting room without comment. She had not reappeared to remove the dirty dishes and Felicity presumed they were still sitting there.

She went into the kitchen and, as she had expected, it was empty; no sign of Mrs Parsons.

Felicity found the tin of muesli and helped herself to a bowlful, added milk from the fridge, poured herself a glass of orange from the carton that stood in the door and took her scratch breakfast through to the morning room.

There was no sun, the sky was once again cloudy but though rain threatened at present the air was clear.

Felicity drank the juice and ate the muesli, refusing to think. That could come later. First, she was going to continue to try and get her body back into reasonable condition. She changed into tennis shoes and took racket and balls down to the court.

Starting slowly, she began to hit a ball against the practice board. Almost immediately she discovered that the exercise had already made an impression. Her legs were stronger, her reactions quicker, her arm more capable of swinging the racket as her mind dictated. Her strokes were good; she found it as easy to take the ball on her backhand as her forehand and her feet automatically moved to the right position. She began to hit the ball a little faster.

Such was her concentration that she didn't notice someone was watching her until she was startled by his voice. 'You could be a good player,' said Sam McLean. His black leather jacket and jeans emphasized his height and his broad shoulders. In a formal suit he had seemed uncomfortable; today he looked formidable.

Felicity stood panting from the effort she had put into her exercise and looked at him in dismay. So much for all her attempts the other evening to mislead him as to how quickly she was recovering from the effects of the accident. It was gloves-off time.

'Were you passing Kingsleigh again?' she asked caustically.

The vestige of a smile twisted his mouth but didn't reach the grey eyes. 'Not really. I'm down here for the weekend and thought that, if you were free, I'd like to offer you lunch.' He looked at the court and added, 'If I'd realized tennis was on the agenda, I'd have brought my racket.' But there was nothing amused about his smile and the grey eyes looked colder than ever.

'The exercise is good for me.' Felicity challenged him to query that. A few drops of rain fell and she looked up at the lowering sky.

'How about it?' he pressed. 'It's not the weather for doing anything much outside.'

There was no point in saying she wasn't up to going out. Mrs Parsons wouldn't be preparing lunch for her and to get away from Kingsleigh and all its ominous associations was suddenly an appealing thought. Quite apart from all that, Felicity felt impelled to try and find out what this man was after. 'All right,' she said, 'you're on.'

It was only later that she realized how dangerous an invitation it was.

'Good!' He held the door to the court open for her then fell into step as she walked towards the house.

Asking him to wait, Felicity went upstairs and had a quick shower. She found another pair of loose trousers and a long-sleeved silk shirt. She added a cardigan then took the back stairs down to the kitchen and knocked on Mrs Parsons' door.

The housekeeper was in an old pair of trousers and a baggy cotton jersey. Behind her Felicity caught a glimpse of boxes and cases littering the short corridor, belongings surrounding them everywhere. Again she felt guilt. Ten years to be packed up in a morning.

'Yes?' Mrs Parsons grunted belligerently.

Felicity quelled the impulse to ask her to stay. 'I shall be out for lunch,' she said. 'If you leave before I return, please lock up and post the key through the letter box. I shall take the key to the side door. Mr Rankin will be making up the money due to you.' She moved off before Mrs Parsons could say anything more.

Sam McLean assisted her into the front seat of his Rover and then helped her to fasten the safety belt. The car moved slowly up the drive, drove a little faster on the minor road then increased speed dramatically when it joined the main highway.

'I hope driving doesn't worry you,' Sam said, moving into top gear after overtaking a lorry. A vehicle coming from the other direction rushed past them.

Felicity gripped the edges of her seat. 'Not much,' she lied.

He eased his foot off the accelerator. 'Sorry, wasn't thinking. Always in too much of a rush, that's my trouble.'

What was it he'd said when he visited her in hospital? That he had been driving too fast along a Devon lane the day he'd come across the car crash? Felicity sat silent in her seat as their speed decreased and she began to relax. He drove well, she decided. He concentrated on the road rather than on idle chatter and didn't become impatient at being stuck behind a tractor but waited for the right moment to overtake. This competence was not reassuring.

'There's a nice pub a little way down the coast with good food and a view of the sea,' he said, turning off on to a minor road.

The pub was low, stone built and crouching on a headland as though protecting itself from prevailing winds. It wasn't warm enough for anyone to be sitting outside but inside there was a cheerful buzz. 'Would you like to sit at one of the restaurant tables or eat in the bar?' said Sam as they entered.

'The bar, I think,' murmured Felicity, deciding the more casual atmosphere was preferable to formal tables laid with mats and red napkins arranged in wine glasses.

'What would you like to drink?'

Felicity asked for half of bitter and found a quiet corner, ignoring the curious glances at her face. Whatever his motives, she had to admire Sam McLean's courage in being seen with her in public.

She told him this when he arrived with their drinks.

His response was straightforward. 'Nonsense. If you imagine your face is something out of a nightmare, I have to disappoint you. You wouldn't win any beauty prizes at the moment but you're no Frankenstein's monster.'

She found herself able to laugh. 'Well, thank you! I suppose that has to be a compliment.'

He directed her attention towards a board where the daily menu was chalked. She chose fresh crab salad and he returned to the bar to place their orders.

Felicity drank some of the beer and looked around her. No one was now looking her way and she wondered if she was too sensitive about her appearance. She realized with surprise that she was feeling almost cheerful. Getting away from Kingsleigh had been a good idea.

'Won't be long, they say.' Sam sat down opposite her and held his pint mug as though a pub bar was a natural habitat.

She looked at his large presence, relaxed and cheerful, and for the first time didn't feel threatened by him. She could almost imagine she was out on a date. Unconsciously she relaxed. 'Tell me about yourself,' she suggested.

'Not much to tell.' Caution edged his voice. 'You know what I do and it's not the sort of job that's interesting.'

'Are you married?'

He shook his head.

'Got a girlfriend?'

'Nothing steady; see too much of a girl and she starts interfering.'

'Always?'

'In my experience.' The fingers of one hand beat impatiently on his knee.

'And what about rugger?'

'What about it?'

'Don't tell me you don't play or I'll accuse you of telling porkies.' And, oh, how she'd have liked to accuse him of that.

'I don't know how you guessed but, yes, I was once a pretty keen player.'

'University team?'

He nodded.

'Where?'

'Edinburgh, and afterwards with the Barbars.'

'The Barbarians?' Felicity was impressed. 'Did you get capped?'

He shook his head regretfully. 'Never made it. I'm too old now and too busy for more than the odd game. Terrible to have to say you're too old for anything in your early thirties, isn't it?'

'What did you study at Edinburgh?'

'Politics and economics.' The fingers had stopped strumming at his knee and he was beginning to sound amused at her interrogation.

'And then you entered the insurance world?'

'You sound sceptical.'

'Somehow I would have thought you'd want a more active sort of a job.'

'They're difficult to get and one has to pay the rent.'

Sam McLean didn't look the sort of man who worried about paying the rent.

'What about your family? And don't say what about them!'

'Mother and father academics in Cambridge, two brothers, one in the army the other in computers just outside Geneva, both married, no children and, before you ask, I get on with my sisters-in-law.'

For a moment he looked like an ordinary man, one she could believe really had been going about his own business when he came across her burning car, someone she should only feel grateful to.

Felicity sipped at her beer and remembered the lies he had told, the sinister import of that little snatch of conversation she had overheard in the Golden Lion. What was she to make of him?

Their crab salads arrived. Sam leaned over to the next table to borrow salt and pepper. The action stretched his sleeve above his wrist and Felicity's horrified gaze caught the raw pink of scars as fresh as the ones she bore.

He caught her eyes riveted on his wrist and pulled his sleeve down to cover it.

'I'm so sorry,' Felicity stammered. 'I never realized you'd been so hurt pulling me out of that car.'

He evaded her gaze. 'It's nothing. I was wearing driving gloves so my hands were undamaged. The scarring will soon fade. Like yours,' he added pointedly.

Felicity flushed and ate some of her salad.

'Now, you've delved into my life. What about yours? Can you really remember nothing?'

'Nothing before the accident.'

'You haven't found anything's come back since you left hospital?'

Felicity shook her head.

'That must be distressing.' He sounded sympathetic.

'In a way. In another way it's really quite relaxing. Someone said the other day that I'd been given a second chance at life; I could start again with a clean slate. I like that idea.'

'What makes you think you have to wipe the slate clean?' He looked at her, his shrewd grey eyes unwavering.

Felicity felt grateful for her dark glasses. 'Don't we all have things we regret we've done?' she asked with a light laugh. 'Things we'd rather forget?'

After a moment he said, 'We're none of us saints. But,' he persisted, 'there must be something in your subconscious that's telling you that's a good way to think of your amnesia.'

Could he be suggesting he knew something about her past? Something she could be ashamed of? Maybe even something criminal?

'Don't you like to be positive about things?' She pushed the remains of her crab salad away. 'I'm sorry, this is delicious but I don't have much appetite yet.'

'You need to play more tennis,' he said slyly. 'What about a sweet?'

She shook her head.

'How about coffee?'

He took both their plates to the bar and ordered two cups, then returned to his seat and stretched out his legs. 'You told me when you were in hospital you could remember things that had nothing to

138

do with your personal life. Can you remember abroad? Holiday places, that sort of thing?'

Before Felicity could deflect the conversation into less dangerous paths, her wayward mind conjured up a picture of Inca ruins in Peru and she heard herself saying, 'Do you know South America?'

'I've always longed to go there,' he said invitingly. 'Some of the sights sound wonderful.'

She couldn't stop herself talking then. Over coffee she found herself describing the delights of the Brazilian Matto Grosso, sailing up the Amazon and the glories of ancient cultures. Sam appeared quite content to listen. 'And it's a marvellous place for souvenirs,' she heard herself saying. 'I bought a lovely alpaca sweater in Lima in wonderfully soft shades.' She stopped abruptly as she realized what she had said.

Sam looked at her, his face very still. 'That was a genuine memory, wasn't it? Not just your travel agent's spiel?'

'How did you know I was a travel agent?' she demanded, her voice low and angry. Behind her anger she was terrified. It seemed the curtain between her and the past was getting thinner. But what was going to happen if it all came back to her while she was sitting with this man? She'd never be able to conceal the fact and then he wouldn't stop until he got what he wanted. Already his face had subtly changed. The grey eyes were hooded, his gaze sharper, he looked hungry, avid. But even as she challenged him, he appeared to draw back. His face lost its predatory expression and became smooth and open again. This was a dangerous man.

'Are you a travel agent? I didn't know, it was the way you were describing everything, just like a brochure.' He made it sound like the truth but she couldn't believe him. Not now.

'I want to go back,' she said in a low voice.

He studied her face for a long moment. 'Have I exhausted you?'

'Despite the tennis, I'm really not very strong yet and sometimes I overdraw on my reserves of energy.'

He nodded slowly. 'I understand. I'll settle the bill.'

He looked very fit and strong standing at the bar, very powerful.

Felicity looked round the pub, at the holidaymakers, at the number of young couples. She wished she'd been here with a boyfriend, someone who'd wanted just to be with her, someone she loved. Who was it, she wondered, that she loved and was he still alive?

Chapter Thirty

For the first part of their drive back to Kingsleigh, Sam McLean was silent. Then he said, 'I'm sure if you explore the past more you'll find other fragments coming back. Then suddenly there'll be a great whoosh and it'll all be there.'

She said nothing.

'Isn't there someone who knew you before the accident you can talk to?'

'Only Belinda Gray, my cousin's aunt, and the housekeeper, Mrs Parsons. Neither of them is exactly sympathetic.'

'All you have to do is speak nicely to them, woo them with your charm.'

Felicity almost laughed. 'Mrs Gray is hardly speaking to me and I've just fired Mrs Parsons.'

'You've fired your housekeeper?'

She glanced at Sam; there'd been something more than surprise in his voice – was it dismay?

The countryside flashed past the car windows as their speed increased. The sensation was not pleasant. She felt her equilibrium, already unsettled, dangerously threatened. She glanced again at her driver. His expression was set and focused. Was it the road he was concentrating on?

Felicity swallowed hard and fought back the urge to beg him to slow down.

They reached Kingsleigh's front door in a spray of gravel.

'Thank you for the lunch,' said Felicity. She undid the seat belt then found herself entangled in the webbing.

'My pleasure.' Sam opened her door, freed her from the belt and helped her out of the seat. 'Would you like to offer me some tea?' he asked.

Only now that she was back at Kingsleigh did Felicity realize how reckless she'd been to go out with him. In his car, in the quiet Devon lanes, she had been at his mercy. How could she have been so foolish?

'I'm sorry,' she held out her hand. 'I really am very tired.'

He gave her a sharp look but seemed to realize he couldn't insist without appearing rude.

'Another time, I hope.' He shook her hand.

Felicity said nothing and after a moment his eyes narrowed slightly.

'Just one thing.' He pushed a hand through his short hair as though trying for an air of sudden inspiration. 'I noticed the other afternoon that there were some photograph albums on the shelves in your sitting room. Looking at photos might jog your memory into place.'

He didn't give up! What was it that was so important to him and how far would he go to get it?

'Don't you have good ideas?' Felicity said, feeling all her aggressive instincts back in place. 'I'll certainly try that. Drive carefully now.'

After that there was nothing he could do but get in his car and leave.

The relief of seeing the vehicle's rear disappear up the drive was so enormous that Felicity felt the weight of years lift from her shoulders.

She took out the key to the side door from her bag and let herself into Kingsleigh.

She went into the kitchen half expecting to find chaos, revenge by Mrs Parsons for losing her job.

All was neat and tidy.

The door to the flat was open. The little sitting room and bedroom were far from tidy but there was nothing left of Mrs Parsons.

Felicity came back into the kitchen, went through to the larder and checked the deep freezes. Again, all seemed to be in order. A check on the door and window locks and bolts confirmed all were fastened.

She made herself a cup of tea, took it through to the sitting room, sat down and listened to the silence. The huge house grew around her. The sitting room seemed as large as the drawing room, that room took on the vastness of a football pitch, the library would take the British Museum's collection of books. The hall was the length of an airport runway.

Felicity fought panic. She would be here on her own tonight and all tomorrow and tomorrow night, until Malcolm Biddulph turned up on Monday morning to drive her to London. Would Sam McLean turn up again before that? He knew Mrs Parsons had gone away, that she was vulnerable. How could she have been so stupid as to tell him that?

Suddenly the privacy that Kingsleigh offered with its large estate, tucked away in this corner of the rocky coastline, became a threat. The police had left and who else was within miles of her?

The nearest habitation was Johnny's cottage. Felicity thought of his surly green eyes and aggressive body. Thought of Johnny circling the house full of mischief and cunning.

And what of the mysterious telephone caller? Was the time he'd said he'd give her nearly up? Would he be coming for her as well?

She couldn't stay here on her own until Monday.

But where was there to go?

Could she ring Belinda Gray and ask to stay with her for a couple of nights?

The very thought was chilling. No, Belinda Gray was not an option.

But Felicity didn't know anybody else.

Except Malcolm Biddulph. Could he, would he, take her to London tomorrow instead of Monday? Even if that wasn't possible, perhaps he'd come over and keep her company for at least some of the time.

Like an alcoholic desperate for a drink, Felicity went to the desk, reached for the local telephone directory then dialled the number she found.

'Hello?'

Even just hearing the pleasant voice was immediately reassuring.

'It's Felicity Frear.' Her voice was tight with tension.

'Felicity, how nice to hear you!' The strain eased from her shoulders as she heard his warm response. 'How can I help?'

There was the tiniest of pauses after Felicity made her request and she immediately said, 'You've got a date! Don't worry; Monday will be fine.'

He laughed. 'Only an arrangement to see my parents for lunch. That's easily postponed. Tomorrow's an excellent day to go to London; we'll avoid all the traffic. Paloma Travel will be closed, of course, but maybe that's better left for another day anyway. We'll find somewhere nice for lunch, make a day of it.'

'Are you sure your parents won't mind?' But already Felicity felt safe, sure he was going to take her.

'They're used to not seeing me. Now, will you be all right this evening? Would you like me to come over and stay with you?'

Before she'd got through to him, Felicity would have given anything for this offer. But now his calm and sensible voice had made her fears seem ridiculous. 'No, I'll be fine,' she said.

'You're sure? Well, then, I'll call for you at eight o'clock tomorrow, if it's not too early?'

Six o'clock wouldn't have been too early for Felicity.

She replaced the receiver then sat looking at the instrument. Was it going to ring? Was she to get yet another of those calls? She waited, her heart thumping uncomfortably.

The telephone remained silent. Around her, the house settled back to its normal size.

Outside, rain had started to fall. The temperature had dropped and the room was chilly. Felicity rose and went across to the fireplace. Behind an arrangement of dried flowers, paper and sticks were ready in the grate.

She lit the fire, determined to banish her remaining feelings of unease.

Supper was a quiche she found in the deep freeze, eaten watching a video of *Casablanca*. Felicity had no trouble remembering practically every line.

She went to bed feeling a sleeping pill wasn't going to be necessary.

In the early hours, something woke Felicity.

She lay with her heart racing, listening, listening. All around were the sounds an old house makes in the dead of night, the odd creaking, the scurrying of tiny feet in the attics.

Felicity lay and heard, moving above her room, treading softly but distinctly, feet that belonged to something much larger than a mouse.

She must be mistaken. She looked at the little clock on the bedside table. Half-past two. A time for the imagination to take fantastic leaps.

She lay and listened again; more steps.

Then she wondered how she could have been such an idiot. How could she not have checked the house properly after Mrs Parsons had left, checked that no one had been let in to wait until all was quiet? But surely no one was up there, surely it was just her imagination? Felicity listened again and now heard nothing. Had it been her imagination? She thought again of the open library window and realized she was faced with two unacceptable alternatives. She could remain lying in bed building the noises into bigger and bigger threats or she could go upstairs and check that no one was up there.

Very slowly and very quietly, Felicity dragged herself out of bed and slipped on her dressing gown. Walking soundlessly on bare feet she went into her cousin's bedroom and picked up a poker from beside the open fireplace. Then she climbed the narrow back stairs to the upper floor.

Quiet as she was, Felicity couldn't prevent the first door she opened squeaking on its hinges. She halted, holding her breath, and listened. Nothing. All the noises seemed to have vanished. Bolder, she switched on the light, banishing the shadows. The sparsely furnished little room was empty. She looked underneath the bed, then opened a corner cupboard. Only a few lonely metal hangers. She left the light on and silently moved on to the next room. Again, nothing.

Her heart thumping at increasing speed, Felicity drew closer to where she thought the steps had been. Once more she could hear creakings. Not footsteps, no, not footsteps. These were the tiny creaks and scratchings she had heard countless times before. But now their sound was magnified by her fear.

Felicity gripped the poker tighter, turned a corner in the twisting corridor and stood outside the door of the room that lay above hers. Very carefully she opened the door, then, with a quick gesture, threw the light switch – and caught her breath in a horrified gasp as she saw a mouse scuttle into the corner, behind the wardrobe.

But mice had tiny feet, minuscule feet. Felicity's throat was constricted, her ears deafened by the beat of her heart. She slowly advanced towards the wardrobe, grasped the handle of the door and forced herself to pull it towards her. Nothing, it was empty.

Carefully Felicity closed the wardrobe and left the room. Lights now blazed throughout half of the floor. Next room, empty, another corner and another empty room, and the room after that and the room after that. There was nobody on the top floor of the house.

Felicity returned to her bed. She lay, sleepless, feeling more alone than ever, refusing to think of the turns in the corridor that could have enabled someone to tread softly ahead of her search, go down one staircase, along the first floor and up the other stairs. There must be some way of ending this nightmare. But until her memory returned, she could think of none.

Until she knew exactly what she herself was involved in, she couldn't approach the police. And there was no one else who could help her. Except, perhaps, Malcolm.

At the thought of the lawyer, Felicity felt her heart lift a little. He would be here in the morning and they would drive to London. Leave this place if only for a day. More than that, they would visit her flat. Maybe, just maybe, the sight of her own things would bring back her memory.

144

Chapter Thirty-One

The long night eventually gave way to dawn.

Felicity dressed in the comfortable trousers she had worn the day before then realized she had no suitable top for the continuing grey weather.

In her cousin's wardrobe she found a pile of sweaters and knitted jackets and chose a matching set in a crunchy linen and cotton mix that was both lightweight and elegant.

Tidying the other sweaters, Felicity found herself looking at a jersey knitted in soft shades. She drew it out with hands that trembled and looked at the label. 'Alpaca from Peru', it proclaimed. She held it against herself and looked in the long mirror. The pinks, dusky creams and delicate browns formed a swirling pattern, flowing around the sweater. Above it her still swollen nose dominated her face with its fringing of pink patches. The large, dark blue eyes surveying the sweater were alive with excited conjecture.

Slowly Felicity replaced the jersey with the others.

Back in her room, she checked she had the set of keys for her flat that Jane from Paloma Travel had sent her, together with some of the money she'd found in the desk. She thought about the lights still blazing on Kingsleigh's top floor. She would leave them on. She couldn't believe now that she had been so foolhardy as to go up there alone. Why hadn't she rung the police? However suspicious they were of her, they would at least have provided protection.

Malcolm Biddulph turned up just before eight o'clock. Felicity was waiting in the hall for him, watching for his car through the bay windows.

The moment she saw it coming down the hill, she made for the front door.

As Malcolm jumped out of his BMW, she was struggling to secure the ancient lock.

He came into the porch with a bounce to his step. 'Good morning! Can I help?'

145

Felicity felt her spirits rise. 'Perhaps I should have used the side door but I thought I'd bolt that and rely on this lock. Ah, that's it.' The old key turned at last and she was able to withdraw it.

'That's really something! How old is it?'

Felicity looked at the heavy piece of ornate iron. 'Eighteenth century?' she hazarded.

'How marvellous it hasn't been replaced by a Yale or a Chubb.'

Inside the house the telephone started to ring.

Felicity moved resolutely towards the car.

'You don't want to answer that?' Malcolm queried.

'They'll ring again.' Felicity felt a marvellous feeling of release to be leaving Kingsleigh behind. Perhaps she'd decide to stay in her flat and not come back here.

Malcolm handed her into the passenger seat. 'Now, have you had breakfast?'

Felicity shook her head.

'I've only just had a cup of coffee, instant at that. We'll stop somewhere and get a proper breakfast.

As he drove skilfully along the smaller roads, Malcolm Biddulph talked casually and amusingly about life in Devon and how he was enjoying its slower pace after the hectic backstabbing of a London office.

'Are Little Chefs beneath you? We're soon coming to one and I thought we could stop there.'

'As long as the coffee's hot and the eggs nicely done, I don't mind anything,' Felicity said.

The restaurant was half full, the other customers holidaymakers with bleary-eyed kids half asleep over eggs and chips.

Malcolm ordered and made Felicity laugh with an observation on the awfulness of family holidays. Then he looked at her, reached out a hand and gently removed the dark glasses.

Felicity felt naked.

'You're looking much better,' he said. 'Your nose is almost normal now and your mouth is relaxed. Even your shoulders aren't as tense. I'm no longer worried you might flake out on me at any minute.'

Felicity took back her glasses and put them on. 'Is that how you felt when I was in your office?'

'I had a hand continually poised to ring through to Mrs James and ask her to bring in the smelling salts.' He smiled at her. 'Now, I have been ringing around on your behalf, chasing up all sorts of information. Do you want a progress report?'

'Yes, please!' Felicity gloried in the feeling of safety she had here in this garish café with ordinary-looking Malcolm.

'Well, the police haven't got any further with finding out who

146

murdered Gordon Rules. Tales are circulating in the village of mysterious strangers seen in the vicinity of Kingsleigh but I think Bob Combe is dismissing most of those as wishful thinking. The locals love a good mystery.'

'Most of the stories?'

'What's the matter? Have you seen something?'

Slowly she began to tell him about the library window and the footsteps she had been convinced she'd heard the night before. Even to Malcolm she didn't want to mention the telephone calls. Not yet.

He looked appalled. 'My poor girl, and you were in the house all alone? Well, you shan't go back there tonight. It doesn't matter whether there was or wasn't anyone, it's enough that you believed there was someone.'

The relief at not being treated as an hysterical female was exquisite and when her breakfast arrived she was able to attack it with an eager appetite.

'What else have you got to tell me?' she asked.

'Well, let's see. Bob Combe seems to have given up any idea that you could have had the strength to hit someone over the head, drag him into the boathouse and lift him into a locker. I've also talked to your aunt, Mrs Gray.' A smile in Malcolm's eyes told Felicity he had enjoyed this part of his job. 'She was shocked you hadn't approached her yourself but said you always were an odd girl. However, she doesn't know anything about your business, except she'd heard that it had grown very successfully since you started it some two years ago, after the death of your mother and in the teeth of the recession. Nor could she help with any banking details.'

The thought of Belinda Gray exclaiming over her situation was disagreeable. 'I wish you hadn't asked her.'

'I'm sorry, I thought it was necessary.'

Felicity pushed away her plate. 'That was delicious. You may quote me as stating that Little Chefs are excellent. I feel replete.' She enjoyed the sound of the word, just as she enjoyed feeling full but not too full of food she suspected she never normally indulged in. She looked across at her companion. Sam McLean was more obviously attractive; Malcolm's ginger hair and freckles were disarming but could never in a million years be called sexy, yet when she was with him Felicity felt some of her nightmare recede.

He insisted on paying the bill. 'Don't worry,' he laughed, 'you'll pay in the end; it'll be logged on my charges. This is just to make me feel I'm in control.'

A little under two hours later they were pulling up outside a small terraced house just off the north-west end of Clapham Common.

The street was on the up and up; at least half the houses had been gentrified: Austrian blinds, chic curtains and smart paint had been liberally applied and neatly tied-back roses rambled over front doors studded with antique coloured glass. In between these signs of prosperity were properties meekly apologetic for their neglected appearance.

Felicity's flat was the upper floor of number eighteen. The paintwork was worn and faded and the decorative stucco work above the ground floor flaking.

The windows of the downstairs flat were beautifully clean, however, and the floral curtains flaunted their patterns to passers-by rather than to the inhabitants.

Felicity found her keys. Inside the front door was a neat little hall. A small table set against the wall held a plastic plant and a pile of mail addressed to her. She flicked through; among the circulars and other junk was what looked like a bank statement.

She showed it to Malcolm before putting it in her bag, dumped the rest then went up the narrow stairs to her flat.

At the top, Felicity paused for a moment, gathering her courage before she inserted the key that would open the door of her home.

Then, suddenly impatient, she turned the key in the lock and pushed at the door.

It wouldn't open; something was in the way. She shoved harder, then Malcolm came alongside and together they forced the door wide enough to enter.

They were greeted by chaos.

The flat had been ransacked. No, it was worse than that. Gutted was the only way to describe what had happened. Cushions had been ripped apart, drawers emptied, cupboards opened, their contents smashed or sent sailing around the flat. Even the television had had its back removed. Hall, living room, the two small bedrooms, all were the same. The kitchen looked worst because here there had been more to fling around. Packets of flour, sugar, beans and pasta had been ripped apart, their contents left littering the floor together with shards of crockery and glass swept from cupboards.

Felicity and Malcolm looked at each other, incapable of speech, shell-shocked.

Then Malcolm found a chair still in one piece and set it upright. 'Sit down before you fall down,' he told Felicity.

She sank on to it, trembling. The violence and thoroughness of the search terrified her. She had no doubt that the voice on the telephone had been responsible. Had he found whatever it was he was looking for? If not, what would he do next?

148

'The bastards must have cut the telephone wires,' Malcolm said, holding out a dead receiver. 'I'll go downstairs and see if I can ring the police from there.'

He seemed to be gone a long time.

Felicity gradually got her trembling under control. More than ever she needed to keep her wits about her. She looked at the chaos. Its anarchic disorder taunted, seeming to reflect her mind, its essential furniture obliterated under layers of debris. No hope now of familiar surroundings restoring her memory.

Malcolm returned. 'The police are on their way. They said not to touch anything. I told them if only they knew just what the damage was they wouldn't say anything so daft.' He looked angry and upset, standing in the doorway, his well-polished brown shoes almost lost in the drift of papers. 'The people downstairs, nice old couple, been here for ever, said they heard a noise last night but just assumed that you'd got back from whatever trip you'd been on. They didn't know you'd had an accident.'

Felicity stared at the broken bits of what had been her home. 'But there must have been a hell of a din.'

'They're both quite deaf. He said he thought he heard music playing up here when he turned the television off just before they went to bed. She said there were odd bumps but she thought you were changing the furniture around or maybe having a party.'

'Some party!'

The police arrived and started taking details. Inevitably they asked what was missing. Malcolm shouldered the burden of explanation.

Then Felicity thought of Paloma Travel.

149

Chapter Thirty-Two

Felicity couldn't make the police see any reason why they should investigate the office but, after they'd had their fingerprints and statements taken, she and Malcolm were allowed to go.

Paloma Travel was in Victoria, in a side street not far from the station. Few cars were around on a Sunday and Malcolm was able to park right outside.

Felicity got out and stood looking at the windows. This was her business, she'd started it and built it up, apparently successfully. It was her child.

Nothing of the agency itself could be seen through the windows. They displayed colourful posters of South America and Spain, together with a collection of native artefacts.

The door was painted a glossy steel grey. Automatically, Felicity tried the large brass handle. 'Hey, it's open!' she called to Malcolm.

It led into a tiny vestibule.

Through an inner, glass door, they could see the agency had been destroyed almost as comprehensively as the flat.

Desk drawers and cupboards had been hastily emptied and the floor covered with a thick carpet of paper. Display racks had been denuded of their contents and brochures scattered everywhere. The lid of a cash box had been ripped off but notes and coins littered the floor. Drawers had been flung anywhere and computer keyboards hung off desks by their wires. At the back of the agency a cupboard door sagged open, its locks forced by some heavy implement and airline tickets swept out to lie like a broken pack of cards.

Felicity and Malcolm waded through the mess. At the back of the agency they found a stockroom. Here boxes of brochures, packets of booking forms and stationery had all been ripped open and scattered. Beside the stockroom was a manager's office which had suffered the same fate.

The telephones were still connected, though, and Malcolm rang the police.

Another team quickly arrived.

More questions. Felicity sat slumped in a chair and let Malcolm deal with them. She was asked for the name of someone who might be able to check what was missing.

'I'm sorry,' she said. 'I only know that the girl running the place at the moment is called Jane.'

The officer in charge looked gloomily at the computers. 'No doubt the records are all inside those,' he said. Then another policeman found a list of telephone numbers taped to a sliding panel in one of the desks. The name at the top was Jane Murray.

A call was put through and Felicity was asked to wait until Miss Murray arrived.

Felicity no longer cared where she was or what she was doing. Her mind refused to cope with this latest obscenity.

Far more real than the confusion around her were the huge South American posters hanging on the walls of the office.

Machu Picchu, lost city of the Incas, its peaceful ruined streets perched on top of a tall green mountain; the crashing falls of Iguaçu that made Niagara look like an ornamental fountain; the Italianate opera house at Manaus in the heart of the Brazilian jungle. They called to Felicity, dulling the tumult around her, drawing her soul into their depths.

All those details she'd given Sam McLean yesterday; how many times had she had to travel there to absorb them?

She couldn't forget the alpaca sweater she'd first described to Sam then found in Fran's wardrobe. Had she bought it for her cousin or for herself? And if for herself, who was she?

Felicity sat thinking over this question until the arrival of Paloma Travel's manageress.

Jane was a neat, competent-looking girl of around thirty with smooth, dark hair and an ordinary face made interesting with skilful make-up. She looked at Felicity and was more appalled by her appearance than that of Paloma Travel. 'My God, I had no idea! No wonder there was no word after the accident.'

Felicity smiled thinly and said nothing.

Faced with the devastation in the office, Jane was unable to confirm whether or not anything was missing. She told the police that the agency had closed at the usual Saturday time of one o'clock and she had personally locked up.

Felicity felt incapable of following the detailed questioning of the police and quite soon Malcolm asked the inspector, 'Do you need Miss Frear any longer? She's still recovering from a very nasty accident.'

Not long after that they were driving away and Felicity lay back in the passenger seat and closed her eyes.

When she opened them, they were once again driving into the Little Chef restaurant.

'I didn't want to wake you,' said Malcolm apologetically, 'but do you realize we haven't had anything to eat since we left here seven hours ago?'

Felicity didn't feel hungry but she was immediately contrite. 'You must be starving. I am sorry.'

'No, I'm the one who's sorry. I had planned a leisurely lunch for us somewhere nice. It's a pity to have to bring you here again but it's too early for a pub and I can't think of anywhere else we can get something reasonably substantial.'

Stiff and tired, Felicity eased her body out of the car and into the restaurant.

Malcolm kept up an easy chatter on nothing at all while they ate hamburgers.

Then he ordered ice cream for himself and more coffee for Felicity and asked, 'The way your flat and the agency were taken apart looks as though someone was looking for something. Have you any idea what?'

Oh, that she could say yes!

Felicity shook her head. 'I just keep wondering what would have happened if I'd been there.'

'Don't even think it! It was done by professionals who must have known you were in Devon.'

It was no comfort. The chill voice on the telephone echoed in Felicity's mind and the possibility that she could be involved in whatever was going on terrified her so badly that she was compelled to suggest, 'Paloma Travel specializes in South America. Don't a lot of precious gems come from there, emeralds and rubies? They'd be easy to hide, especially in bags of flour or a box of forms.'

Malcolm placed a hand over hers. His was warm, pulsing with life, hers was cold as death. 'You may not be directly involved,' he said soothingly. 'Someone may have given you something to look after, or perhaps hidden a packet in your flat. You may not have known anything about it.' He hesitated a moment than added, 'Precious gems, though, are not the most likely prospect. These days Customs and Excise are far more worried about mules bringing in drugs.'

'Mules?'

'Carriers of illicit goods.'

Malcolm removed his hand from hers and Felicity watched the square, spatulate fingers take out a packet of cigarettes and light one. He had said out loud what she'd feared.

She wanted to tell Malcolm not to get involved with her, that it could be dangerous. Gordon Rules was dead and someone was secretly, quietly, searching Kingsleigh. It was the only explanation that made any sense. 'That gossip about a stranger being seen near Kingsleigh; it's not just rumour, is it?'

Malcolm tapped the ash from his cigarette and avoided meeting her eyes.

'Rules disturbed whoever it is. That's why he was murdered.'

Malcolm looked at her squarely. 'I'm afraid it's a definite possibility.'

'So why did the chief inspector remove his men?'

'I can't answer that one.'

Felicity's mind was beginning to work again, putting together the bits and pieces she knew. They added up to little more than that someone was trying to find something she had hidden. Was there anything else she could discover without her memory?

Sam McLean had been trying to help her recover it.

Sam McLean's car had been so close behind the car that had crashed that he'd been able to pull her from the burning wreck.

Sam McLean had turned up at the hospital and then at Kingsleigh.

That first afternoon Mrs Parsons had shown him into the library and left him there for several minutes. Long enough to open the window? The security key had been in the middle drawer of the desk, quite easy to find. Had she done the housekeeper an enormous injustice?

'What is it?' Malcolm asked urgently. 'Have you remembered something?'

'Yes,' Felicity said slowly.

'What?' He stubbed out his cigarette and leaned forward. 'What have you remembered?'

'The man who rescued me from that burning car, Sam McLean, keeps coming to see me.'

Malcolm looked ludicrously disappointed and Felicity realized he'd thought she'd recovered a part of her memory. She detailed all the grounds for her suspicions and by the time she'd finished, his expression had changed. 'You mustn't be alone with him again, Felicity. Promise me?' His hand squeezed hers compellingly.

Felicity's blood chilled. If sensible, level-headed Malcolm was worried, she really was in trouble. 'You think he could be dangerous?'

'Whoever trashed your flat and the agency wasn't messing.'

'But Sam was with me on Saturday.'

'He could have driven straight up to London after leaving you. When you'd made it clear you wouldn't co-operate.'

'Then it couldn't have been him on the top floor at Kingsleigh; he couldn't be two places at once.'

Malcolm looked at her, his eyes very steady. 'Are you quite sure you heard someone up there?'

'Yes!' Felicity shot the word out. But almost immediately she wondered how she could be so sure. In the middle of the night, woken out of a deep sleep, in an old house full of creaks and groans, anything was possible.

Then the obvious candidate for prowling round the house came to mind. 'It was Johnny,' she said, almost with a note of triumph. 'He must have been involved in the theft of the horses even if not in Rules's murder.' She told Malcolm about the groom.

'He does seem suspicious,' he said slowly.

She hadn't told him the most unpalatable fact of all: Felicity Frear's involvement.

Felicity liked nothing about the sort of person she seemed to be. Uncaring, unthinking, aggressive, that was the picture being played back to her. Was she really like that? Maybe her people skills were a little rusty but they did exist. There had been times in the last few days when Mrs Parsons had almost been co-operative and at one stage even Belinda Gray had seemed sympathetic. She had outfaced Sam McLean, and Malcolm Biddulph seemed more than happy to help in any way he could.

Once again she thought of the alpaca sweater.

'Could there be,' Felicity asked Malcolm, 'any doubt that I am Felicity Frear?'

'What do you mean?'

'I'm not really sure,' Felicity confessed. 'It's just that both Felicity and Frances were travelling in the car and they were apparently quite like each other and I wondered how I was identified.'

'You were seen getting into the back of the car at the station and Frances's body was wearing a wedding ring. Unless you can think of a good reason why you should have changed places and Frances should give her ring to Felicity; then according to Bob Combe, the identification seems quite certain.'

'You've spoken to him about it? Did you think there might be a chance the police had got it wrong?'

'Let's say as your lawyer I wanted to explore every possibility.' He gave her a consoling smile. 'You look disappointed. Why shouldn't you want to be Felicity Frear? It's not as though you haven't got possession of Kingsleigh.'

That was the sort of remark Felicity would have expected to hear from Belinda Gray, not Malcolm. 'Wouldn't you prefer not to be involved in some sort of criminal racket?' she asked with a certain heat.

'Don't condemn yourself before you know what the facts are.'

'How am I going to find them out?' Felicity asked him bitterly. She finished her coffee, looked round the brightly lit café and said, 'I think we should get on.' But her reluctance to leave this safe haven came through.

'Look, you mustn't go back to Kingsleigh tonight,' said Malcolm. 'Come and stay with me or, if you prefer, book in to the local hotel.'

Would that be the Golden Lion where Sam McLean could be staying?

'No,' Felicity said, surprised at her decisiveness. 'I'm not going to be driven out of Kingsleigh. I've got to sort out my life whether or not I get my memory back. What will you do if I do turn out to be a drug smuggler?' she asked abruptly.

'Why, hand you over to the police,' he said lightly. 'Then defend you in the courts. But I don't believe you're any such thing, any more than you do. Look, if you're determined to go back to Kingsleigh, I think I should stay with you.'

She smiled. 'I was hoping you'd say that.'

'Just let me make a telephone call.'

He walked away from the table and Felicity sighed with relief. Then her body tensed. Had Johnny known that Kingsleigh had been left empty all day?

155

Chapter Thirty-Three

Felicity clutched at Malcolm's arm as he drove down the hill towards Kingsleigh.

'There aren't any lights on!' she breathed.

He corrected the car's swerve and drew up outside the house. 'It's only half-past eight, it's not dark yet. And who would put them on anyway?'

'You don't understand. I left all the lights on on the top floor!'

He looked doubtfully at her. 'Are you sure?'

'Of course,' Felicity said impatiently.

He looked up towards the top of the house. 'Don't misunderstand me, but you're only just recovering from a pretty dreadful accident. Mightn't you have forgotten turning them off?'

Once again, Felicity began to wonder. She thought back to her search the previous night. Had she, in the end, turned the lights off? She grew impatient and the only thing she could be sure of was that she wanted to check that Kingsleigh hadn't been taken apart like the flat and the office. Dashing out of the car the moment it stopped, she retrieved the large iron key from her bag, turned it in the lock of the heavy front door, lifted the handle and pushed. The door creaked back on its huge hinges and revealed a dark hall.

Felicity switched on the lights and breathed a quick sigh of relief. Nothing seemed changed from the morning. She ran through the hall to the library, then to the drawing room and the sitting room, flinging open the doors, relief flooding through her as she saw that they, also, looked undisturbed.

'This is just the most incredible place!' Malcolm, following at her elbow, sounded stunned.

Felicity looked round the elegant vastness of the drawing room. She saw it through Malcolm's envious eyes and realized, with a shock of surprise, how readily she had accepted Kingsleigh's magnificence, as though it had always been hers by right.

'I think we should check the rest of the house,' said Malcolm.

She felt what little courage she had leak away. 'What if someone is here?'

156

'We need to arm ourselves.'

Felicity picked up a poker from the hall fireplace. 'There's another one in the sitting room,' she said.

Malcolm looked at the piece of iron. 'Doesn't Kingsleigh have a gunroom?'

Why hadn't that thought occurred to her? 'Of course it must.'

They found it at the kitchen end of the house. An unimpressive room, it had a battered old desk sitting under a barred window and a long, green painted dresser. Opposite the dresser, two gun cases were mounted on the wall. Glass doors fronted the cases and inside a padlocked bar secured the guns. They found the keys hanging on a hook at the back of the dresser. Malcolm undid the padlock on one of the cases.

The wooden stocks of the guns gleamed softly and the steel was sheened with a fine coating of oil. 'All in superb condition,' he said. He took one out, laid it against his shoulder and took aim out of the window. Then he inspected it more closely. 'A Purdey,' he said reverently.

Felicity meanwhile was opening drawers in the dresser and pulling out cartridge cases.

'We don't need those!' Malcolm sounded shocked.

'What use is an unloaded shotgun?' asked Felicity.

'Deterrent value. If it's loaded, you might shoot someone.'

'I thought that was the idea. I mean, if anyone is there.' She swallowed hard.

Malcolm shook his head. 'If you killed him, you'd be in real trouble. The law is very strict about what you are allowed to do to defend yourself, even in your own home.'

He took down a second gun, broke it to check it was unloaded, brought the halves back together and handed it to her.

Felicity felt the gun's weight, holding it with both hands as she might a cudgel. 'Well, it's heavier than the poker.' Her voice was bright and determined.

'We can always go to my place.'

'No,' she said very firmly.

They went through to the hall. 'We should each take a different staircase,' Felicity reluctantly suggested. 'Then no one could slip down one while we went up the other.'

'Good idea.' Malcolm sounded almost enthusiastic. 'Shall I take the main one and you the back stairs?'

'Let's start with the top floor, the fact the lights have been turned off doesn't mean no one's there, there aren't any on anywhere else. It's a rabbit warren up there, all different levels and odd corners.'

157

'See you up there.' Malcolm grasped his shotgun and set off for the other end of the house.

The thought of yet another search along the top corridor was terrifying and only the knowledge that Malcolm would not be far away allowed Felicity to climb the narrow stairs to the top of Kingsleigh.

The gun was clumsy, got in the way. She held it awkwardly, feeling like a cheap gangster in a second-rate movie but relieved that there was no possibility it might go off.

At the top of the stairs she paused for a moment to catch her breath. Had Malcolm already started checking the rooms at the other end of the house? Could she just wait here until he'd worked his way all along to this end, holding the shotgun like a keeper waiting for a terrier to flush out an animal from his burrow?

No, that would be cowardly. Taking a firmer grip on the weapon, Felicity forced herself to start opening doors, switching on lights as she went.

Once again the rooms were empty.

She met Malcolm at the room that lay above her bedroom. He shook his head in response to her unspoken question and laid his hand on the door knob.

A moment later they were looking at yet another empty room. Felicity slowly released her breath, walked jerkily across the room and yanked open the wardrobe. A clutch of wire hangers hung untidily from the rail. There was nothing else.

'So, do we check the next floor down, too?' asked Malcolm in a whisper. He had an air of suppressed excitement.

Felicity nodded.

She again took the back stairs then started working her way along the carpeted corridor. The rooms here were bigger and offered more hiding places so progress was slower.

Felicity was standing in the main bathroom as Malcolm entered. The moment he saw her, he came across. 'Felicity, don't look like that. It's all right, I'm here.' He put an arm round her shoulders. 'What's the matter? There's no one else here, it's empty!'

She gulped helplessly. 'Someone's had a bath recently, look!' She pointed at the long streak of water at the bottom of the old-fashioned bath.

Chapter Thirty-Four

'It's not possible,' said Malcolm. 'An intruder searching the house, yes. Having a bath, never!'

'It does sound ridiculous.' Felicity felt her terror lessen. But she went over and fingered her big fluffy white towel. It was definitely damp.

'That's from this morning. It's been such a dreadful day, it hasn't dried,' Malcolm insisted. 'Switch on the towel rail.'

'You think I'm paranoid, don't you?'

'I just think you've had a long and very difficult day and you are, quite rightly, worried. Come home with me.'

Felicity shook her head. She looked again at the bath and the towel. Perhaps Malcolm was right and she was allowing things to get to her. The very idea of an intruder taking a bath had to be laughable.

'We'll go and have a drink.' She led the way out of the bathroom to the main staircase.

As they passed the landing, Malcolm glanced at the small flight of stairs leading to the solar room. 'Shouldn't we check up there?' he asked.

'You do it. I'll wait for you here.'

It took no more than a moment for Malcolm to fling open the door, glance in, then rejoin her.

'Strange room,' he said. 'The only window is one looking over the hall.'

She didn't comment. The solar room was developing into a major problem. She no longer liked even to look up at its window.

'What shall we do with these?' she asked, lifting the shotgun that was weighing heavily in her hand.

'Keep them with us.'

That wasn't reassuring.

Felicity led the way into the sitting room and waved towards the butler's tray with its load of drinks. 'Will you give me a whisky and help yourself?'

Malcolm poured generous measures from the decanter into two cut-glass tumblers. 'Water with yours?' he asked.

'I'm sorry. I'll get some from the kitchen.'

'Don't worry, I'm there already,' he said and disappeared, leaving his shotgun by the drinks table.

He was gone a long time. Then, just as Felicity was wondering if she should go and see if something had happened, he was back. 'Sorry,' he apologized breathlessly. 'I got carried away by the kitchen. Isn't it amazing? I had to do a bit of exploring. No wonder you don't want to leave this house.' He poured water into the glasses and brought one over to Felicity. Then he saw the photo albums she had placed on the large coffee table in front of the sofa. 'What have you got there?'

'They are full of pictures of my cousin and me when we were growing up. I thought we might go through them.'

'See if they jog your memory? Great idea!' Malcolm sat beside her on the sofa and placed his drink on the table.

Felicity swallowed some of her whisky and moved a little closer to him. The thought of what might lie behind the veils that were cutting her off from her past made her hands sweat and her pulse race faster than Concorde but with Malcolm beside her she felt she might be able to cope if her memory should suddenly return.

She opened the earliest album. There, in snapshot after snapshot, each subject neatly identified underneath the prints, was her lost childhood. There were the two girls, Fran and Flick, there Thomas and Jennifer Dashwood, Sarah Frear.

Felicity looked eagerly at the shots of her mother.

Sarah had been a most attractive woman, with all Jennifer's loveliness plus an added vivacity that was most appealing. Her clothes were always slightly outrageous, skirts either trailing voluminously or desperately short and tight, swimming costumes indecently crocheted, palazzo pants in wildly patterned silk. Her hair changed colour and style from shot to shot but her dark blue eyes, identical to her sister's, never changed. Her nose was straight, too.

Felicity worked her way through the snapshots without any sense that she was reaching out to a world that was hers.

Then she turned a page and a new figure appeared, posed in the garden, drink in hand. Alexander, said the caption underneath.

Flick's father!

Denise had said he had charisma, had been devastatingly attractive. She'd talked about him in the same way she had about Mark.

The snapshot showed a fair-haired man with well-cut features, lean and easy, laughing into the camera, raising his drink in a mock salute. His eyes were crinkled against the sun but Felicity thought she could catch a glint of blue. His teeth were very white. There was a hint of

160

the pirate in the way he flashed his smile and leaned nonchalantly against the garden wall. Felicity thought she could see exactly what Denise had meant. Then she found another one of him, with his daughter. Alexander's arm was around the young Flick, her small face turned to his, looking incredibly happy. There were no more shots of him in that album and only one or two in the next.

How often had Flick seen her father? Had there been photograph albums in her flat of her life outside Devon? With Alexander playing a larger part?

The years sped by. The girls grew up, Sarah came less and less, then, when Flick was in her early twenties, she also vanished except for the very occasional snap, always alone, posed in some part of the garden. Had they been taken by Jennifer Dashwood? It must have been after Philip Bishop's death, after Fran had severed relations with her cousin.

Felicity looked at the pictures of the grown-up Flick. She seemed little changed in spirit from the sassy youngster who'd ridden, sailed and played tennis with her cousin. What had she been up to?

As the last year or so of Jennifer Dashwood's life was painfully captured, Flick again appeared frequently in the snapshot record but Felicity didn't linger over these pages.

While she studied the photographs, Malcolm sat quietly by Felicity's side, occasionally making a comment. 'What a pretty girl you were,' he said but Felicity thought how much prettier the straight-nosed Fran had been. 'Isn't that a marvellous yacht? You must be in the South of France there. Oh, yes, it's labelled "Cannes harbour". Can you remember it? Look, you and your cousin have won some sort of tennis trophy. Don't you both look pleased? You must remember that!'

But none of it jogged her memory.

Then came a book that was taken up with South America and here, for the first time, was Mark Sheldrake, who was soon turning up in nearly every shot, most taken with herself, almost certainly by Fran. Then there were some of him with an exceedingly happy-looking Fran that maybe Flick had snapped.

On the final page was a snapshot labelled 'Mark, Flick and Alexander in Lima'. The two men were laughing together and Felicity got a strong impression of camaraderie. Flick didn't look at all happy, her expression had lost its bounce and confidence. Had she been sulking for some reason? Could she have been upset that Mark's attention had been turned away from Fran and herself? Felicity looked at the snapshot for a long time before closing the book.

The last full album covered Fran and Mark's wedding.

Felicity recognized Belinda Gray, self satisfied in a purple silk two-piece and an all-feather hat. There was Flick in a very short bright red coat dress and no hat at all, with an expression that seemed resolutely happy. There was Alexander, with the air of a man who has drunk slightly too much champagne, more attractive than ever in morning dress. Thomas Dashwood, with Fran on his arm, was suddenly looking much older. Fran looked exceptionally lovely in a simple white silk two-piece with a short veil and a bouquet of cream roses. Then came pictures of the happy couple together, Mark Sheldrake, looking twice as distinguished in morning suit as he had in casual holiday clothes, wearing a triumphant smile.

It had been a small wedding but obviously very happy.

There remained only the half-full album that she had looked through with Denise.

'Is that all of them?' asked Malcolm as she closed the unfilled pages.

'Yes.'

'And they haven't brought back anything to you?'

'Not a thing.'

He put his arm round her shoulders and gave her a quick hug. 'Don't despair. Your subconscious might be working even now.'

'We'd better get you a bed organized,' Felicity said brightly and gathered up the books of photographs.

He helped her put them back on the shelves then Felicity went upstairs.

She found a linen cupboard with sheets and pillowcases and made up a bed in one of the spare guest rooms. 'Hope it's aired,' she said doubtfully to Malcolm.

'It'll be fine.'

She went back to the cupboard and found him towels. 'I'll get you some pyjamas and a razor from Mark's dressing room.'

'Thanks. Tell you what, I'll make you a hot drink to help you sleep.'

Felicity thought she was so tired she'd drop off the moment her head hit the pillow but the idea of Malcolm making her a goodnight drink was somehow comforting.

In Mark's chest of drawers she found a pair of grey silk pyjamas with maroon facings. Felicity picked them up with a slight smile. Very suave! Her smile vanished when she saw what had been hidden beneath the pyjamas.

The gun had a dull, efficient gleam to its metal. It was a revolver, the kind that had a clip of bullets napped into the handle rather than a barrel that was loaded individually. She stood gazing at it, hypnotized. Why would Mark have had a hand gun? She heard Malcolm coming along the corridor and quickly closed the drawer, picked up the electric razor and Noël Coward-smart dressing gown she had also found and went to meet him.

He was holding a hot drink.

'You use the main bathroom, I'll use Fran's,' she said. She placed the night gear and razor on the chair and rescued her towel. He handed her the mug, his freckled face serious and concerned.

'Many thanks for this.' She raised it in salute as she spoke. 'And thank you very much indeed for all your help today. I don't know what I would have done without you.'

'My privilege,' he said simply. 'Now, don't worry about a thing. I'll be here tonight and in the morning we'll talk about what we should do next.'

For a moment she thought he was going to kiss her and she half raised her face but he gave her a quick smile instead and disappeared into the bathroom.

Had her appearance put him off?

Felicity put a hand to her scars and remembered the attractive girls in the photograph albums.

Chapter Thirty-Five

Felicity put the hot milk on her bedside table, looked at the shotgun she'd placed on the bed and carefully rested it against the side instead. She undressed, slipped into a négligé, and went into Fran's bathroom.

After she'd washed and cleaned her teeth, she took the revolver out of Mark's chest of drawers. Once back in her own room, she worked out how to release the safety catch, secured it again and then slipped the gun under her pillow. Finally she got into bed and drank the milk, still warm and sweet with honey. It had been a nice thought.

There wasn't much that was pleasant going round Felicity's mind at the moment but her last coherent thought before she slipped into a deep sleep was how good it was not to be on her own any longer.

Felicity's night was disturbed.

She dreamed she heard more footsteps above her head. Then that they were in her room. Someone was whispering, urgent, sibilant whispering that echoed around and around her head. Words cracked across her consciousness, angry words. Fire, she heard, and flames. Fire and flames, fire and flames. She dreamed of the car crash, of being trapped in a burning car.

In the morning Felicity had to struggle to pull herself out of sleep. She lay for a long time half conscious, trying to retrieve her dreams. They eluded her; insubstantial as mist, the images melted away as her mind gradually woke. Cautiously, she explored her memory, half expecting to find it had returned, so disturbed did she feel. But there was nothing new. Only yesterday flooded back, loading her mind with despair. She turned in the bed, curling herself up into a tight ball, then slipped a hand beneath the pillow, felt for the pistol and remained there for a long while, feeling the metal, heavy with latent violence. Her brain felt muzzy, stuffed with a rat's nest, and there was a headache behind her eyes.

She felt as though she had run miles and put it down to the whisky she had drunk the previous night. Malcolm had poured her out far too large a glass.

With an immense effort Felicity dragged herself out of bed and threw back the curtains. The weather had improved; the sky was clear and the sun was shining weakly. She washed, went to Fran's wardrobe and chose a long-sleeved loose shirtdress in a blue that almost matched her eyes. She added her dark glasses and went and knocked on Malcolm's door.

He was already up. 'How did you sleep?' he asked, his eyes anxious, searching what he could see of her face around the glasses.

'Like a log.' She smiled at him. 'How about you?'

'Fine,' he assured her. 'I meant to stay awake, to listen for intruders, but I went off almost at once, never heard a thing. You haven't remembered anything, I suppose?'

She shook her head, then wished she hadn't. 'I'm not going to worry about it. What do you want for breakfast?'

In the kitchen they found some bread, made toast and coffee and ate sitting at the big pine table, arguing.

Malcolm wanted to stay with Felicity at Kingsleigh. She wanted him to go into his office.

'There's no point in you staying here. I'm sure nothing's going to happen in daylight; there are too many people around.'

'But didn't you tell me you'd fired Mrs Parsons?'

'There'll be one of the other women who work at Kingsleigh coming this morning. And all sorts of callers, the postman, newspaperman, the butcher, you have no idea.' She smiled at him. 'Come back this evening. I'd prefer not to be on my own then. I'm sure there's lots you should be getting on with at the office.'

'I'd crossed the day out. We were going to London, remember?'

'There's something you could do for me.' Felicity had brought down the bank statement she'd found at her flat and now laid it on the table between them.

'Look, here are all my banking details. You could contact the manager and see about getting me another cheque book and cash card.' She handed the statement over to Malcolm. 'Not much money in there but at least I'm not overdrawn.'

'There could be other accounts,' he said, studying the figures.

'You really are trying to make out I'm a criminal, aren't you?' she said gaily.

He flushed and she regretted her words.

'Then you could talk to your friend Bob Combe and see how the police are getting on with solving Rules's murder and finding the stolen horses. You could mention we think there might have been an intruder here.'

'I could do all of that from here.'

Felicity looked at him and began to give up the idea of being strong and independent. If it had been Sam McLean who'd been searching the house yesterday and he'd failed to find whatever it was he wanted, would he call again today? Had Johnny supplied him with a key or helped him break in without leaving a trace? Would the two of them gang up on her?

She was just about to say that perhaps she'd like it if Malcolm did stay with her when the telephone rang.

She went into the morning room and approached the instrument with every nerve tensed. She picked up the receiver and waited to hear the cold voice.

Instead the caller asked for Malcolm Biddulph.

She gave him a shout.

He appeared quickly. 'I rang my partner from the Little Chef last night,' he said quickly, in response to her silent query as she handed him the instrument. 'I thought someone should know where I was.'

Had he indeed! Felicity went into the kitchen garden and found Johnny forking up new potatoes, stabbing the earth as though it was an enemy. Felicity asked if his aunt had managed her move to his cottage without too much trouble.

He hunched his shoulders over the fork. 'She's not staying with me,' he said truculently.

'Where's she gone?'

'Dunno, but she said she'd post you a letter with where to send her money!' He wiped away the persistent drip from the end of his nose and jabbed the soil, spearing the small round globes that gleamed through the brown earth. He looked as though he would like to tell Felicity exactly what he thought of her but wasn't prepared to lose his job in defence of his aunt.

Felicity looked at the wounded potatoes, told him to be more careful and asked for a box of them to be left by the back door. Her heart was thumping but she turned away before she could betray her unease.

Even though the sun was shining, the air was fresh. Felicity wrapped her arms around herself and walked slowly back to the house.

Malcolm was hastily finishing his breakfast. 'That was my office. I'm sorry, some sort of crisis has blown up and I've got to go in. Unless, that is, you've changed your mind about being happy here on your own?'

Felicity swallowed. 'No, I'll be fine. I can always ring if I need anything.'

'Look, why don't you come in with me? You can explore the town or do some shopping and I might be able to get away for lunch.'

She shook her head. Something was telling her not to leave Kingsleigh.

Felicity saw Malcolm off and went back into the house, feeling its emptiness reverberate around her. She returned to the kitchen to stack the dishwasher and found one of Mrs Parsons' helpers had arrived. The woman was startled to see Felicity. 'I thought Mrs Parsons said you wouldn't be here, miss! Never mind, I expect I can find something for your lunch. Do you know where Mrs Parsons is? I can't find her anywhere.'

'She isn't working here any more, Mrs Fry. Can you follow your usual routine this morning? I'll get something sorted out soon.'

The woman gave her a curious glance and Felicity hurried away before questions started coming.

She should get a locksmith to change the locks but she felt oddly lethargic and reluctant to make the effort. Then the thought of Johnny with the power to come and go as he pleased made her find the Yellow Pages. When the job had been explained, the man said he'd come immediately.

Felicity went upstairs with a feeling of satisfaction and found her tennis shoes. The buzzing in her head was worse now and she thought exercise might drive it away.

While she was putting on the trainers, the front doorbell sounded.

Her heart started thumping. It was too soon to be the locksmith. Sam McLean; it had to be him. And Malcolm had gone.

She thought about the revolver under her pillow but her dress didn't have a pocket. Instead she picked up the shotgun from beside her bed, took it with her downstairs and leaned it against the hall table, hoping it looked quite natural there.

Mrs Fry had already reached the door. 'You should take that round the back,' she said sharply to the caller. 'These delivery people never want to go the extra distance,' she complained to Felicity as she went back towards the kitchen carrying a box. 'This is the china Mrs Sheldrake ordered months ago. She said the set was badly down.'

Felicity went to find racket and balls with a ridiculous sense of anti-climax.

Exercise was no help to her today. Every thud of the ball against the wood board sent a hammer swinging inside her head. Her feet wouldn't move and the racket soon felt too heavy to hold. She left the racket and balls on the court, walked instead down to the beach and stood watching the rolling waves, feeling their rhythm echoing inside her head.

Soon she collected the tennis things, went back to the house and took a couple of aspirin, then went into the sitting room. She switched on the stereo and chose a disc at random. It was the Mozart symphony she had heard in the hospital and she sat and listened to the compelling, complex music, trying to be swept along by the force of its melodies.

She must finally have fallen into a doze because she came to with Mrs Fry knocking on the door.

'There's a man here says he's come to change the locks,' she said, looking at Felicity strangely.

Felicity went and showed the man what had to be done.

He scratched his head. 'I can do half of them now but I'm afraid the rest will have to wait until tomorrow. I didn't realize what a big job it was. I've got something else on in the afternoon that I can't change.'

'I did explain on the telephone,' Felicity said wearily.

'Yes, well . . .' He left the sentence hanging. A combination of desire for the job and certainty that she must have been exaggerating, Felicity decided.

She didn't feel up to starting again with someone else.

'Do as much as you can,' she told him.

By the time he came and said he had to go now, gave her the keys for half a dozen new locks and said he'd be back the next day to do the rest, the morning was over.

As the locksmith left, Mrs Fry came up. 'I've finished my time, Miss Felicity. There's chops and vegetables in the slow oven and I've made a nice salad for your supper. I got one of Mrs Parsons' jam tarts out of the freezer for your pud and put that in the slow oven as well. By the time you've eaten the chops, it should be just ready. You'll be all right, will you, miss?'

'Fine, thank you, Mrs Fry.'

The woman stood looking at her uncertainly. 'Don't know how you're going to manage without Mrs Parsons but no doubt Mrs Gray will be organizing something.'

'We'll be fine, Mrs Fry, don't you worry,' Felicity forced herself to say through the renewed throbbing in her head.

She locked the back door behind the woman with one of the new keys then stood in the kitchen feeling naked and vulnerable. The house seemed larger than ever.

Chapter Thirty-Six

The chops and their vegetables looked dry and unappetizing. Felicity wrapped them in some newspaper and threw them in the rubbish bin. Instead she ate the melon Denise had brought, its flesh sweet and juicy. She must remember to congratulate Charles when she eventually met him.

If she ever met Charles Comstock! She went through to the sitting room with a tight feeling round her heart, as though she'd offered a hostage to fortune. Again she put music on the CD player then lay back in her chair, listening to more Mozart, trying to summon the energy to take more aspirin against the throbbing in her head.

The sound of the door bell brought her head up with a jerk. Cautiously she rose, went through to the hall and, standing well back, looked through the bay window.

On the gravel stood Sam McLean's car.

She thought quickly and picked up the shotgun that was still leaning against the hall table and opened the door.

Sam McLean's easy smile faded as he saw the gun and his body stiffened. 'Quite a welcome!' The distinctive timbre of his voice was flat; his tough guy face was still.

'Come in, why don't you?' Felicity said in a cordial voice and stood back to allow him in.

'Shouldn't you be carrying that broken?' he asked, looking at the shotgun as he stepped inside.

'You know your way to the library, I believe.'

He glanced at her. She remained with her back straight, the gun held across her left arm, waiting.

His eyes narrowed, then he walked through the hall, past the staircase and into the library without further comment, his steps firm, positive.

In the library he advanced to the big table that stood in the centre of the room, turned towards her and leaned against it, thrusting his hands in his pockets and waiting, watchful but at ease.

As Felicity remained standing by the door, holding the gun, he said, 'My dear Miss Frear, can you be holding me at gunpoint?'

'Hardly that; the gun is not, as you can see, pointing anywhere near you.'

'It looks horribly businesslike, though. I would feel much easier if you put it down.'

'I expect you would. But I'm not going to. I know why you're here now, you see? Why you've been trying so hard to trigger my memory.'

Something flared in his watchful eyes. 'Do you indeed?'

'You've been looking for my hiding place, haven't you?'

Now tension was clearly visible under the carefully relaxed pose.

'And I want to tell you that you won't find it. Not even if you take this place apart the way my flat and agency were taken apart.'

'So where is it?' he asked, very softly.

Felicity settled the gun a little more comfortably over her arm. 'That is my secret and it is going to remain my secret. There's nothing you can do that will make me tell you.'

'Nothing?' The very softness of the word was menacing.

She shook her head. 'It's all I've got left. My cousin has gone, Alexander, Jennifer and Thomas Dashwood, everyone I ever cared about. Even my looks. Take this away and I really will have nothing left.'

'And with it?' Again that menacing softness.

'With it the world is my oyster.'

'Without it you'd still have Kingsleigh.' His glance encompassed everything about the room from the oriental carpet to the plaster ceiling with its ornate decoration.

'You think I should just sit here and admire the view?' Felicity managed an ugly laugh. 'You have very little imagination, Mr McLean.'

'I like to think I have quite a considerable one. Even so, I find it difficult to work out how you are going to ... how shall I put it? Liquidate your assets? I'll be watching you every moment.' His eyes never wavered, boring through the protective dark glasses until Felicity felt they must reach her innermost secrets.

'I shall wait for my moment. I think you'll find it difficult to keep quite such a close eye on me, you and your grubby little colleagues. And it's no use your trying to hang around Kingsleigh any longer. The windows in here and in the other rooms are now checked every night. And if Johnny's supplied you with any of the keys, I have to tell you the locks have been changed. Did you enjoy your bath yesterday? I hope so because it's the last one you will have in this house.'

The eyes watching her narrowed again but their expression was different.

He walked slowly over to her. With one swift movement he removed her glasses. Felicity stood blinking and cursing herself for going that bit too far. Until she'd started on the keys and the bath, she'd had him. Now she'd blown it and didn't know why.

'Miss Frear, I don't think you've recovered your memory at all. I don't think you know what you're talking about.' Before she could sense his intention, he grabbed the gun from her and broke it, checked the barrels, then tossed it on to the chair next to her. 'Well, well, we are being careful, or perhaps just foolish!'

Felicity's mind was racing. She was on the right track, she knew it. Until she'd made the mistake of accusing him of breaking into Kingsleigh, he had accepted everything she said.

She looked straight into his eyes. 'You can't deny it,' she said hoarsely. 'You want what I've hidden; that's why you were chasing us and why you pulled me from that car.'

Again that narrowing of the eyes, that considered gaze, as if he was wondering what her game was.

But her headache was suddenly overpowering and her belief that this had been a way to shake him off her trail faltered. She felt herself swaying; the room seemed to be alternately expanding and contracting. She reached out for the chair beside her and had her wrist grasped in an agonizingly strong grip. 'No you don't,' Sam McLean said grimly. 'And don't pretend you feel faint. That's not going to work a second time, not after I've seen you playing tennis.' His last words faded away as the world went black.

Felicity heard someone groaning as she came round. Only gradually did she realize that the groans were hers. She was lying on the library floor and Sam McLean was bending over her with the look of a man who thought he'd held a high poker hand only to find it was, in the end, worthless.

'Will you be all right if I leave to get you a glass of water?' he asked.

'Yes,' Felicity whispered. She closed her eyes again as he rose to his feet and left the room. She felt dreadful, drained and exhausted with a hydraulic drill working hard at destroying her mind.

He was back within minutes. 'Here, I've brought you some brandy as well as the water.' He helped her to sit up, propping her back against a chair.

Felicity spluttered as the brandy fired its way down her gullet. On an empty stomach, it wasn't going to do much for the steadiness of her head, but its warmth brought comfort.

'Better?'

She nodded, put the brandy on the floor and reached for the glass of water he still held. He was hunkered down on his haunches, a big man neatly balanced. She shivered at his total control of the situation.

'So, you weren't faking this time.' His voice was only marginally less menacing than when she had been facing him with the shotgun.

Think, Felicity told herself fiercely, think!

'Thank you,' she said, placing the glass of water beside the brandy. 'Could you possibly help me upstairs?'

He suspected nothing. Half lifting and half letting her climb the stairs, the big man made light work of assisting her to her room. He pulled back the cover on the bed then settled her easily and smoothly.

Felicity turned on her side and, as naturally as she could, trying to give the impression she could hardly keep her eyes from closing, she slid her hand under the pillow and reached for the pistol.

It wasn't there.

'Is this what you're looking for?'

Felicity's eyes flew open, to see Sam McLean standing by the bed, holding the gun in his hand.

'Leaving it on the bedside table for anyone to pick up is not the best of ideas.'

Felicity understood immediately what had happened. Mrs Fry had made the bed and removed the revolver, leaving it on the bedside table. Just as though it were a handkerchief or a book! No hope now of holding him at gunpoint and insisting he told her what he was after.

'You can't possibly have a permit for this,' he said, removing the ammunition clip. 'Nice little weapon. Smith and Wesson, American. Just how did you come by it, I wonder.'

Felicity shut her eyes in frustration.

'I think I'll take it with me, just in case you get the idea of hastening me on my way.'

All she could feel was relief that he appeared to be leaving.

'But don't worry, I'll be back! When you're a little better, we'll resume the interesting conversation we were having in the library.'

She kept her eyes closed and heard the bedroom door click shut behind his departing footsteps. She felt weary beyond words. She knew, somehow, she had made an enormous mistake. Long minutes later, in the far distance, she heard a car start and climb the drive. At least he'd gone. Felicity felt her body relax and failed to remember the unlocked front door. A few minutes later she slid into sleep.

When she awoke the sun was low in the sky and there was a man sitting in her bedroom chair.

Chapter Thirty-Seven

Slowly Felicity pulled herself up and stared at this man who had invaded her room.

He was in his mid-fifties. His hair was an odd shade of brown, his eyes glinted at her, a sharp blue that danced with light. His mouth smiled with a hint of whimsicality. Recognition came gradually as she remembered the photographs from the album. The hair colour was all wrong but, despite the impossibility of the fact, it was surely Alexander.

'Darling, you're awake,' he breathed, his voice full of repressed excitement.

'Father? Alexander?' Neither name sounded right, any more than the fact that he was sitting in that chair was right. Could he have some sort of double? After all, that hair should be golden.

He rose and came towards her.

'But you're dead!' protested Felicity.

He gave her a wide smile. 'I'm no ghost, I promise you.'

He sat on the bed beside her, his body pulsing with life. 'The boat did indeed explode, taking poor Thomas with it, but I was saved. I apologize for the hair; my own was too recognizable so this came out of some bottle. Terrible colour.'

Felicity saw his eyes taking in her appearance, his smile fading.

'I was in an accident,' she said, her fingers hovering around the swollen nose and scarred skin.

He gently took her fingers in his own, kissed them and laid them on the bed. Then he kissed the scars and the nose with light, butterfly touches. 'My poor darling, how you have suffered.' He studied her profile, turning her face away from him with a finger under her chin. 'Mmm, like the new outline, you were always so worried about your nose, said it spoilt your looks, but you've always been beautiful to me.' He lifted his finger away from her chin and ran it gently down the new bridge of her nose. 'The main thing is that you're alive and I'm alive and now we're together again.' He kissed her mouth, a longer but still gentle kiss, then continued down her neck into the open collar of her dress, his fingers struggling with the buttons. 'This is a terrible garment; it matches your eyes but that's its only merit.'

Felicity lay listening to the laughter in his voice and feeling the warmth of those tender kisses. She didn't ask herself where this was leading. It was enough that, for the first time since she had regained consciousness in hospital, someone had appeared who loved her. She hadn't realized until now how starved of affection she had been.

'My poor angel.' Alexander had drawn down the dress and seen the scars on her back and arms. 'How you have suffered.' Another series of light kisses.

Felicity found tears were streaming down her cheeks. Alexander wrapped her closely in his arms and rocked her gently. 'Everything's all right now. I'm here and you're safe,' he murmured. Then he kissed her ear. She felt the wet tip of his tongue exploring its curves before his mouth moved on to her eyes, kissing shut the lids and tasting the salt of her tears as it worked its way once again down to her lips, the caresses gaining in intensity until his mouth closed on hers possessively.

His hands were soothing her body, gentling her as he might a nervous horse, but his lean length was hard against her and his breath was coming faster as he pulled off and tossed away her dress then expertly reached for the fastening of her bra.

Felicity fought against the languor that was stealing over her body, the desire that was rising in response to his. With an effort she raised her hands between them and pushed him away.

Alexander lay back on the bed beside her, breathing quickly, his eyes questioning, his hands still. 'Did I hurt you?'

Felicity looked at him in shock. 'You're my father!'

Her words took him aback; for a moment he looked lost. 'You mean it isn't a trick, that you really have lost your memory? I didn't believe Johnny.' There was an odd echo of something in his voice.

Felicity edged nervously away from him and tried to gather up enough strength to get off the bed. 'It's no trick!'

He reached out a hand to her hip, his white teeth flashing. 'Come on, now, whatever else, you can't have forgotten your father isn't your father!'

She lay watching him, her mind trying to work this out.

His smile faded a little. 'I. Am. Not. Your. Father.' He separated the words as though he were speaking to a child or an idiot.

Through confusion rose hope. 'You mean I'm Fran, not Flick?'

Consternation hit his face. 'What are you talking about?'

'I've felt so odd, not knowing who I am, and people have been so strange to me. I can't tell you how awful it's been.' The words came in soft, gasping groups. 'I don't like being Flick and I thought maybe we changed seats in the car; perhaps Flick took my wedding ring? There's no bump in my nose, nothing to say I'm not Fran.' She laid the propositions before him like a child offering some carefully assembled project for approval.

And he promptly blew the whole thing up by roaring with laughter. 'My darling, do you think I wouldn't know you? Of course you're not Fran. You're my darling Flick. Not my daughter, never my daughter, just the dearest thing in my life.'

Felicity lay her head back on the pillow and looked at him, doubt and disappointment and renewed exhaustion flooding through her in equal measure.

Was this Alexander? She looked at the brown hair, remembered the golden man from the photographs, not only his hair but his skin a glorious colour. This man's tan had faded but it was dark enough to show up tiny white creases fanning out from the corners of his vivid eyes; such a pale blue yet so intense, they were blue ice if you could accept that ice could hold flickering fire in their depths. The clear-cut bones of his face matched those in the photographs, though they hadn't shown the slacking skin under the chin or just how thin the mouth was.

'You look at me as though we've never met!' His voice was all wonder.

'If you're not my father, who is?'

'Ah!' He raised himself on an elbow, the laughter fading from his eyes. 'I believe you know that but it's more than I do. Your mother kept her secret. When we met she would only tell me it was someone in Kenya, that he was married and she wanted a father for her child.' There was a little ironic twist to his mouth. 'I thought she was rich and I needed money. It seemed a perfect recipe. And she was attractive, God, she was attractive in those days. Almost as beautiful as you were when you grew up.'

'How long did I believe you were my father?' asked Felicity, remembering how both Belinda Gray and Denise had shown no doubt but that Alexander was her parent.

'Until your mother lost her temper with you even worse than usual one day and, jealous of the way you loved me, said I had no claim on you.' He reached out his hand again and laid it on Felicity's leg, where it lay on the bed beside him. 'You contacted me on one of your trips to South America, shepherding a troupe of tourists, and asked me if it was true.' There was a reminiscent smile in his eyes. 'And that was the start of everything for us.'

'But my real father,' protested Felicity, her mind refusing to accept what he was suggesting.

'I had my suspicions but your mother always denied them. She said she'd let you know after her death. I believe she wrote you a letter but you never told me what was in it.'

'So I do know? If only . . .' whispered Felicity.

'If only you could bring back your memory,' agreed the man. He slipped his hand up her leg. 'And I have the perfect recipe.' He gathered her towards him in arrogant confidence.

At first his touch was loving, passionate. Then Felicity realized what was happening and began to fight. Alexander became rougher, laughing at her attempts to free herself, still confident he could turn her struggles into sweet surrender. Finally, as she scratched and screamed and pushed and kicked, anger became one with the passion, a hot, abusive anger that laid waste her feeble strength; one of his hands anchored both her arms with contemptuous ease, scorching the new skin; his legs pinioned hers, preventing their pitiful thrashing, and his free hand forced them apart so he could take her with savage thrusts, his face contorted into a brutal mask that contained no hint of love or tenderness.

When it was over, Felicity lay shaking uncontrollably. Pain was everywhere. Not as it had been in hospital; that had been an honest pain compared with this, this sullying of her very soul. It consumed her, made it impossible to think, to speak, even to cry.

Alexander swung himself off her. He was panting, all rage gone. 'Girl, you shouldn't have made me do that.' There was regret in his voice but, stronger than that, there was also triumph. She turned away, drawing her violated body into a foetal curve.

Roughly he pulled her back to face him. 'Now, don't say you still can't remember me after that. I'm Alex, your lover! Alex, whom you've always loved. Alex who loves you.'

A hot hate began to fill Felicity. 'You can do that to me and say you love me?' Contempt filled her eyes and her voice.

'I don't know what game you're playing but I tell you now – forget it!' Alexander leaned urgently towards her, grabbed her wrist. 'You're going to tell me where you've hidden the stuff. And don't think you can fool me you don't know what I'm talking about. Mark told me you'd hidden it but the fool didn't know where.'

It was a horrible travesty of the way she'd tried to deceive Sam McLean earlier. But this could be no bluff.

A tiny area of Felicity's mind registered that evening was here. Soon Malcolm would be back.

'I don't know what you're talking about,' she gasped.

Alexander's eyes narrowed to slits. 'You know! Now, where have you hidden it?'

'If I'd hidden it, don't you think you would have found it by now?

176

You've been looking for days, haven't you?' She spat out the words. So much was becoming clear to her. 'You're desperate, aren't you? Was it you who organized Johnny into stealing the horses? To raise some cash?' She saw she'd hit the mark.

He released her wrist in a violent gesture. 'You think it's easy to find anything in this bloody house? It's got more odd corners and possible hiding places than a bank has deposit boxes.' He rose from the bed in a single, fluid movement and walked to the window, adjusting his clothes. For a moment he stood looking out towards the sea. Then he swung round and leaned against the windowsill. His attitude had lost its belligerence, had changed to one of reason, even appeal. 'Look, you've got to understand. I've put everything I own into this consignment. If it's lost, I'm ruined. Not only that; you don't set up a deal like this on your own – I'm part of a cartel. If I can't produce the goods, they're going to be after me. I'll have no future. Now do you see?'

'But everybody thinks you're dead anyway. You can just disappear, nobody will be after you.'

There was nothing even faintly amusing in his smile. 'They already know I'm alive. I had to have somewhere to go after the boat went down. But I'm on my own as far as extra cash is concerned. There is, you see, no alternative to your producing the goods.' There was an ugly twist to his mouth.

'So Sam McLean's a member of your cartel.'

'Sam McLean? You mean he's been snooping around here?' For an instant rage returned to Alexander's face and Felicity shrank back on the bed; then he regained his composure. 'So you're in trouble as well. One way or another your secret has to come out.' He looked over his shoulder towards the sea again, at the sun that was blazing gold and streaking the sky with red. 'I think it's time to try something a little more drastic.'

Chapter Thirty-Eight

Alexander picked up the blue shirtwaister and tossed it towards Felicity. 'Get dressed.'

He didn't try to help, just watched as she fumbled with the buttons. Through pain, exhaustion and the bedlam in her brain shot fear that fuelled adrenalin, strengthening her weak muscles, sharpening her reactions. Malcolm would soon arrive but would he be a match for Alexander? Johnny was in the background somewhere as well. And Malcolm would be unprepared. If only she had been cleverer over the revolver or had one of the shotguns, even if it was unloaded.

Felicity drew down her torn panties, threw them in a corner and went towards the chest of drawers. Alexander was there in an instant, barring her way.

'I only want some pants.' She managed a steady gaze, appalled at the quickness of his reactions.

He opened the drawers, found a pair of white cotton pants and tossed them to her.

'Do you think I keep a gun with my undies?'

'I can't trust you.' He watched while she slowly drew the pants on underneath her dress, wincing at the bruising and other witnesses to his rape. 'I never thought we would come to this!' Through his voice came confusion.

Felicity liked that even if she didn't like the implication of what he was saying.

'When I think of how you used to help me as a child in my little ploys.' The memory seemed to restore his confidence. 'Such a sweet little girl you made yourself out to be, it quite melted the hearts of those rich middle-aged women waiting to be charmed out of enough money to prime my pump. None of them realized just what a sharp confidence trickster you were.'

'You corrupted me early.'

'Still saying you remember nothing?'

Felicity felt somewhere, deep inside her, veils were shifting, dissolving. For days, weeks, she had been fighting to tear them down, longing

178

for her memory to be restored, to be able to find her identity. Now the past terrified her. More than that, she was afraid that once she had remembered the secret of whatever hiding place it was, she wouldn't be able to keep it from this man. If she knew nothing else, she knew that. And that, whatever he had once been to her, she had no desire to hand over to him whatever it was she'd concealed, even though she still didn't know what it was. Didn't know, but her suspicions were crippling her.

Felicity slowly smoothed down her dress and adjusted the top button.

Alexander moved impatiently towards her. 'That's fine. We're going downstairs. And don't have any ideas about trying to run away. Johnny's outside the house and you wouldn't get far.'

He grabbed her wrist again and, with a quick movement, twisted it round, bringing her arm back in a painful half-Nelson. 'Now you haven't much option.' He gave Felicity a shove towards the bedroom door. She staggered, then recovered. Half pushed, she moved out into the corridor and towards the big main staircase.

Halfway down, she thought she heard the sound of a car coming towards the house. Malcolm!

Alexander hadn't seemed to hear anything but his grip on her arm was just as tight.

Felicity pretended to stagger, pulling him just a little off balance, then, grabbing the banister with her free hand, she jerked a leg behind her and thrust it between his.

Caught by surprise, Alexander fell. Felicity pulled free from his hand, fled down the stairs and across the hall.

She reached the front door and flung it open just as Malcolm arrived in the porch.

She threw herself at him. 'Alexander!' she panted. 'He's here, he's still alive!'

Malcolm caught and steadied her, his arms holding her gently, his freckled face anxious. 'What's going on? What's happening?'

'We've got to get away,' Felicity panted. 'Now!' She tried to pull him with her towards the car and safety.

It was too late. Alexander was in the door, a shotgun in his hands. 'I don't think you're going anywhere,' he said.

'Come on, Malcolm,' she pleaded. 'You know that gun's not loaded.'

'Does he?' said Alexander, holding it steady. 'Do you think I would rely on a weapon I hadn't checked?'

Malcolm's arm round her, Felicity looked towards Alexander and focused on the gun. Her heart sank as she realized it was different from the one she'd used earlier. He must have raided the gunroom while she slept. The disappointment was so intense she slumped against Malcolm and buried her head in his shoulder. Now they were both at Alexander's mercy.

'Anyway, you don't think young Malcolm would have carried you away, a white knight rescuing his lady, do you?' Alexander jeered.

Felicity drew back. Malcolm dropped his arm apologetically and blinked behind his glasses.

'Malcolm has been a colleague for a long time now. Who do you think it was helped your mother bust that trust? I sensed the corruption beneath the Savile Row suiting the first time I met him after he'd taken over as trustee. It only took a lunch and the suggestion of one or two little ploys and your mother had all her problems solved, some of mine vanished as well and Malcolm didn't go short either.'

Felicity fell back against the jamb of the heavy oak door. The only thing she understood, the only thing that was important, was that Malcolm was not her ally.

Alexander waved the shotgun and Malcolm put his hand round her shoulders again to guide her indoors. Indignantly she pushed it away.

'Malcolm likes money, you see, and I've been able to offer him the chance of real riches. Anyway, Devon's getting too hot for him; he's been playing fancy games with some of the accounts down here and his partner's closing in on him. He needs his share of the consignment, you see, very quickly.'

The lawyer flinched as Felicity looked at him in despair. 'But I came to you for help! I thought you were on my side!'

'I am, Felicity, really I am. I want to help you and if only you can remember where you've hidden the consignment, we'll all be fine.'

'He couldn't believe it when you walked into his office,' Alexander said, motioning her through into the main hall with another wave of the gun. 'I'd told him to dream up some excuse for approaching you. I thought if anyone could get to the bottom of exactly what you were up to he could and, just as he was dithering about wondering exactly how he could manage it, you walked into his arms.'

Despairingly Felicity remembered surveying the solid, old-fashioned-looking firm and deciding it was exactly what she needed. Had there been any others she could have gone to in the town or had that been the only one?

Alexander waved the gun again. 'Come on, into the garden.'

Malcolm took her arm, gently. 'There's no need to frighten the life out of her, Alex! Felicity understands the score, don't you?' He guided her through the hall and into the drawing room. 'She knows

180

that if she tries anything, you won't hesitate. After all, you won't be much worse off than you are now, will you?'

Malcolm's voice was gentle and utterly reasonable, exactly as she had come to expect from him. Hopelessness eating at her soul, Felicity allowed herself to be guided, stumbling, across the huge expanse of Aubusson carpet, to the open sash window that led out on to the terrace.

All around her, it seemed, were nothing but enemies.

On the lawn, she stopped suddenly. Malcolm staggered and almost lost his grip on her arm. 'I don't know where you're taking me but what makes you think it's going to do you any good? I'm never going to tell you the hiding place. Alex.' She faced him. 'You know me; say whether I'm speaking the truth or not.'

To her horror, he smiled, lowering the shotgun. 'I know how determined you can be, my darling. I also know that, when you remember everything, you'll want to tell me.'

Fresh despair flooded through Felicity. Malcolm renewed his grip on her arm and pushed her over the grass. 'I was always convinced it was down here. But Alex said we had to make sure; he said he'd searched everywhere and you could easily have taken it up with you. So I had to organize that search, all to no avail,' he added through gritted teeth.

'You're quite sure your friends did the job properly?' asked Alexander.

'If you'd seen the result, you wouldn't ask that,' Malcolm said, pushing Felicity faster towards the beach. 'Not that you made things any easier,' he hissed at her. 'Insisting we went up on Sunday instead of Monday. I knew you'd want to check the agency as well as the flat, even though you didn't have any keys. I had to tell the boys to be out by noon. But apparently they'd finished long before then. Said they'd covered the whole place and not a trace.'

'Can you trust them?' came Alexander's voice from behind. 'They won't have nabbed the stuff and pretended it wasn't there?'

'They might help themselves to a little but they couldn't market that much without us knowing. No, you can be sure it wasn't there.'

The three of them had reached the end of the lawn and the start of the path leading through the scrub to the beach.

'Help!' shouted Felicity. Her voice sang out into the emptiness around them. The setting sun was striking the sea with fiery rays that traced a dazzling path through the water and lit the clouds with glorious colour that turned them into an antechamber for heaven. But all this glory was just for the three of them. There was not another soul within miles.

Except one. Up from the beach came Johnny, an anticipatory smile

181

of glee on his sullen face. Felicity knew he was paying her and everyone else back for the hours of vegetable digging, the injustices of an unkind world.

Malcolm gave her another push that propelled her over the soft, dry sand, studded with dead seaweed and pieces of driftwood, that edged the beach. Felicity staggered as her feet sank into its capricious, shifting surface. It was hard work to reach the firm, wet sand of the beach proper, where she was halted with a jerk at her arm.

The tide was out; a wide reach of darkly golden sand, curved like a half-moon, stretched down to the crashing rollers. White foam ran up the sand then was sucked back with greedy noises as the sea gathered itself for a renewed onslaught.

In the centre of the beach was arranged a pile of hay bales. Near to where Felicity had been forced to stand was a low trailer.

'Now, my sweet,' said Alexander. 'In you get.'

Felicity stared at him, uncomprehending.

'Into the trailer,' he said impatiently. 'Malcolm, help her.'

Malcolm pushed her, not unkindly, in the direction they wanted her to go. Felicity stumbled a few steps then stopped. He took a firmer grip of her arm, digging painfully into the flesh. She resisted, pulling the opposite way, her flat shoes biting wet depressions into the sand.

'For God's sake, Malcolm! Do I have to do everything myself? Take this!' Alexander handed Malcolm the shotgun, grabbed Felicity's right wrist and twisted it backwards into another half-Nelson. 'Shout if you want to,' he said sardonically as she yelled with pain. 'There's no one to hear. Scream to the fishes, it won't do you any good.' He forced her to climb into the trailer, making her put one foot on the wheel axle then jerking a knee under her buttocks to flip her on to the cart's flat bed.

Felicity fell with a cry of pain as her shins caught the wooden sides. She landed in a heap at the bottom of the swaying trailer. At once Johnny was forcing her down, tilting the trailer so that her head was almost on the sand. A harness was forced around her shoulders, the hard leather straps cutting into her flesh, preventing her from struggling.

'Right,' Alexander said, tilting the trailer back level and supporting it. Johnny forced Felicity into a sitting position and Malcolm held her there as the groom took one end of the harness and fastened it over a hook in the trailer side. He twisted it around and around, making sure it was secure, then went and repeated the action on the other side. Alexander tested the straps. Felicity was as secure as a baby in its pram.

'Right!' Alexander said again.

Johnny ran towards the bales. At one side of the semicircular arrangement were several cans of petrol. Two were on their sides, the caps gone. Johnny took the last and doused the topmost bales. Then he tossed the empty can aside and took out a box of matches.

'No!' Felicity's cry curved out in a high wail that fell uselessly towards the sea. She yanked at the straps that held her in the cart; once again the leather bit cruelly into her flesh without giving an inch.

Johnny lit a match and offered it nervously to the nearest bale, leaping back the moment the straw caught. There was an almighty whoosh and the whole crescent of petrol-soaked bales was aflame.

'Now!' shouted Alexander and started pushing the end of the trailer. Malcolm leapt beside him and together they trundled the cart towards the fire, gaining speed across the resilient sand.

Felicity saw the wall of flame coming closer and closer, heard the roar, felt the heat. All around her was fire and terror. Her heart was racing so fast she thought it would explode; her breath felt as though it had been sucked out of her body but she could hear someone wailing in an excess of fear and knew it was herself. Ever nearer came the wall of fire. Sparks were falling on her hair and dress, there was the smell of singeing, back came the agony of the burning as the fire crackled greedily at her.

Chapter Thirty-Nine

Suddenly Felicity was no longer in the cart, she was in a car. In the front were Mark and her cousin and they were hurtling towards a huge lorry. They hadn't been able to avoid the lorry as they'd veered round the corner because Mark had lost control of the car the way he'd lost control of the situation.

Mark had lost control because he was terrified.

As the car, its brakes screaming, hit the lorry, she was thrown against the back of the passenger seat. She felt the crunch of gristle as her nose impacted, heard her cheekbones crack with the force of the collision. The pain would come later; now all she felt was panic as she heard the lorry explode, felt the fire advance. Her cousin was beating at the flames that were licking towards her face, trying to free herself from the safety belt and open the car door. And all the time she was screaming, unintelligible, helpless screams.

Then the burning figure in the front seat that had been Mark turned around, his face a contorted, macabre mask, in his hand the heavy torch that lived next to the driver. He raised the torch and produced a howl that was outrage, hate and white fury wrapped into one incandescent ululation. His words were indecipherable, his burning hand a claw riveted to his weapon with demonic power. She shouted his name as she saw it swing towards her then buried her head in her arms as the flames leaped up to consume them both and the world went black.

Now her throat was on fire, she was choking, drowning in smoke and flames.

Hauled through semi-consciousness back into awareness, she opened her eyes. The bales of straw were burning less fiercely; their core glowed red and odd stalks flamed briefly on the sand before being blown away and out; black debris surrounded the dying pyre.

The trailer had been drawn back, her harness removed and she herself was supported in Alexander's arms. He had a flask of brandy and was gently applying it to her mouth, the liquid trickling down her burning throat.

'You bastard!' she screamed at him, knocking away the flask. He dropped the brandy and grabbed her wrist. 'You bastard!' she cried again, then broke down in racking sobs. Alexander tried to hold her in his arms but she wrenched herself free from him, dashing away her tears with the palms of her hands in angry jabs.

'You've remembered,' he said softly. 'It worked.'

She longed to be able to deny it, to tell him the veils hadn't been wrenched apart, that there had been nothing so gentle as a dissolving, but, perhaps from something in her face, she knew he recognized that the past for her was now one with the present.

'Tell me,' she ground out, looking at the black smears on his face, the small holes burned into his sweat shirt, 'just how far did you push me into that inferno?'

'Not far,' he said soothingly. 'Not far at all.'

'Bloody far enough,' burst out Malcolm resentfully. He was in the same state as Alexander, soot disfiguring his face, tie adrift, his smart suit ruined. 'You said a short trundle towards the flames would be enough. As it was you damn nearly took us all into the centre before I managed to haul her back.'

'*We*, Malcolm, *we* hauled her back. Everything was under control. And it worked, just look, she remembers everything.'

'Yes!' she spat at him, abandoning any attempt to deny it. 'I remember everything.'

'And now you'll tell us where you hid the cocaine.'

'You can go to hell first.'

'You haven't, I trust, any hopes of marketing it yourself? I have to warn you retribution would be swift, if not from me, from my associates.'

'Come on, Felicity, tell us,' pleaded Malcolm, pulling at his tie. 'Can't you see he'd do anything to get that consignment? Without it he's dead meat, we're all dead meat.'

'Don't call me Felicity,' she hissed. 'My name isn't Felicity.'

'No, it's Flick, always Flick.' Alexander was confident, so confident.

'Are you sure?' She looked at him with her straight nose and her scarred face, her dark blue eyes bright and steady. The dark blue eyes that belonged to both Frances and Felicity, Fran and Flick.

She saw doubt flare in his face. Where he had been so sure before, now there was uncertainty.

'You have no power over Fran, have you, Alex? She never fell beneath your spell; was never seduced into assisting with your ugly trafficking. Oh, there've never been any secrets between us, I know everything about Flick and everything about you.' Her voice dropped. 'How many lives are you going to ruin with the contents of your "consignment"?' Her voice dripped disgust. 'You think I would help

185

you market your dirty drugs? When you killed Philip? Got Sarah hooked? And no doubt it was you who persuaded Mark Sheldrake to help you in your foul trade.

'Did you tell Mark about the Kingsleigh heiress? Did you suggest she could provide a cosy berth for him? Did you tell him about the estate, with its harbour that was so perfect for your purposes?

'You knew all about the trip we were taking through Brazil and Peru. You could set Mark up with the perfect seduction scenario. Oh, you've a lot to answer for, Alexander.'

It was the use of his full name that convinced him. 'Fran!' he said in wondering disgust.

Malcolm looked at her in astonishment. 'So you really are the cousin, not Felicity at all!' Then he saw Alexander move towards the shotgun. 'No!' he shouted. 'No, Alex, you can't do that!' He stumbled over a low rock in the wet sand, nearly fell, recovered his footing and continued towards the other man.

But Alexander had reached the shotgun and raised it, aiming straight at Malcolm. 'Stay there, Biddulph, don't come any closer.'

Malcolm, his face white in the last of the light from the dying sun, obeyed. He looked back in despair towards the girl he'd known as Felicity.

She faced Alexander. She knew he wouldn't hesitate to kill her. To get the cocaine there was nothing he wouldn't do. There must be at least ten kilos there. All in the two holdalls Mark had been carrying when she had met him coming up from the boathouse that evening, the night *Seawind* exploded.

Mark had been full of some crazy story about Alexander and his father-in-law quarrelling then making up and deciding to go for a sail, to do some fishing. She had known it was nonsense just by the shiftiness of his eyes, the way he wouldn't look her straight in the face.

Oh, why hadn't she seen him for what he was in South America? How could she have been taken in like that?

Now he was trying to pretend it was their overnight gear in the holdalls, as though she didn't know exactly what had been taken on board during his and Alexander's long sail.

She'd challenged him, asked him if he really thought she was that stupid. Then he'd changed his story, said it was something Alex had asked him to take care of. Something precious that needed to be hidden.

OK, she'd said, she would hide it, leave it all to her, she knew the perfect place. He should have known Alexander would never have allowed that to happen without insisting he be shown exactly where. Mark had just been pathetically grateful.

He'd broken down completely when they'd heard the fate of the *Seawind*. Anyone would think his father had been on board.

It wasn't until later that he'd wanted to know where the holdalls had been hidden and it was when she'd refused to tell him that the nightmare had really started.

'Back off, Malcolm,' Alexander said now, his voice clear and deadly, the cold voice of the telephone calls. 'Right off, the other side of what's left of those bales, beside Johnny, where I can keep an eye on the two of you.'

She watched Malcolm move slowly backwards, giving the odd glance behind him to make sure he knew where he was going. There wasn't going to be much help from that quarter. There was another person she'd been taken in by. Really, she'd been a complete idiot.

'Come on, Fran, be sensible,' Alexander said to her. 'You must realize that keeping one consignment of cocaine out of the drugs market is like removing a bucket of sand from this beach. It means nothing in the sum total of things. But several million pounds cuts up a lot of ways and I'm sure Kingsleigh could use a roofing fund; all that lead will need replacing one of these days.' His voice was cajoling but the shotgun was held steadily, aimed at her.

She glanced towards Malcolm and Johnny but saw that she could expect no help from that quarter; they were too frightened of Alexander.

Well, there wasn't much of her life left anyway. Kingsleigh could never compensate for the people she'd lost, for the love that had turned to ashes.

'Tell me, God dammit, tell me!' Alexander cursed and swore then, as he realized she wasn't going to tell him what he needed so desperately to know, he raised his gun. 'You've had your last chance.' It was too dark now for her to see his eyes but she knew they were full of anger and there was enough light to recognize the ugly twist of his mouth and the way his finger began to tighten on the trigger.

Suddenly she wanted very much to live. In a desperate dive, she flung herself into the bottom of the trailer and it tilted beneath her weight so that she slithered down its length, splinters catching and tearing at her clothes and skin as she was somersaulted out on to the wet sand.

There was a shot followed by a cry of pain that wasn't hers. Then confusion broke out on the beach and there were people everywhere.

There was shouting and orders barked against the never-ending boom of the surf that was gradually advancing up the beach.

A slick of water ran across the sand and kissed the top of her head before being sucked back. Then a hand was outstretched towards her. 'Are you hurt?' asked a voice that was horribly familiar. A hand reached towards her and she looked up to see Sam McLean, larger than ever in his black leather jacket.

She shrank back with a cry, pulling herself underneath the trailer, trying to get away yet knowing there was nowhere left to go. She had no idea how he'd got there or what his connection was with Alexander; she only knew that her ordeal still wasn't over.

More commands and the trailer was pulled away, leaving her exposed.

Sam grabbed her hands. 'It's all right, Felicity,' he said urgently. 'I'm not going to hurt you.'

She gritted her teeth, resolved to keep her secret no matter what he did to her. 'It's no use, you know!' she forced out. 'You can't make me say where it's hidden. I wouldn't tell Alexander and I'm not going to tell you. I'm not giving that cocaine to anyone but the police.'

He smiled, a warm, amused smile that reached his eyes and transformed his face. 'I am the police! Look around you.'

Then, through the dusky gloom, lit by the still glowing bales, she saw that the beach was filled with blue uniformed officers.

She looked back at Sam McLean, unable to believe her eyes. 'You don't have to worry any more,' he said and gently brushed away sand from her battered face.

It was too much. She burst into tears.

He helped her to sit on one of the wheels of the trailer and produced a handkerchief. She blew her nose and wiped her eyes, trying to regain some semblance of dignity, disgusted at her lack of control.

'You're allowed a small breakdown, Miss Frear,' Sam said. 'You can't be brave all the time.'

'Not Miss Frear,' growled Alexander.

She looked at him. Once he'd rivalled a bronze god; now he'd shrunk. The brown hair was limp and dull, his face grey and drawn. He was holding his shoulder and blood dripped through his fingers. On either side of him were two large policemen and one was trying to organize a makeshift bandage.

'She's Fran Sheldrake,' Alexander ground out through clenched teeth. 'Not my Flick at all. Flick's dead.' There was desolation as well as pain in his face.

'You're wrong.' She looked straight at him, this man she had once adored. 'I'm not Fran. I lied.'

'Flick?' He sounded disbelieving. 'You really are Flick after all?'

'No!' She rose, using Sam's arm as a support, then managed to stand on her own, straight and tall. 'I'm Felicity.'

Chapter Forty

'Well, Felicity Frear, you've led me quite a dance,' said Sam McLean.

She couldn't work out his tone. It was severe, almost condemnatory, yet, underneath, there was a hint of something else, something less impersonal.

They were in the sitting room at Kingsleigh. Sam was seated at the desk, his chair skewed round so he could survey the room. Felicity was not in her usual armchair but the one opposite, so she could face him. There were also what seemed an amazing number of police popping in and out or hanging around.

Alexander, his expression agonized and defeated, had been escorted to hospital to have his wound seen to. Malcolm and Johnny, both wearing looks of profound disbelief, had been taken off to the local police station.

Felicity, bruised, battered and deeply apprehensive, decided on attack. 'Don't you think I should know exactly who you are?' she demanded. 'And I need brandy rather than this . . .' She indicated the cup of hot sweet tea that had been provided for her. She was shivering. On the beach, the heat from the holocaust of burning bales had blunted the chill of the evening air; now reaction had set in and uncontrollable tremors were shaking her body. She pulled the torn and scorched dress closer around herself.

'I'm Detective Chief Inspector Sam McLean of the Drugs Squad,' he said, going across to the tray of drinks. He found the brandy decanter, poured some into a glass and brought it across.

'Sir, what she really needs is a hot bath and a change of clothes,' said a policewoman, a lone female amongst all the male officers that milled round Kingsleigh.

Sam stood in front of Felicity and looked at her. His expression was hard to read but it seemed as though he was registering the full extent of her condition for the first time. How far could he see? Down to the dirt that was inside?

'Take her upstairs, constable, and see she has everything she needs.' He made it sound as though she was under arrest.

Felicity kept hold of her brandy glass and allowed the WPC to take her upstairs. The WPC's name was Jackie Wright. 'You wouldn't believe the jokes I get,' she said as she ran the bath. 'I'm just grateful my dad isn't called Wrong!' She tested the temperature. 'I think that's about right now; you don't want it too hot, not after all you've been through. Have a nice long soak and, remember, if you want to see a doctor, if you don't feel up to being questioned or want a lawyer present, all you've got to do is say.' Her eyes were sharp and bright as she helped Felicity slip out of the clothes that smelled of burning straw and other odours even more repugnant.

'What would your boss say?' Felicity gently lowered her aching limbs into the warm bath.

'Don't you worry about the chief inspector,' the girl said cheerfully. 'You've got your rights and you can't allow anyone to take them away from you. Will you be OK for a moment? I'll go and find you something comfortable to put on. That'll save you having to think.'

If only Felicity could stop thinking!

She told the girl which her room was, drank a little of the brandy and felt its warmth start to quell her inner turbulence the way the heat of the water was dispelling her shivers.

She slipped further into the comfort of the bath and rested her head on the little cushion Fran had provided for guests.

Never again would Felicity share anything with her cousin. Had she ever actually said how much she'd appreciated the gift that had been Fran?

The realization of all that had gone from her life was sinking into her mind like acid burning through metal.

How blessed had been the loss of her memory that it could spare her this pain. And what she felt now was nothing to what she knew would be coming as the full extent of the tragedy sank in.

The one benefit gained from Jennifer Dashwood's last, bitter illness had been Fran's renewal of their friendship and her acceptance that Flick hadn't encouraged Philip. She had even admitted that Flick had done her best, not only to make him realize how valuable his relationship with Fran was, but also to lead a more sensible life.

But Felicity hadn't realized until after Philip's death just what dangers he was running. If only she'd known he had been taking cocaine as well as marijuana, perhaps she could have helped him more. She'd cursed herself for her ignorance, just as she had cursed herself when her mother's addiction had been revealed at the autopsy after her death. How, Felicity had asked herself bitterly, could she have lived with her mother and not known? But she'd been away so often and Sarah had been very cunning.

Almost as cunning as Alexander.

Here was cause for more bitterness.

How devastated she had been at the news of *Seawind*'s explosion. Both Thomas and Alexander killed. She'd felt orphaned and bereft, all joy and any sense of stability gone from her life.

For so many years, Alexander had been the centre of her world. First as beloved father, then, after the divorce, as freewheeling childhood companion. He had had a habit of descending on Clapham or Kingsleigh and whisking her off for a week or so's excitement. Then he'd deposit her back, to be ignored by Sarah or comforted by Fran. Whatever the heartache involved, he'd added an extra, much needed, dimension to the schizophrenic existence she led between school, Clapham and Kingsleigh.

The little con-tricks Alexander had pulled had never seemed very reprehensible to her young eyes. As he'd said, the women had too much money for their own good, more than enough to be able to share a little with him. And in return he gave them a wonderful time.

Later, when she found out that Alexander wasn't her father, it had seemed a dream come true. The man who had always been the most attractive she had ever met wanted her as a woman. She had flown into his arms like a bird coming home. Philip could never have competed against Alex, even if he hadn't been engaged to Fran.

The bathroom door opened and Constable Wright reappeared. 'I can't find anything much in your wardrobe,' she said doubtfully, a pair of brightly coloured leggings and a big sweater over her arm. 'This is about the best I can come up with.'

'Look in my cousin's wardrobe; the room next to mine. You'll probably find something more suitable there.' Felicity started to wash herself. 'We were exactly the same size.'

Throughout their adolescence, she and Fran could have swapped clothes but rarely did, their tastes were so different. They'd shared so much but there had been more it had been impossible to share.

Oh, how she'd envied Fran her life. The mother who was everything a mother should be: kind, caring and understanding, who never seemed to suffer from the tantrums, selfishness and self-pity that Sarah was prone to. Then there was Kingsleigh; it wasn't Spain but it offered riding, sailing, tennis and marvellous fun, so different from dingy, gloomy Clapham. Most of all, though, Kingsleigh offered Fran herself, kind and loving like her mother, staunch and courageous, the best friend any girl could have; no sister could have been better.

Growing up at Kingsleigh hadn't been all fun, though. Warmly as Jennifer and Fran treated her, Felicity had soon sensed that as far as other people were concerned, she was a poor relation. The Dashwoods were surrounded with the aura of Kingsleigh. Its history and wealth gave them a social position which Felicity could only share in by association and then only if she behaved herself. She found it all too easy to infringe conventions she was hardly aware of and difficult to understand the disapproval she aroused. It had seemed a blessing when she discovered her ability to startle people into an awareness of herself as a person. She'd quickly decided it was easier to condemn others before they looked down their noses at her. She developed her flip manner and armoured herself in disdain. Every time she incurred someone's contempt, she told herself she'd actually won a battle. Until in the end she'd convinced herself she didn't need anyone but Fran and Alexander.

She'd lost Alexander first, then Fran.

Constable Wright was back, triumphant. 'I've found the perfect thing.' She held up a soft, beige cashmere robe that tied around the waist with a thick sash of amber satin. 'And lovely silk underwear; you'll hardly know you're wearing it.'

That must be from Fran's trousseau. Felicity had a sudden memory of buying lingerie in Knightsbridge with a deliriously happy Fran.

'Would you like a longer soak? Do you feel like a cup of tea now?'

Felicity shook her head. Her trembling had stopped. She'd washed away the surface dirt and nothing could make her feel clean inside. She might as well face Chief Inspector McLean, the man she knew as Sam, and get her interrogation over with. It wasn't going to be easy and at the end he would almost certainly have to arrest her but it didn't seem to matter greatly now.

Jackie Wright handed her a towel. Felicity wrapped its thick pile around herself and remembered the damp towel she had found here on Sunday evening. What an incredible risk Alexander had taken and how like him!

A thought struck her. She opened the bathroom cabinet. The bottle of sleeping pills she'd brought back from the hospital had several missing. So much for Malcolm's kind action in bringing her a hot drink! No wonder she had felt so dreadful all day.

Jackie helped pat Felicity's scarred skin dry. She appeared to be enjoying herself. 'I can imagine the days when a house like this would have had ladies' maids.' She handed Felicity talcum powder without a trace of embarrassment. 'I think I might quite have liked a job like that.'

'You don't think it would have been demeaning?'

'Not if you didn't look on it that way yourself. It's a job like any other, needs a lot of skills, I should think, and you could have enjoyed luxury by proxy, as you might say. As long as you've got pride in yourself and the job you're doing, that's all that matters. That's what I think.'

Pride in yourself; would she ever have that again?

'Sit down.' Jackie drew forward the bathroom chair. 'I'll brush your hair. You look completely done in. Are you sure you don't want a doctor? You can postpone the chief's interview.'

Felicity shook her head. All she wanted was to get it over with.

Jackie Wright had brought brush, comb and lipstick into the bathroom with the cashmere robe.

'There,' she said after she'd finished. 'Quite a transformation.' She made Felicity look at herself in the mirror.

A small, upstanding collar provided a flattering frame for her neck and head. The nose was now almost normal size and her hair curled round her face, deflecting attention from the scars. The dark blue eyes looked exhausted and shadowed but the centre panel of her face was clear, the skin fair and fine. Felicity tried turning up the corners of her severe mouth then decided she was incapable of producing a smile. The newly straight nose mocked her and she felt a lingering regret for the bumpy version she'd always hated.

Her dark glasses were on the table beside her bed. She was about to ask Jackie if she would mind fetching them, when she decided they could stay there.

She would face her interview with Chief Inspector McLean without protective devices.

Chapter Forty-One

Back in the sitting room, Chief Inspector Sam McLean was writing at the desk.

Now that she knew, Felicity could recognize his air of power for what it was. How could she have missed it before?

He looked up as the two girls came into the room. 'Feeling better?' he asked Felicity. There was little about his manner to suggest he was actually anxious about her state of health.

She sat in the chair and didn't answer. The cashmere robe fell in graceful folds around her legs, caressed her skin, made her feel elegant. She couldn't ever remember wearing anything so soft before. It gave her courage.

'I think I have a case against you under the Trade Descriptions Act,' she said severely.

Almost it seemed he might smile but his face quickly resumed its steely quality. He came and sat in the chair opposite hers and signalled for another officer to take notes. 'Some day I'll ask you to forgive me. Now, are you well enough to enable us to hear your part in this story?' Again, there was no hint of real concern about his request.

She gave him a brief nod. 'I had nothing to do with the cocaine shipment.'

He met her eyes. 'So you said on the beach.'

'You were there and didn't stop Alex? You let him drive me into that inferno?' She couldn't believe it.

'No!' At last a personal note entered his voice. 'Believe me, I'd never have let him do that. When we arrived the trailer had been pulled clear of the burning bales. And our marksmen took Frear out before he could fire at you.'

She found it difficult to accept his reassurance. 'You were as desperate as Alex to know where the cocaine was. I don't believe you would have stopped at anything.'

His grey eyes were very still as they looked at her. 'You make me sound quite ruthless.'

'Oh, you are! Why didn't you put a stop to the fun and games when you arrived at the beach?' She challenged and answered him in the same breath. 'Because you wanted as much information as you could get; my safety was incidental.'

'I was there to save you,' he said quietly. 'Our little chat this afternoon convinced me that Frear was not only searching the house but that he was very close to declaring himself to you. Otherwise he'd never have risked taking a bath here. I decided that if I waited any longer for your memory to return, you would be in extreme danger.' His face hardened. 'Your behaviour all along in this case has been suspicious, to say the least, but after *Seawind* exploded it became positively self-incriminatory.'

Felicity heard the censure in his voice and felt the defences she had so newly abandoned start to build themselves around her again. But before she could utter any of the words that rose so readily to her tongue, he continued. 'Yet the more I talked to you, the less I believed you could really be in partnership with Frear. It was impossible, though, to risk giving you the opportunity to blow the whole investigation wide open. All I could do was apply for a search warrant and organize the team. It all took precious time and we didn't arrive until you were just getting into your stride.' He hesitated for a moment then added, 'You seemed to be declaring your innocence and it seemed a pity not to let you put us straight on that.'

Declaring her innocence – did he really believe that? But there was so much more she had to tell him. What would he think then?

'Are you sure you weren't waiting to hear if I'd tell where the cocaine was hidden?'

'There was a marksman trained on Frear the whole time. You were never in danger.'

'I think I have my own opinion as to that.'

He ignored this. 'So, are you ready now to tell us about the cocaine?'

Felicity closed her eyes and took herself back in time.

'It was the night *Seawind* exploded.' She opened her eyes, lay back in the chair and fastened her gaze on the bowl of roses arranged on one of the tables. She couldn't have said what colour they were but she couldn't bear to look any longer at that steely face. 'Alex and Mark were out sailing. They'd been out overnight and were due back that evening.

'Fran and I were with Uncle Tom in this room. Fran hadn't been feeling well and was just thinking of giving up waiting for them to return and going to bed when we heard the front door bell. Mrs Parsons was off by then so Uncle Tom answered it. When he didn't come back, we reckoned he must have taken whoever it was into the library. It was quite late but he was a magistrate and every now and then he'd be asked to sign a warrant at odd hours.' She broke off and gave a brief glance at Sam. 'I suppose you had to get your warrant signed by some other magistrate.' Felicity didn't wait for an answer but ploughed on with her story, her gaze once again on the roses. Now she remembered the scent of roses that had come through the window that evening. Fran lying here on the sofa, doing tapestry.

'He was away a long time and eventually Fran asked me to go and see if anything was wrong. I'd got as far as the stairs when the library door opened. You know the layout of this house and how the stairs come between the passage from the sitting room and the library. So Uncle Tom couldn't see me and I couldn't see him or his visitor but I could hear what they were saying.'

'And what did you hear?' he asked as she paused.

'The other man said something like, "I don't want them alerted, sir," and Uncle Tom replied, very stiffly, "You can be quite sure, Chief Inspector. I know my duty. But you are mistaken; Sheldrake and Frear can have nothing to do with this matter." I could tell he was very upset. Then he took the inspector through to the hall and I heard no more.

'When he returned from letting him out, I asked what was going on. He was absolutely furious with me.' Once again Felicity broke off, her mind distracted from the main story. 'It was strange. When I first came to Kingsleigh Uncle Tom was so nice; both he and Aunt Jennifer seemed to love me like a daughter. Then, about two or three years later, he changed. My mother had been on a visit. They never seemed to get on but that time was worse than usual and after she'd left it was as if his dislike of her had been transferred to me. After that I could never do anything right as far as he was concerned.' She thought about it for a moment then gave a brief shake of her head.

'That night he accused me of being an interfering busybody and said he wouldn't be at all surprised if I wasn't at the bottom of everything. It was just the sort of thing he'd say and I ignored it and tried to get him to tell me what was going on. He just said he was going back into the sitting room and forbade me to say anything that might upset Fran.' She looked again at the policeman. 'Was it you that night? There has always seemed something familiar about your voice.'

He nodded. 'We'd had both Frear and Sheldrake under surveillance for some time. Sheldrake had been convicted of a drug offence several years before; he'd spent time in prison, then we heard he'd gone abroad, to South America. A little while ago, Scotland Yard had an enquiry from the Argentinian police about Frear; some well-connected rich widow had lodged a complaint. He'd apparently made off with a sizeable sum of money and she wanted her revenge. She couldn't produce sufficient evidence for a prosecution, though, and she followed up her initial complaint with an accusation of cocaine dealing.

'That was when I was brought in. Cocaine smuggling into the UK has greatly increased over the past few years. Crack is an increasing problem and we're battling to identify and cut off the main suppliers. Once again, though, there was no evidence and it looked like a feeble attempt by a scorned woman to get her own back. Then we found Frear was in contact with Sheldrake, so we took a closer look at his connections back here. What did we find but that you, his stepdaughter, were making regular trips to South America in connection with your travel business. You were on record as being involved with two cocaine addicts, Philip Bishop and Sarah Frear, and suddenly it began to look as though we might have something.'

Felicity remembered all too vividly the interrogation she had undergone, first after Philip's death then, even worse, after her mother's. And last time she had returned from South America she had been searched. No ordinary search, either. Her luggage had been taken apart, the clothes she was wearing had been removed and taken away, her body subjected to the ultimate humiliation. They had found nothing and eventually she had been allowed to go. At the Clapham flat, the cream leather holdall waiting in her bedroom had seemed to leer at her as, exhausted and violated, she had sunk on the bed.

'When we heard that Sheldrake had turned up at Kingsleigh, married to your cousin, Customs and Excise started keeping a watch on the *Seawind*. It was perfectly placed to pick up consignments from vessels sailing from Colombia to Europe.' He broke off and looked searchingly at Felicity. 'How much do you know about the smuggling of cocaine into Europe?'

She shook her head. 'Very little. I know most of it comes from Colombia and that the main drug baron there, Escobar, was killed about a year ago, but that's all.'

'I wish I could say Escobar's death has solved our problem. But until a legitimate crop can take the place of the cultivation of coca in Peru and Ecuador and the economy of Colombia can free itself of drug money, the situation appears hopeless. The main channel for the cocaine itself is America but over the past few years Europe has been opening up. Much of it comes on ship into Amsterdam, smuggled past none too vigilant customs officers in ports like Cartagena then off again the European end. But some of it gets off-loaded during the trip, specially packaged to float, wrapped in a waterproof covering. A rendezvous is arranged and the package thrown into the sea. A homing device makes it possible for it to be picked up, a pleasure boat sails back to its moorings and everything is set for a big killing on the UK market.' He paused a moment then added, 'Twice Customs and Excise boarded the *Seawind* and searched her, without result. Did you know that?'

'None of us did. If Uncle Tom had been told, we'd never have heard the end of it. The ignominy, the outrage, that one of the most respected magistrates in Devon, Chairman of the Bench, ex-High Sherriff of the county, could possibly have his yacht suspected of smuggling.'

'I had all that fed back to me, the unlikelihood of it pointed out. But all I could see was that he provided the perfect cover! I was convinced Frear was the key to the whole thing and I thought a late-night talk with Thomas Dashwood might be productive.

'But he refused even to countenance the idea that either Frear or his son-in-law could be involved in any way with drugs. I could see, though, that he'd been shaken by the information that Sheldrake had been in gaol and eventually I got him to promise to let me know the next time *Seawind* was taken out for a long sail.' Sam dropped his gaze to his feet. 'I blame myself for not realizing just how protective of his family he was or that he could be concealing the fact that *Seawind* was out at that very time.' He banged the arm of the chair in frustration. 'If only I'd managed to get his confidence, we could have been waiting as the cocaine sailed back into harbour, wrapped the whole case up that night and he, your cousin and Sheldrake would still be alive.'

There was silence for a long moment.

Felicity thought of her uncle. 'He adored his daughter. Fran was everything to him. If he thought there was any chance of salvaging her happiness, he'd have made a pact with the devil. I think, in fact, that that was what he had in mind. He told Fran he was going down to the harbour to see if *Seawind* had returned and that she should go to bed. I could see he was under a great strain but I knew it was no use offering to go with him.'

She looked straight at Sam. 'I'm not a complete idiot, you know. I had my own suspicions regarding those long sailing trips when women weren't welcome.'

He returned her gaze levelly. 'I have the highest regard for your intelligence. Why do you think you were high on our list of suspects?'

Felicity shivered.

'Apart from the other considerations, there was the mystery over where you'd got hold of the capital to start your business. All we could find out was that the money had suddenly appeared. Drug profits seemed all too likely a source.'

Felicity looked at his stern eyes. She was going to have to tell him exactly how she'd been involved. What would he think of her then?

Chapter Forty-Two

Felicity took a deep breath and continued her story.

'I persuaded Fran to go to bed and took her a hot drink. Then I set off for the boathouse, about an hour after Uncle Tom. I met Mark coming up the cliff steps carrying two holdalls and shaking like a leaf.

'All he could say at first was that Uncle Tom and Alex had had a row. When I asked why, he tried to backtrack, said it hadn't really been a row, more of a disagreement but that they'd made up and decided to take the *Seawind* out for some fishing.

'I could hardly believe him. Uncle Tom hated sailing with Alex and hadn't taken a boat out at night for ten years or so. But when I looked towards the harbour, I could see *Seawind* was moving out. No sails were up, the masts were bare and she was motoring. There was just one figure at the helm. The moon shone on silver hair and at that distance it could have been either of them, but I thought it was Alex.' Felicity's gaze fell and she started fiddling with one of the buttons on her robe. 'I was sure then that something very odd was going on. Later when I'd found out more, I decided that there had been a fight and Uncle Tom had got killed. Alex and, maybe, Mark had decided the best thing to do was to take his body out to sea and stage an accident but that the plan had gone wrong and Alex had got blown up as well.' She glanced up at Sam and said bitterly, 'My capacity for self-deception has always been astronomical. Anyway, there I was and there was Mark and *Seawind* was sailing out of the harbour. So I asked him what was in the bags.

'He tried to tell me it was just their things from the boat. Mark was such a fool,' she added contemptuously. 'Fran had made special bags to take off dirty clothes and linen and the rubbish was always left in the boathouse for collection. They never needed holdalls like the ones he was carrying.

'So I told him to knock it off and eventually he broke down and told me Alex wanted him to hide the bags and I was to say nothing about them to Fran.'

Felicity brought her gaze back to Sam and forced herself to look steadily at him. 'I told Mark I knew a perfect place to hide them and that he was to go to Fran and tell her the story he'd told me but to make it sound ten times better.'

'You are not trying to tell me you didn't know what was in the bags?' Sam broke in.

She shook her head. 'I opened them before I hid them, of course. It was pretty obvious to me what was in the packets.'

'So, if you were innocent, why didn't you turn them straight over to the police?'

Felicity sighed. She was feeling very weary, as weary as she had that night when she'd stood looking at the open bags and trying to work out the best course of action. 'The money to start my travel business came from my aunt, Jennifer Dashwood. She gave it to me after my mother died and we found out she'd got round my trust fund and spent all the money. It was secret because she didn't want Uncle Tom to know.'

'She must have loved you very much,' Sam commented quietly.

Felicity blinked hard. 'I think she did but she also told me she felt guilty that my mother had ended up with so little and she had so much. It wasn't her fault; her father had tried to treat them equally but Jennifer was the sort of person who made money grow and my mother was the sort who spent it, unwisely. But in the final analysis it still meant that I had nothing and Fran had a great deal. She knew she was very ill and she persuaded me she wouldn't die happy unless I was settled. In return I promised her I would look after Fran. Fran's never been as fly as I have, she's always been too trusting.'

Felicity closed her eyes briefly as she remembered her feelings that night. 'When I saw that cocaine I knew I had let down both my aunt and Fran. On the face of it, Mark Sheldrake was both a drug smuggler and a fortune hunter. But, you see, I wasn't certain. I wasn't prepared to expose Fran to losing everything before I knew exactly what had been going on. Maybe Mark had become involved by accident and there could be some way of keeping him out of it. Nor did I know how deeply Alex was implicated. After he and Uncle Tom returned, perhaps I could persuade him to turn both himself and the cocaine in. That had to be the best thing he could do.

'So I decided to hide the bags where I was absolutely certain no one could find them and try and sort things out.'

'You seem to have been very confident that the cocaine would be safe.' Sam sounded sceptical.

'Oh, yes, I was.' She looked at him with bright eyes. 'Alex has spent weeks, ever since the horses were stolen, searching this house

202

without finding it. In fact, he started to wonder if I hadn't taken it up to London.'

He held her look for a long moment. 'You'd hidden the cocaine; what happened next?'

'When we heard that *Seawind* had exploded, Mark went demented. He kept on talking about gas smells and how it must have been something to do with the stove. Both Fran and I found that hard to believe. Uncle Tom knew all the dangers of gas seeping into the bilges and lying there, waiting for an electric spark or an unwary match. But Fran was distraught and in no state to raise objections and I couldn't see what good it would do.

'Mark kept begging me to tell him where I'd hidden the bags. I began to realize that someone else was involved and that they were threatening him. I came in here one day when he was on the telephone. He was saying that he'd got things under control, to trust him, when it was patently obvious no one could trust him, he was in such a state.'

'You didn't know who he was talking to?'

Felicity shook her head. 'I tried to get him to tell me just how deeply he was involved and who with but he wouldn't say anything, just kept begging me to tell him the hiding place. Then he started threatening me, saying if I didn't tell him I could say goodbye to my looks.' Felicity snorted. 'As though I'd ever been beautiful!'

'He didn't intimidate you?'

'He was pathetic! I knew he wouldn't do anything to me and I was so sorry for Fran. Not only had she lost her father, her husband was a broken reed. So I decided I had to go to London and make some enquiries.'

'Such as?' Sam was sounding sceptical again.

'I rang Alexander's house in Argentina. You knew about his ranch? He raised polo ponies, very successfully according to him, though lately he'd hardly seemed to spend any time there. When I asked him if the business wasn't going to pot, he claimed he had an excellent manager. Anyway, I discovered that Mark Sheldrake had been there several times before he met Fran and me in Brazil, the last time only a couple of weeks before our trip.

'When I heard that, I was convinced our meeting with Mark had all been arranged by Alex, so that Mark could ingratiate himself with Fran and so give Alex access to *Seawind* and the harbour. If he'd been in touch with Kingsleigh at all, with Johnny, say, he'd have known about our plans for the trip. And that we would be following one of the itineraries my company was offering. Once he'd found out our departure date, he could work all the rest out too easily.

And the plan worked beautifully,' she added bitterly. 'Not only did Fran fall in love with Mark, she agreed to become his wife.

'After that I went to see the pharmaceutical company Mark had told us he represented in South America. I pretended to be a long-lost cousin who wanted to get in touch. They told me he had only worked for them for a very short time. I got the impression it wasn't the first enquiry they'd had for him and that they wished they'd never heard of Mark Sheldrake.'

'We could have told you all that, if you'd only come to us.'

'Yes, well, it's too late now. The day after I got back to London, I began to understand why Mark was so afraid. The phone rang and it was Alex.

'At first I thought it must be someone playing some sort of sick joke. But his voice has a particular timbre that I don't think anyone could imitate.' Felicity stumbled briefly over her words then recovered. 'When I realized that he was alive, that he had survived the explosion and was now in hiding, I began to get afraid. I was certain he had organized Uncle Tom's death and would now allow nothing to get between him and the drugs.' She broke off, dropped her gaze and started playing with the buttons of her robe again. 'You probably know that Alex wasn't my real father.' She glanced up at Sam, could read nothing in his face and forced herself to continue. 'I can't explain what he meant to me as a child and a young woman. He was like a god and when, a few years ago, I learned he wasn't my real father and he then told me he loved me, it was as though heaven had been handed to me on a plate.' She swallowed hard. The eyes of the man opposite her were calm and dispassionate, gave no clue to his thoughts. 'Later, well, disillusionment set in and it's been some time since we've been lovers. When Fran, Mark and I ran across him, by chance as I thought, in Lima, it was the first time we'd met for a considerable while.' She sighed. 'I was very cross, I thought he'd spoil everything but he was as charming as only Alex can be and he and Mark got on so well. Fran was delighted. She'd always liked Alex and by the time the tour moved on we were at least friends and I didn't mind Fran asking him to the wedding.' She swallowed hard. 'I couldn't forget the past but it seemed there might be something worth salvaging from our relationship.'

Her eyes suddenly narrowed. 'But when I had that first telephone call from him, on top of what I'd learned since coming to town, I realized he'd planned everything like a military campaign and I was disgusted. I told him so. Then he changed his approach and I knew even our relationship had been a sham. He tried to tell me I had meant something to him. He was almost convincing and at first he was quite reasonable. He said if I handed the bags over and kept quiet, everything would be all right.'

Again Felicity looked straight at Sam. 'I told him I wouldn't, that I was going to call the police. Then he dropped his attempt to make me believe he cared anything for me. He took up the threats where Mark had left off and this time I did get scared.' Felicity's dark eyes were enormous in her pale face. 'I thought I could cope with anything but the calls never stopped coming. Any time of the day or night. I couldn't unplug the phone because it was the emergency line if any of my clients was in trouble. But I couldn't sleep. I knew the telephone would ring and there would be that cold voice suggesting another little way he could make life unpleasant for me.' She attempted a smile. 'I never realized how fond one could become of one's body!'

'But you didn't tell him where the cocaine was?'

She shook her head. 'I told him he had three days to come to his senses and for him and Mark to give themselves up. If not, I'd go to the police.' She thought for a moment. 'I should have realized he was never going to do that.' Her voice trailed away, exhausted. It was as if she couldn't bring herself to say anything further.

Sam McLean gave her a sharp look then got up and went across to the drinks table. He poured her out some more brandy, added a good splash of soda, brought the glass across and gave it to her.

'And then?' he prompted after she'd sipped at the drink.

'Then I had another of his little calls in the middle of the night. I screamed at him to let me alone. I told him that he'd never get me to change my mind. He just said, in that expressionless voice he'd adopted, that his patience was at an end and if I didn't tell him where the cocaine was Fran would be the one who'd suffer.'

'And you still didn't come to us?'

'I decided then I had to. I couldn't risk Fran getting hurt. I couldn't stop her finding out about Mark without giving Alex the cocaine and I knew that was too high a price. I'd try and help her cope with the truth and perhaps one day she'd realize she was better off without him. So, early next morning I rang, told her I was coming down and asked her to meet me at the station, and said I had something serious to tell her.

'I was going to explain everything then and there and suggest we went to the police together. It never occurred to me Mark would be at the station as well.'

Felicity paused but Sam said nothing. The note-taking sergeant glanced at his watch.

'I knew Mark would do anything to prevent us going to the police and I was going to wait to get Fran on her own before I told her what had been going on. But no sooner had we started back to Kingsleigh than she demanded to know what I was going to tell her. She was in a real state and finally I gathered that she thought Mark and I might be going off together. She was so beautiful and good and kind and yet she never really believed she was anything much. She always thought men only liked her for her money.

'Anyway, she accused us of having an affair and nothing I or Mark could say would convince her it wasn't true. Finally Mark lost his temper and told her the only thing between us was the fact that I'd hidden something very valuable of his and wouldn't tell him where it was.'

Felicity drew a tired hand across her eyes. The full horror of those last moments before the crash filled her. 'She laughed and said if that was all it was she knew exactly where I would have hidden it and she'd show him as soon as we got back.

'I was so angry, with her for being so stupid, with Mark for coming to the station and being such an idiot, with Alex for being, well, Alex and getting us into this mess. I was so angry, it all started to spill out: how Alex had contrived our meeting with Mark in Brazil, the drugs they'd brought to Kingsleigh, *Seawind*'s accident, everything. All the time, Mark was shouting at me and at Fran, telling her not to believe anything I was saying, that I was just jealous of them, that I'd always wanted him. He was paying no attention to his driving at all. That's when we went too fast round the corner on the wrong side of the road and met the lorry coming the other way.' She stopped bleakly. 'The rest you know.'

Felicity stared at Sam for several minutes. Neither said anything. She still couldn't tell anything from his face. Did he believe her? Did he realize there was something missing from her story?

'I still don't know, though, how you managed to be following us.'

He lay back in his chair, the one Tom Dashwood had always sat in, steepled his fingers together and addressed them rather than her. The gesture put a distance between them that chilled Felicity. 'After the *Seawind* blew up, we applied for a phone tap. We had to know if it was accident or deliberate. Frear appeared capable of anything and I was sure that if the cocaine had been landed, Sheldrake would need instructions.

'The day after the tap was installed, Frear rang and spoke to Sheldrake, so we knew both that he was alive and that they'd landed the cocaine.' There was the minutest hesitation in his voice before he added, 'And that you were the only one who knew where it was. It sounded to us as though you were part of the cartel.' His voice was level, emotionless. 'I nearly asked for a search warrant then but this place looked like a nightmare to find anything in and even if we did locate the cocaine we still wouldn't have Frear. You seemed to be the key to everything. You never noticed the man we had following you in London?' He looked at her then and raised an eyebrow. Felicity shook her head but the information failed to surprise her.

'We did wonder what you were doing at the pharmaceutical company, and when we learned you were coming down again I was sure it was to link up the cocaine with Frear and that you were going to fill in Mrs Sheldrake on the whole situation. I even thought you might bring the stuff with you. So I was at the station as well. By then I'd been told you didn't have a case with you, not even a small overnight bag, but I still thought you might lead us to Frear.'

'I had everything I needed at Kingsleigh,' Felicity interposed.

'So I and another police car followed Sheldrake's, taking it in turns. I was behind when the crash came.' Sam fell silent and she knew they were both remembering the flames, the burning, the funeral pyre. He raised his gaze from his fingers and looked again at Felicity. 'With Sheldrake gone, you were our only lead to Frear and the cocaine.'

'I knew when you visited me in hospital that you weren't there just to see how I was getting on!' she burst out.

'All those bandages were a pretty horrifying sight.'

She didn't know if he was apologizing for his deception or his acting skills but for the first time since they'd come up from the beach she thought she could sense a thaw in his manner.

'You must have had a shock when you heard I'd lost my memory!' Despite her desperate situation, Felicity couldn't help being amused at the thought of his consternation. 'Did you believe me?'

'Put yourself in my position. Would you have believed you?' Once again there was the merest suggestion of an answering warmth beneath the official manner.

'Yet you brought me flowers, flowers that smelled so beautiful.'

'It seemed the right thing to do,' he said simply. 'And I've never seen a more pathetic sight. Wreathed in bandages and blind; if you'd tried to organize a more disarming situation you couldn't have managed better.'

'I think you managed quite well not to be disarmed.'

'I found it more difficult later, when I was finally convinced you really had lost your memory.' He paused then said, 'I'm as cynical as the next detective but even when you were doing your best to mislead me you seemed so straightforward. Despite all my best endeavours, I began to believe you were as much a victim of Frear's machinations as the rest of the family.'

'But if you'd kept your phone tap, you must have known I was innocent when Alex rang.'

He shook his head. 'We went over and over the calls. They were frustratingly short. We couldn't get a fix on where Frear was and everything that was said could be interpreted several ways.'

Felicity wouldn't let herself think again of those chilling calls. 'Have you found out yet where Alex was hiding?'

'We think he escaped from the *Seawind* in her inflatable rubber dinghy and motored down the coast to his friend, Frank West. He's someone else we've had an eye on for some time. He had an extravagant lifestyle with little to explain how he supports it. He left a London firm of stockbrokers, where Frear was a client for a time, under a cloud but with enough money to buy a large estate just south of here. We suspect he provides financing for men like Frear, leaving them to do the actual organization and marketing.'

'A friend of Fran's told me Alex sailed into Kingsleigh harbour with a couple of friends just before my aunt died. Perhaps he was checking things out.'

'More than likely. I'm hoping Frear can provide us with the evidence to put West away as well.'

'I can't see Alex taking the rap alone if someone else is involved.' Felicity thought back over the events of the last few days. 'And was he responsible for Gordon Rules's murder?'

'We think by then Frear was sleeping in the boathouse, with the connivance of the groom. The gardener probably got suspicious of Johnny in some way. Maybe he followed him to a meeting and Frear discovered and killed him, perhaps in the woods above the harbour. We'll be going over that area with a fine toothcomb now, searching for traces of blood. Johnny would have helped him take the body down to the boathouse and they may have planned on taking it out some dark night in the smaller yacht, the *Seabreeze*, and throwing it overboard. Except you got there first.'

'Why weren't you involved in the investigation? You must have known what it was all about.'

'I wanted it to look a straightforward murder case. I left all the formalities to Combe and managed to persuade him to move his men out of here as quickly as possible. While they were around there was no hope of either Frear coming back from wherever he'd disappeared to or you making a move towards the cocaine.'

They sat in silence and the sergeant taking notes eased his cramped fingers.

'Well,' said Sam at last. 'Are you going to show us where it is?'

Chapter Forty-Three

Felicity led a small procession out of the sitting room. Sam McLean was close behind her, the note-taking sergeant behind him and Jackie Wright brought up the rear.

They went up the main staircase to the landing with its balcony overlooking the hall.

There Felicity paused and opened a small cupboard in the panelling by the stairs. She took out a camping gas lamp, placed it on a small table and lit it. Then she picked it up and led the way up the little staircase, into the solar room.

'When electricity was first introduced into Kingsleigh, no one wanted to spoil this room. They thought the panelling was so perfect,' she said as she entered and placed the gas lamp on the torchère that stood just inside the door.

The flaring gas highlighted the carved wood, throwing the linen-folds into relief and making the polished oak glow darkly.

The police came into the empty room, looking about them curiously. Jackie went over to the window and looked down into the hall, moving back quickly as she realized how high they were.

Felicity stood in the centre of the room, her hands clasping her upper arms just below her shoulders, her arms crossed over her breast. In the long cashmere robe with its high collar she could have been a ghost from the medieval age as she closed her eyes and opened herself to the room's atmosphere. Once again she felt that terrible sense of despair. But now she knew the reason for it.

She resisted the room's power, opened her eyes and went over to the panelling opposite the door, on the outside wall. She stood and scrutinized it for some time.

'Fran and I spent nearly the whole of one Christmas holiday looking for a priest's hole,' she said slowly. 'Fran researched in the library and I explored the house, matching rooms to old plans, trying to eliminate everything that had been built since the seventeenth century. Eventually I decided that, if it still existed, it had to be in here. I dragged Fran out of the library and we spent days tapping and pressing all the panelling. Uncle Tom thought it was the funniest thing ever; he said it was all a myth and that if the hole did still exist, he and his sister would have found it when they went through exactly the same exercise when he was our age.

'With all the confidence of youth, I was sure they hadn't tried hard enough. I thought of the complicated lock on the lid of that medieval chest in the hall and decided the secret wouldn't yield to anything as simple as pressing in one place.'

Felicity stood in front of the panelling, frowning. Nobody said anything and the only sound in the room was the slight flare of the lamp. Then she advanced to the wall and pushed sideways at one of the linenfolds. It moved just enough for her to be sure she'd got the right one. She held the panel in its new position and pushed at another, adjacent one.

There was a collective intake of breath from the watching police as a whole section of panelling moved slightly back and to one side, leaving a gap of about an inch some four feet high.

Felicity slipped her fingers round the open edge and pushed the section sideways. Slowly, creaking, the panel section started to move, then it gained momentum and suddenly shot back. There was a scream from Jackie Wright.

Revealed for them all was the legend of Kingsleigh made fact.

The hidden space was tiny, just enough room for a man to sit on a stool and have a pot, a jug and a plate on the floor beside him. A slit in the stone behind provided air and, during the daytime, probably a narrow shaft of light.

On the stool sat a man.

He had been dead a long time. The body leaned against the wall, his death's head grinning at them with hollow eyes and yellow teeth. The bottom jaw had dropped into his lap and lay like an abandoned piece of ancient dentistry, the teeth horribly real. The fine cloth of his Cavalier's dress was faded, the lace and rosettes ghosts of their former glory. The long bones of the hands lay open, as if in supplication.

Sam stepped closer to Felicity and Jackie Wright breathed, 'Who is it?'

Felicity turned to her. 'I think he's Sir Edward Dashwood, who fought for King Charles in the Civil War. There's a history of the Dashwoods and Kingsleigh in the library. Fran was reading it just before I dragged her up here. Apparently, Sir Edward escaped after a major Royalist defeat; I forget which one, history was never my strong point. Parliamentary soldiers came to Kingsleigh looking for him. Lady Dashwood swore on the cross he hadn't come home and then she had a sort of seizure. Something like a stroke, I suppose. She couldn't move or talk, or even write, but the soldiers thought she was faking and kept on questioning her. Eventually she died. They never found Sir Edward and he was never heard of again.'

'You mean he was shut in here and couldn't get out?' Jackie's voice was horrified.

'Fran and I never tried but we reckoned the panel can't be opened from the inside. Probably the secret was handed down from father to son and only Sir Edward and Lady Dashwood knew it. He must have known something had happened but didn't dare make a noise in case the soldiers heard him. Perhaps he hoped they'd soon leave and then he'd be able to get someone to hear him and let him out.'

Felicity looked at the skeleton and remembered her fright when they'd first found the panel, then how aghast she'd been when Fran had related the story. To know the man you loved was starving to death and not be able to do anything about it seemed to her so awful that she didn't see how anyone could have borne it. Perhaps that was why, in the end, Lady Dashwood had died.

'And you never told anyone you'd found this place?' Sam asked.

Felicity shook her head. 'Fran wanted to but I thought it would be sacrilege. I couldn't bear anyone else to know how Sir Edward and Lady Dashwood had suffered. Fran finally agreed. So we shut the panel and, as far as I know, it wasn't opened again until I put the cocaine in.'

They all looked at what the panelling had concealed. Beside the stood with its skeletal occupant, incongruous, sat two modern hold-alls, one identical to Felicity's cream leather case, the other a striped one of some strong, lightweight material.

Felicity took a deep breath. Now she had to make her final confession and she wasn't at all sure how it was going to be received. She indicated the leather bag. 'That was the key to Alex's first smuggling efforts. He gave me an identical one after we met in South America one time.' It was when they'd become lovers. It had been filled with small presents for her and she had been so touched.

'Before I had my own company, I couriered for another travel organization specializing in South America and every time I came back from a trip, Alex appeared in Clapham. He said he'd come to take me somewhere.' They'd go to some luxurious hotel in the country, make love, ride, play tennis, swim, all the things she loved to do with Alex. She unwound from the stresses and strains of shepherding tourists around, sorting out their problems, rescuing them from their idiocies.

'I was so stupid! I thought he wanted to see me, to take advantage

211

of the days off I got after each trip.' She swallowed hard. 'It took me a long time to realize he was using me as a mule. The cases have false bottoms. He would get someone to fill mine with dope in Peru then he'd switch cases with me at this end, repeating the operation each trip. I finally found out that I brought in about a kilo each time.

'After my mother died, when I discovered that she had been a cocaine addict, so many things fell into place and I suddenly realized what Alex must be up to. I tackled him and he admitted everything. He said he wanted to set me up in business, tried to persuade me we could make a great team, that we'd make our fortunes and could do anything. I told him no, everything was finished between us.'

There was silence as she finished speaking. The police – Sam, the sergeant and Jackie – remained looking at her.

What was it they wanted her to say? Why she hadn't gone to them at that stage and told them everything she knew? Surely they couldn't be that stupid?

'Well, there it is, the cocaine everyone's been searching for.'

The sergeant moved forward but Sam put out a hand and stopped him and Felicity understood.

Gracefully she bent down and reached for the holdalls.

As she did so, some draught or change in the atmosphere caused the skeleton to move and it flopped forward, the arms moving round Felicity's shoulders in a macabre embrace. She stifled a scream and for a moment the two of them remained like that, then the skull rolled off her shoulder to lie, rocking, on top of one of the bags, grinning its spectral smile.

As though a spell had been broken, the three police officers moved forward. Sam was there first, freeing Felicity from the remains of the dead Cavalier, then raising and holding her tightly against him as she watched the sergeant pick up the remains, the stuff of the clothes disintegrating, the bones coming apart and falling with a grisly musicality back into the chamber. Lastly he picked up the skull from the holdall and added that, too, to the little pile.

Felicity hid her face in Sam's shoulder for a long moment. Beneath his leather jacket she could feel the steady beat of his heart. Still he said nothing. Then she gathered herself together and gently pulled away.

He held her by the shoulders and looked closely at her. 'Are you all right?'

She took a step backwards, freed herself and rubbed at her eyes. 'I'd have given anything in the hospital to have known who I was. Now I think I was lucky to have remembered nothing of what happened.'

'I think you've been extraordinarily brave,' Sam said at last.

She shook her head. 'Courage doesn't come into it. The most shocking thing of all is not anything I've remembered but how I gradually came to realize what people thought of me. With my memory gone, I'd lost all the reasons why I'd erected so many defences against the world. All I had left was the reputation I'd gained. I felt naked in a raging storm. Earlier, you said if only you'd managed to gain Uncle Tom's confidence, his, Fran and Mark's deaths could all have been averted. Now that I can remember everything, I know that most of the tragedies connected with this place are my fault.'

'It wasn't your fault Frear got involved in cocaine dealing,' said Sam quietly.

'If I'd been brighter, I wouldn't have allowed him to use me as an unwitting mule. Then perhaps he would have worked harder at making his ranch a success and not needed to become a drug trafficker. If I'd helped Philip Bishop more, maybe he wouldn't have become an addict and would be alive today. If I'd understood my mother better, perhaps I could have helped her as well. I should have seen through Mark and protected Fran.' Slow tears silently slid down Felicity's face. She made no effort to wipe them away.

Sam said nothing, just stood watching her, his eyes very steady. Behind her the other two police were also silent.

'If I'd handled Mark better in the car, we wouldn't have crashed and Fran would be alive and probably Gordon Rules as well. Everything I've touched has turned to dust and ashes. And if you tell me I only did what I thought was best, I'll hit you!'

'We have to live with what we are,' he said slowly.

'Isn't that the truth?'

Sam said nothing more.

Felicity looked again at the two bags standing next to the small pile of bones. She bent down and grasped the handles. A moment later she had lifted them out of the secret chamber and placed them at the detective's feet.

Sam McLean hunkered down and unzipped each case. Inside were clear polythene packets of gleaming white powder. He took out a penknife, cut a small slit in one, licked his finger and tasted the powder. After a moment he looked up. 'This seems almost pure cocaine. Turned into crack, its street value could run into millions.'

With a swift movement he closed the zips and handed the bags to the sergeant. 'Both of you take these downstairs and guard them with your lives. I'll be down in a few minutes.' Carrying the holdalls, the sergeant and Jackie Wright disappeared.

Felicity looked at the secret chamber, at the collapsed skeleton, the shredded bits of decayed cloth that had once clothed a Cavalier. 'I think it's time this poor soul was laid to rest. Is there some way we can arrange for him to be properly buried?'

Sam nodded. 'I'll get on to it first thing in the morning.'

She couldn't relax, not yet, but she gave him a small smile that held a hint of wickedness. 'After you deal with the cocaine, of course!'

He smiled back at her. 'What are you going to do now?' he asked.

For a moment she didn't understand, then she drew in her breath in a quick gasp. 'You mean, you're not going to arrest me?'

He shook his head, never taking his eyes from her. 'Your co-operation now outweighs your unwitting actions earlier. The details will, I'm afraid, have to be sent to the Director of Public Prosecutions but, in the light of the value of that cocaine, I shall be very surprised if a case is pursued against you.' His grey eyes were serious as he added, 'Trust me.'

Felicity felt that the guilt of years was lifted from her shoulders. Until then she hadn't realized how heavily it had weighed. Was her long nightmare at last at an end?

'I hope I can do better in the future. As soon as I can find out where she's gone, I'll offer Mrs Parsons back her job. It isn't her fault Johnny is her nephew and I really can't blame her for supplying him with food for Alex; she always had a soft spot for him. I don't know what story he spun her but I expect it sounded very plausible.' She looked round the room. 'Then perhaps I can think of some way in which Kingsleigh can be used to help drug addicts, perhaps as a rehabilitation centre. It's far too large for just me. I think Fran would have liked that.'

'I think all that sounds excellent. And if I can help in any way, I'll be delighted.'

She raised an eyebrow at him, searching his face for some hint of his true feelings. 'There is one more secret, one I'm only going to share with you.'

He waited.

'Thomas Dashwood was my father.'

He said nothing.

'You don't seem all that surprised. I'm sure he knew, too. I think my mother told him that weekend his attitude towards me changed. I think he refused to believe it; she said he told her she was trying to con him.'

'How did you find out?'

'After she died, my mother's lawyer gave me a letter from her. In it she told me I had been conceived when Uncle Tom and Aunt Jennifer went out to Kenya to visit her. My aunt had just become pregnant and she wasn't at all well. So Sarah took Uncle Tom on safari by himself. She said in her letter she couldn't resist the opportunity to prove how attracted he'd been to her but that afterwards she realized she'd made a terrible mistake, that they would never have been happy together. She said she hoped Jennifer never guessed what had happened.'

'Do you think she did?'

'Yes, I think so. She didn't blame Thomas or her sister, she just felt guilty because they'd fallen in love after Sarah had thought she was going to be the one.'

'But why did your mother finally tell your uncle – father?' He stumbled over the right term for a moment. 'I mean, tell Dashwood that you were his child after such a long time. How old were you?'

'Twelve. You never knew my mother. She was so quick tempered. She'd drink too much, get annoyed about something and then lash out with her tongue. She had an unhappy knack for choosing the words that were going to hurt the most. She wasn't a happy woman.' Felicity felt a wave of depression hit her as she remembered just how difficult Sarah could be. 'But even though he refused to believe I was his daughter, I think ever afterwards Uncle Tom saw me as a reminder of his weak moment, the one time he'd betrayed my aunt. No wonder he disliked me so much!'

She sighed and ran a finger down her straight nose. 'I think Belinda Gray suspected, too; her nose and mine were identical before the car crash. That's why she couldn't stand me. I was proof her beloved brother wasn't a verray parfit gentil knight after all.' She squared her shoulders. 'Somehow, since my accident, I can understand so much more than I did before. It's as though I had to be blind before I could see.'

Carefully she pulled the panelling back into place. 'I'm glad there aren't any more secrets now and I'm glad Kingsleigh is still owned by a Dashwood, even if nobody knows it but me.'

'I do,' Sam said and smiled at her, his strong face at last relaxed, the watchful look gone from his eyes.

'So you do.' She gave him a shy little smile that was sweet with promise.

Then Felicity looked back at the panelling that concealed again Kingsleigh's long-held secret. 'Tomorrow?' she said to Sam. 'You promise?'

'Tomorrow, I promise.'

She stood as she had when they'd first entered the room, tall and straight, head up, eyes closed.

After a long moment she opened her eyes and smiled at him. 'I think we've laid the ghosts to rest. This is just a room now.'